THE CREEPING DEAD
BOOK TWO

EDWARD P. CARDILLO

SEVERED PRESS
HOBART TASMANIA

THE CREEPING DEAD: BOOK TWO

Copyright © 2017 Edward P. Cardillo
Copyright © 2017 by Severed Press

WWW.SEVEREDPRESS.COM

ISBN: 978-1-925597-77-6

Acknowledgements

I would like to thank my wife, Sandra, who has been my editor, coach, and agent. I would also like to thank Alan Basso and Charlene Nunez for their extra sets of eyes, braaaains, feedback, and support. Thank you to Trevor Smith for his knowledge of military procedure and equipment. Thank you to my son, Alexander, who helped me compose some key scenes. Thanks again to Gary Lucas at Severed Press.

Thank you to my readers, who made the first book a success.

This novel is dedicated to my readers, who made The Creeping Dead a success and have been patiently asking for a sequel for two years. I hope you enjoy it.

ACT 1
RESILIENCE

CHAPTER 1

Clinging to the carousel horses for dear life, the remaining survivors in the Blackbeard's Pier Arcade were weary from sleep deprivation, a diet of candy and soda, and exposure to the elements.

What had made matters worse was that the pounding of the zombies outside never ceased. At times, it had slowed, but it always returned full blast. In the daylight, they could now see the searching fingers reaching under the hem of the bent security gates. Nancy wouldn't allow the children to look at it.

Vinnie, Mike, and Holbrook dismounted their horses and went to the edge of the arcade. The water had receded, and the beach below was littered with debris.

And zombies.

They were everywhere. They reached upward for the humans hiding within the arcade.

"Son-of-a-bitch," said Vinnie. "I swear, there's got to be more of them."

There was the scraping of metal, and Alessandra screamed. All three men turned around to find the security gate being shoved off its track. Zombies wriggled in the gap, eyes wild, desperate to reach their prey.

Nancy and Dharma grabbed the children and pulled them off the carousel.

"We're trapped!" said Vinnie.

"There's a ladder to the roof!" said Nancy, pointing to the right of the shooting gallery.

The gang didn't need to be told twice. They sent Dharma up first to open the hatch up top. Both children followed closely behind.

"Hurry!" shouted Vinnie. "They're coming in!"

Mike and Nancy insisted that Vinnie go up next.

Dharma pulled the children up onto the flat roof. It was sagging and dilapidated from storm damage and having a third of it torn away.

"Go ahead," said Holbrook, gesturing to Nancy.

"You first," she said.

"There's no time to argue," said Holbrook. "Ladies first. I insist."

Nancy grabbed the rungs and began her ascent. She'd done this a few times before to shovel the snow off. It had to be done with a flat roof, or it would cave in from the weight.

"Come on, Mike. You next."

A few of the zombies had made it under the gate and were inside the arcade. Mike shook his head. "You're a family man, Chief. You first."

The zombies who made it in were getting to their feet, while the next wave squirmed under the gate. Mike looked around at all of the ruin. Everything that made him happy, his whole purpose in life, was destroyed.

Holbrook recognized the look in Mike's eyes. He knew a suicidal person when he saw one. "I have to insist. Hurry up, or we'll both die."

Nancy stuck her head through the hatch. "Jesus Christ, Michael! Stop lollygagging and get your handsome ass up here!"

That remark hit Mike like a hard slap to the face. He snapped out of his funk and grabbed a rung of the ladder. "You'll be right behind me?" he said to Holbrook, more than asked.

"Not unless you move your ass," said Holbrook.

Mike climbed the ladder, and as promised, Holbrook was right behind him. Holbrook climbed just high enough as a zombie swiped at his foot, missing it by mere inches.

"Let's hope they don't know how to climb ladders," quipped Mike as he reached the hatch.

When Holbrook pulled himself onto the roof, aided by Vinnie and Dharma, he stood and got a good view of Smuggler's Bay.

Or what was left of it.

Parts of the boardwalk were missing. Ripped-up boards littered the remaining parts and the beach. Sand was everywhere, even on the streets beyond the boardwalk. Storefronts were ruined, gates bent inward with debris hanging out.

He looked to the left and saw that half of Blackbeard's Pier was indeed missing. The top of the iconic Albatross roller coaster poked out of the ocean, the rest of it submerged like a metallic iceberg.

The group was stunned into silence. They were all taking in the destruction of their home, their livelihood.

Nancy held the children close.

Dharma hugged Vinnie, sobbing.

Holbrook looked down the ladder. None of the dead appeared to know how to climb. However, they were surrounded on all sides on top of a damaged structure that was on the verge of collapse.

They were screwed.

Holbrook took his cell phone out of his pocket. It was on its last bar. He wanted to call Lena and Robbie to tell them that he loved them very much. He wanted to say goodbye.

Suddenly, the air echoed with the popping of gunfire. Holbrook's cell phone rang, and he answered. "Chief Holbrook…yes, we're on the roof of the Blackbeard's Pier Arcade…we lost a man…I don't know how much longer this building is going to hold up…Okay." He hung up.

Mike, Nancy, Dharma, Vinnie, and the children looked at him expectantly.

"The National Guard is coming to get us."

"We're saved!" yelled Nancy. "It's about damned time!"

Within minutes, they saw the National Guard advance up the boardwalk, taking out zombies with well-placed headshots. When they reached the arcade, a man who identified himself as Sergeant Miller called out to them on a bullhorn, telling them to stay put. As if they had a choice.

They surrounded the arcade and fired into it, dispatching the hoard of zombies within. When the arcade no longer moved with the dead, they entered and helped everyone down from the roof.

On the ground, Sergeant Miller immediately approached Holbrook and introduced himself. They discussed the state of the Bay, the CDC, and how the infection appeared to be contained on the barrier island, with only a few isolated incidents in neighboring towns.

The Bay, however, was trashed. The flooding had not only destroyed the boardwalk and many of its businesses. There were houses that were shifted off their foundations, inundated with water and sand. Boats were deposited randomly in the middle of roads and between houses.

The federal, state, and local authorities closed Smuggler's Bay for the next six months. They cut the power to the barrier island. The military swept the town, dispatching the last of the dead wandering around. The CDC tagged and bagged the dispatch dead, sending them to laboratories for analysis of tissue and bodily fluids.

After the island was secured, engineers and inspectors were sent in to assess the damage and any safety concerns regarding building structure, gas lines, and the power infrastructure. Sewage and waste concerns were also investigated and addressed.

To the government, the wait was necessary, as a matter of caution. The event was unprecedented, and they needed time to assess and develop a plan to secure and reopen the island.

To the residents and business owners of Smuggler's Bay, the wait seemed like an eternity. The government closing the island meant that reconstruction would be delayed. To add insult to injury, FEMA and insurance companies were dragging their feet in paying out claims.

With the next summer approaching, Smuggler's Bay would be in shambles. Although the dead had been wiped out, their effect on Smuggler's Bay lingered, leaving the community weakened and its economy sick. To make matters worse, the town would now have to grapple with the stigma attached to it. Once a family resort, it was now ground zero for the world's first zombie outbreak.

Motels changed ownership with the changes in the tide, and to stay open, many were now converting some of their rooms into low-income apartments. Social workers stocked the rooms with ex-cons and recovering drug addicts, further hurting the town's reputation as a family resort.

Damaged by the dead and the politics of the living, Smuggler's Bay had become a town of second chances for many. Only time would tell if the community would be able to rebuild. Only time would tell if Smuggler's Bay would survive, and in what version of itself.

Only time would tell if the dead stayed buried.

* * *

Two Years Later

Mike Brunello opened his eyes as his metal trash can toppled over outside. He sat in his recliner in front of CNN, half in, half out of sleep as he found it more and more difficult to sleep in his own bed. There was something stirring between his bungalow and the next.

He sat up, his back creaking, and rubbed his eyes, his vision clearing as his body began to pump adrenaline. Fight or flight. Two years ago, it would've been flight. However, after narrowly escaping being eaten alive by zombies, he decided that it would henceforth be fight.

He turned, reached behind his recliner, and produced a shotgun he kept for such occasions. It wasn't just for his protection. It was also to protect those he loved, just as he did two years ago when a horde of land sharks invaded Smuggler's Bay.

The trash can rolled around outside as his motion detector light went on, casting a moving shadow across the curtains of his living room. Mike pushed himself to his feet, careful not to bang his shins on his glass coffee table, and raised his shotgun.

He trained the barrel on the shadow moving across the curtains as he crept towards the window. Horrifying images flashed through his mind of the cloudy-eyed, screeching dead, snapping their jaws like some novelty windup teeth that Nancy had in her prize counter at the arcade.

Mike leaned forward, brushing aside the beige curtain with his left hand while holding the shotgun with his right. He peered out the window, his finger itchy on the trigger.

He relaxed his shoulders when he saw yet another feral cat stalking around his side yard. Not realizing he had been holding his breath, Mike let it out in a long, weary sigh.

"Mike, what are you doing?"

Startled, he wheeled around, nearly pulling the trigger. His heart was in his throat. "Damn it, Nancy! I almost blew your head off!"

Nancy put her hands on her hips and bared her teeth. "You better stop pointing that gun at me, Michael, or I'm going to shove it where the sun don't shine."

Mike quickly lowered the shotgun. "I thought I saw one of them outside."

"Jesus, Mike, there hasn't been one seen in Smuggler's Bay for two years. The damned storm washed 'em all out to sea."

Mike walked back to his recliner and placed the shotgun back behind it. "Yeah, well, the military didn't get them all. It's not inconceivable for any of them to return."

Nancy shook a rebuking finger at him. "This is why I told you that you need to sleep at my place in Lakeview."

Mike planted himself back down in his recliner, waving a dismissive hand. "Now, Nancy, I already told you that I'm not ready for that yet."

"For crying out loud, your wife is long gone. You have a right to move on. To be happy."

"Oh, is that what this is?" quipped Mike.

"I don't believe in half measures," she insisted. "At some point, you're either all in, or I'm all out."

"I don't know what more you want from me. I'm with you, aren't I?"

Nancy threw her hands up in defeat and shuffled back into Mike's unoccupied bedroom to salvage the night's sleep. "You'd better get some sleep, or you'll be useless at the arcade tomorrow."

To sleep meant to dream of cannibalistic monsters, so Mike remained in his living room, his skin still tingling from his fright with the feral cat.

Tara told him that he should see a shrink. When she saw that he wasn't responding to her suggestion, she turned to Nancy. Once Nancy got on his case about it, Mike found one that took Medicare just to get Nancy off his back.

Acute Stress Syndrome, the head shrink called it. After a bunch of months, the shrink started calling it Post Traumatic Stress Disorder. But, Mike wasn't the only one in Smuggler's Bay suffering with it. Half the Bay had it after the dead had attacked their little town.

His therapist, Dr. Mondavi, wanted him to 'take ownership' over his fear by facing it head on, empowering himself. He interpreted that as buying a gun and learning to shoot at the range in Stonewall.

A gun-owner herself, even before the zombie attack, Nancy supported him fully, going with him to the range and taking every opportunity to show him up. She was a regular Annie Oakley, while Mike was more of a Mr. Magoo, but he was improving.

Wired, Mike sat there in his recliner, half paying attention to Anderson Cooper prattling on about something in the Middle East as he waited for the sun to peek over the horizon and sneak between his curtains.

* * *

Sunrise was Morty Sandberg's favorite time of day in the Bay. The ocean sparkled like liquid diamonds, and the beach and boardwalk were completely empty.

With his granddaughter, April, by his side, he enjoyed the cool breeze as he swept his metal detector over the sand. Close by, his fishing rod stood, planted in a PVC tube that he had driven into the sand. They had already salvaged seventy-three cents in change and a gaudy pinky ring, so he was off to a good start.

Satisfied with his morning's findings, he placed the metal detector in the sand. "Grandma wants us to find shells for the house."

April smiled at this, as she was getting bored of sifting through sand for change. He took her small hand in his, and they shuffled to the water's edge. The beach sloped downward towards the water, and the sand became wet and packed solid beneath their feet.

April looked down and smiled at little holes produced by air bubbles. Grandpa had explained they were baby clams lurking beneath, momentarily safe from the hovering seagulls.

She looked up at him, squinting her eyes against the sun. "Grandpa, why does Mommy think you should move?"

Morty frowned at this. Obviously, his daughter had been discussing his predicament in front of the little one, something he estimated to be poor judgement. "Well, it's not so simple, honey."

"Why?"

"Because I am waiting for the insurance company to issue me my check so I can continue to fix my house."

"Grandpa, is it true that monsters wrecked your house?"

Normally, Morty would have no compunction about assuring April, or any child, that there were no such things as monsters. However, after the dead invaded Smuggler's Bay two summers ago, he could no longer convince himself that was true.

"The superstorm damaged my house. But, I was lucky. Others had their houses destroyed."

April recalled houses shifted completely off their foundations, some sitting right in the middle of the road. "Kinda like the Wizard of Oz?"

Morty chortled. "Kind of, except it wasn't a tornado, and there was no Wicked Witch or flying monkeys."

"Grandpa, are the monsters all gone?"

"I think so. We haven't seen any since the attack two years ago. Chief Holbrook seems to think we're okay, but he and the police are on the lookout, just in case."

As if on cue, a helicopter fluttered overhead, scanning the water. Morty remembered when they used to look for sharks.

"Besides, Smuggler's Bay is my home. I love the town and everybody in it. Well, almost everybody."

"I wouldn't want to move from my home," said April in commiseration.

As cold June water washed over their toes, Morty, grateful for the opportunity to change the subject, pointed out intact shells, and April collected them. They picked out one or two large clam shells and a couple of tiny fan shells. He threw away a few that were chipped or broken, and April tossed a hollowed crab shell into the surf.

Morty shoved the shells into the large left cargo pocket on his shorts. As they walked further into the icy water, picking up more shells, the growing collection clinked in his pocket. April found a couple of shards of sea glass, the edges worn smooth by surf and sand particles.

"Grandpa, keep these for me." Sea glass was her absolute favorite. She had her own collection back at the house.

She handed Morty the shards, and he accommodated her, placing them in his right cargo pocket, so as not to mix them with the shells.

Looking over his shoulder to check that his metal detector hadn't grown legs and walked off, he decided to wade into the surf up to April's knees. As he held her hand firmly in his so she wouldn't be pulled by any undertow, April squealed with delight as the cold water splashed up, wetting the bottom of her shorts.

However, her squeal turned into a cry of pain as she picked her foot up, recoiling from the sand underneath the waves.

Morty bent down and looked at April. Her face was contorting, as she was on the verge of tears. "What happened? Are you okay?"

"I stepped on something sharp," she said, allowing herself to cry.

Morty picked her up in his arms—an easy task as she was tiny, even for a six-year-old—and carried her back to shore. When they were just out of reach of the surf, he sat her down in the damp, hard sand. She wiped her tears with the backs of her arms as he inspected the bottom of her right foot.

As he squeezed it, blood trickled out of a small cut on the bottom of her foot, and April winced.

"Honey, I think you stepped on a sharp piece of sea glass."

She stopped crying for a moment. "I thought sea glass wasn't sharp."

As a wave washed up, Morty scooped up water in his cupped hands and drizzled it over her foot. The blood washed away, revealing a small white cut. The cold water offered her some relief. "Well, it is sharp if it was just broken. It takes time to grind it down and make it smooth."

The truth was, since Superstorm Randy, all kinds of debris had been washing up on shore—pieces of the Albatross roller coaster, fragments of bathroom tile, small chunks of concrete, and even splinters of the old boardwalk.

Little April considered this for a moment, frowning. "I wanna go home now."

Morty smiled. "That's right. We'll put some peroxide and a band-aid on that cut of yours, and your foot will be as good as new."

April scrunched up her nose at the mention of peroxide, knowing it would sting. Morty leaned in close. "If you don't tell Grandma about the seventy-three cents, I'll split it with you."

April's frown turned upside down. "Deal!" Her attention immediately shifted to something on the beach. "Look, Grandpa! You caught something!"

Morty turned to find his fishing rod bent. Something was pulling the line. Hard.

"Let's go!" Morty helped her to her feet, and they raced over to where the fishing rod was planted. It was bending, then straightening, then bending again.

Morty bent down and snatched it up. It was almost torn from his grip. "Golly, I've caught something big."

Forgetting her injured foot, April jumped up and down, squealing and clapping her hands in excitement. "Get it, Grandpa! Get it!"

"Get back, honey." Morty struggled with trying to reel it in as April backed away. Whatever it was, it was taking an awful lot of his line. He leaned backwards, pulling the rod with him as it bent nearly in half.

"That's a big fish, Grandpa! You caught a whale!"

Morty knew it wasn't a whale, but it was a sizeable fish. Hell, the way it was fighting, he figured he might've caught a small shark. Maybe that was what the helicopter was looking for. "Get back, April," he said again, and she took several more steps backward.

There was a strong pull, and Morty was yanked forward off his feet. He went crashing face-first into sand, and he let go of the rod. It was dragged towards the water in staccato bursts. Something was reeling the rod in.

April ran over to Morty. "Grandpa! Are you okay?"

Morty pushed himself up with both hands, spitting dry sand out of his mouth. He saw his fishing rod sitting twenty feet in front of him on the wet sand. He had to move quickly.

He pushed himself to his feet, his joints creaking and back complaining, and he lurched over to the edge of the water. As he stretched down for his rod, it was pulled just out of his reach.

April, losing interest quickly, began to play with the sand in front of her, creating a small mound that she fancied to be a grand palace housing a princess.

Morty splashed through the water, which was now up to his knees, and he reached down, his fingertips just barely touching his rod. The thought crossed his mind that this was a lost cause. Before he could straighten up, a hand reached out from the surf and latched onto his wrist.

Morty's eyes bugged out of his head, not just because he was taken by surprise, but because the pale, green hand was swollen, and its flesh was torn.

He was immediately pulled into the water face-first, as another hand clamped itself down on his neck, pulling him further out. He struggled to push his face above water to catch his breath, but the hands held him down as waves crashed over his back.

April.

Morty knew he had to fight, not for his life but for April's. If this zombie got him, she would be next.

He thrashed around in the surf as the hands pulled him away from shore. Soon, his knees were no longer scraping the pebbles and sand. He felt buoyant, as he had been dragged out to deeper water, but he wasn't being allowed to float.

Morty forced open his eyes, the salt stinging them. In front of him, there was nothing. Below him was one of the dead, its eyes feral with hunger. It was bloated and discolored, no doubt from spending a couple of years at sea.

Running out of oxygen, Morty's vision began to fade as shadows crept from his periphery, looming over his vision. He was about to lose consciousness when he felt teeth clamp down on his right calf.

He let out a silent scream of pain as more teeth sunk into his left thigh and right shoulder. Sea water rushed into his lungs, and they burned as the life leached out of his body.

On shore, April, oblivious to the disappearance of her grandpa, was immersed in a game with her sand castle. She had made a drawbridge out of an old piece of boardwalk, shorn away by the superstorm two years ago. She positioned a cigarette butt upright and adorned it with dry seaweed. It was Princess April of the Bay, and she sat on a throne fashioned from a small shard of bathroom tile.

While she oversaw her kingdom made of detritus, she did not notice the staggering figure rising up from the surf and sloshing out of the water. It zeroed in on her, reaching out, trying to screech, but its lungs were filled with sea water.

April saw a tall shadow looming over her sand castle. "Did you get your rod, Grandpa?"

There was a muffled grunt in response.

"What's the matter, Grandpa? Cat got your tongue?" She turned around and screamed as swollen fingers seized her in death's embrace.

* * *

Vinnie Cantone stood at the edge of the boardwalk, peering out at the broken Blackbeard's Pier. Nancy had reinforced the remaining portion of the pier and replaced the half of the arcade that had broken off into the ocean. The Classics Room had been replaced with claw machines, which Vinnie thought to be a travesty, but Nancy insisted they made her money. She was in the process of extending the pier with money she scraped together from her other, smaller businesses while she waited for the insurance company and FEMA to fight over who was going to pay out first.

There was construction equipment sitting dormant in the morning sun next to piles of wooden pilings. Dozens of feral cats hid amongst the construction equipment. There had been an infestation of them since the superstorm. The town even started a grassroots movement to neuter and feed them.

It all seemed ridiculous to Vinnie when tons of families were still displaced from their homes, some of which had been condemned. Some of those fortunate to receive an insurance check began renovations, while others elevated their homes on pilings as a precaution against future floods.

As he looked at Blackbeard's Pier, Vinnie thought back to that night when he, Dharma, Mike, Nancy, Alessandra, and Salvatore were trapped inside the arcade during the storm. He remembered the dead fingers probing underneath the bent metal gates, searching for them.

He shook his head, as if doing so would clear the mental image away, and redirected his attention to a child throwing pieces of toast from breakfast to the seagulls. His daddy broke off small pieces and handed them to the little boy, who then chucked them, giggling as the seagulls caught them in midair.

"Boo!"

Vinnie jumped out of his skin when Dharma snuck up behind him and tickled his ribs. He shot her a look.

She slipped an arm around his shoulders and kissed him. "Jesus, I'm sorry. I forgot."

"I don't know how you can be completely unaffected by…what happened."

"Vin, it was two years ago. And that's not true, anyway. I was affected by it."

Vinnie glanced down the boardwalk at the shuttered businesses. The signs above, many of them now hand-painted, read things like: Shoot the Zombie, Whack-A-Zombie, Water Gun Apocalypse, and The Creeping Dead (a zombie-themed haunted house). "It's kind of hard to move on when the whole Bay has become Zombie Central."

Dharma pulled him closer, putting him in a loose headlock. "Oh, come on. This is how some people choose to deal with it. I, for one, think it's constructive."

Vinnie arched a dubious eyebrow. "Constructive? Try morbid. And in poor taste."

Dharma looked down the boardwalk at the signs and smiled. "All this is bringing in much-needed dollars. Without it, the town may have gone under."

Vinnie drew his attention back to the little boy, who was now pitching his pieces of toast straight down into the sand. The smaller, black-headed seagulls swooped down first to try to claim their prize. However, the larger ones swept down, chasing them away. Might made right. Law of the jungle.

"I just don't know if it's good for all the kids. You know, the little ones."

Dharma smiled at the little boy and his father. "This is just a phase. In a year or two, the zombie obsession will fade, and we'll go back to being a quaint, boring little beach town."

Vinnie thought that Dharma was right. This was just a phase, like that time that goofy reality show was shot in Smuggler's Bay, the dating show with the goofy Bennies, as if Bennies actually lived here.

Dharma looked concerned. "Have you given any thought about talking to Tara?"

Vinnie frowned. "I don't know if that's such a good idea."

"Why not? You're obviously having some difficulty getting past what happened."

"*Past* what happened? How does one get past his hometown being invaded by blood-thirsty zombies?"

Dharma turned her back to the beach, leaning her back against the temporary fence. "I think she's the perfect person to speak to."

"She lost her husband," said Vinnie. "He tried to eat her and her son."

"She understands what happened," said Dharma. "At least your family is safe. You didn't lose anyone."

"I lost friends, remember?"

Tara wanted to swallow her words. "Vin, that's not what I meant."

He looked down at the boardwalk. "It's not that I'm depressed or anything. Dharma, I'm not sleeping at night, and when I do, I have horrible nightmares."

"About the zombies?"

"Yes. Every night. Whenever a balloon pops at the water gun race, or a car honks its horn, or inconsiderate people sneak up on me…" Dharma shrugged her shoulders, looking sheepish. "…I jump out of my skin."

Dharma put her hands up in mea culpa. "Hey, hey, I said I was sorry."

"What if…what if they come back?"

"But they haven't come back, Vin. It's been two years, and no sign of them whatsoever."

Vinnie began to shift back and forth on his feet. "What if the military didn't get them all? You know how many got washed out to sea…"

"Exactly. They're floating around somewhere out in the ocean."

"What if they're walking the bottom? What if they're making their way back here?"

Dharma chuckled. "Why would they come back here? What's so special about Smuggler's Bay?"

Vinnie leveled his gaze at her. "Jaws always came back to Amityville."

"That was only in Jaws 2," corrected Dharma. "Jaws 3 was set somewhere completely different, as was 4. And they're just movies, Vin."

Vinnie frowned. "Until two summers ago, I would've said that zombies were only movies."

Dharma frowned too. "I see your point."

"Maybe I should call Tara."

"I think you should schedule an appointment."

"I will," resolved Vinnie.

Dharma stared him down.

"What, now? It's too early in the morning."

Dharma smacked his forehead. "There's a new invention, doofus. It's called voicemail."

Vinnie pulled his cell phone out of his shorts. "You want me to make an appointment. Fine. I'll make an appointment."

He called up her contact information in his phone. Dharma made him enter it and save it on his phone as a contact, step one in her relentless intervention. He pressed the call button, and it began to ring.

"Dr. Bigelow."

Vinnie hadn't actually expected her to answer. "Uh, hi, Tara. It's Vinnie Cantone."

"Oh, hi, Vinnie. How are you?"

Vinnie hesitated, but Tara was nudging him with her elbow. "Well, that's why I was calling. I was wondering if I could schedule an appointment to talk."

"What, like a session? I'm not really supposed to see people I know socially."

She had a point. Although Vinnie wouldn't consider her a close friend, she was a friendly acquaintance, and one he survived the almost-apocalypse with.

"I-I figured you might be able to…offer me some perspective, seeing as how you went through…that thing we all went through two years ago."

"Are you having a tough time with it?"

"I haven't been sleeping, and I get these crazy bloody nightmares when I do. I'm real jumpy, too." Vinnie didn't like appearing vulnerable, and it was clear in his voice.

Tara hesitated on the other end, considering the prospect. "Well, I guess we're not technically friends, so I guess it's okay. Besides, if you told another therapist about your difficulty getting over a zombie attack, they might lock you up."

Vinnie hadn't considered that. Even though the attack had been all over the news, it was still difficult to swallow for outsiders.

"Take a breath, Vinnie. I was just joking."

Vinnie exhaled.

"I'm dropping Tyrell off at Marie's store, then I'm heading to work. I'm seeing a client at four on the boardwalk. How about we meet at your pizzeria at five o'clock?"

"Sure. That would be great."

"Great, I'll see you later then." Tara terminated the call.

Dharma was hanging all over him in anticipation. "Well? How'd it go?"

"I have an appointment at five o'clock."

She kissed him on the cheek. "That's great!"

Vinnie was starting to feel a little better when the little boy tossed a piece of toast a little too close to the boardwalk. A seagull landed nearby and waddled over to where it rested in the sand. As he bent to snatch it up in his beak, two feral cats leapt out from under the boardwalk, tackling it. One cat grabbed its neck in its mouth, while the other grabbed its wing.

The seagull lay there helpless, its wings splayed, one of them broken, and the cats dragged it under the boardwalk to be eaten alive.

The little boy began to squeal in terror as his father pulled him away from the fence and down the boardwalk, away from the scene of the crime.

Vinnie and Dharma stood there, flabbergasted, unsure if they really saw what just happened.

"Fuck," gasped Vinnie.

Dharma laughed. "Like I said, boring." She grabbed a shocked Vinnie by the arm and pulled him away from the fence. "I'm hungry, let's get some breakfast."

Vinnie looked at her in revulsion, allowing himself to be pulled away from the fence. "How can you possibly be hungry after seeing something like that?"

Dharma punched him in the arm. "Hey, I just thought of a new name to help your dad's pizza shop to capitalize on this whole zombie craze."

"God, no. Please, don't."

"World War Ziti."

"Oh, Jesus Christ."

She snapped her fingers. "I've got it! The Walking Bread!" She put her arm around his shoulders as they walked and shook him. "Get it?"

Vinnie shook his head. "This is going to be a long summer."

* * *

"Hurry up and get dressed!"

Tara waited by the front door. Tyrell was dragging his feet, as all children do when off during the summer. However, what he—like all children—failed to appreciate was Tara still had to go to work.

He finally materialized, pulling a T-shirt on as he shuffled to the front door.

"Double time it, mister."

He yawned as he slipped his feet into his sneakers that were laced up loose enough for easy access, but somehow tight enough to stay on his feet. "I'm coming. I'm coming."

Tara grabbed him by the wrist and guided him out the front door, which she promptly slammed and locked. The morning sun felt warm on their faces. It was late June, but it felt like late July.

She marched him to the car, and they slipped inside. Within minutes, they were parked behind Marie Russo's store. As Tyrell slowly exited the vehicle, Tara was already halfway up the ramp to the boardwalk. "Tyrell!"

However, she didn't wait for him. When she reached the boardwalk, she saw that Marie had already opened the security gate. When Tara peeked in, she saw Salvatore and Alessandra unpacking boxes. She took note of how different they looked from when she first met them two summers ago. Although Alessandra was a bit younger than Salvatore, she was beginning to catch up to him in height. Both children looked older, more mature.

Salvatore was the first to see Tara peering into the store. "Hi, Mrs. Bigelow."

Alessandra called out to her mother, and Marie emerged from the stock room in back, her skin already glistening with sweat. She smiled when she saw Tara. "Hey, there."

Tyrell had finally caught up, walking into the store and immediately diving into the task of helping the other two kids unpack boxes of T-shirts.

Tara smiled back. "Hey, Marie." She looked at Tyrell working, an abrupt change in mode from five minutes prior. "I wish I could get as much work out of him as you do."

Marie glanced over her shoulder at the three kids working together seamlessly. "Oh, he's a good kid, and he's been a big help."

With Marie's husband, Mario, gone, she needed all the help she could get. Tara understood. They were both zombie widows.

Tyrell opened up a fresh box and pulled out a T-shirt with a big, ragged zombie on the front clutching a surfboard. In blood-smeared lettering above, it read 'The Zombie Shore.'

Tara couldn't help but frown. Marie winced at her reaction, feeling bad about Tara's loss of her husband in the attack.

Tara, sensing Marie's reaction, was quick to smooth it over. "Oh, come on. You need to make your money and feed your family."

Marie shrugged, shamefaced. "You don't think it's in poor taste?"

Tara waved a dismissive hand. "Honey, this whole town is in poor taste." She saw the clock on the wall. "Dammit, I'm running late."

Marie hugged her and gently ushered her out of the store. "I've got him. Go, go."

Tara darted to the ramp leading back to her car, but she took a moment to notice the other shops opening up, some already open. The 'Shoot the Zombie' booth two storefronts down was already spewing creepy music with screams, like a haunted house. In June.

Before she boarded the wooden ramp, flashing lights caught her eye on the beach. The lifeguards were all mobilized, converging around one spot on the beach. Chief Holbrook was there. She shook her head, as she estimated that someone had tried to go for an early morning swim and had gotten into trouble, and then she headed for her car.

CHAPTER 2

As Chief Holbrook was standing over the chewed-up remains of an apparent swimmer, two things bothered him. Firstly, the man was thick in the middle with skinny arms and legs and a tuft of gray hair flopped over a vast bald spot on a half-eaten head. His nose and one eye were missing, and claw marks on his face made him unrecognizable. However, one thing was clear—he was an older gent.

The second thing that bothered Holbrook was his attire. He wasn't wearing swimming trunks. Instead, he was clad in shorts and a Hawaiian print shirt. There was still a sneaker on his right foot, which was dangling by the thread of sinew.

"This was no swimmer," he said to Mac Cochran, the Beach Captain.

Mac scrunched his face as he viewed the remains. "Shark attack?"

Holbrook gave a heavy sigh. "God, let's hope so."

Mac knew exactly what he meant by the remark. A shark was the better scenario.

Holbrook looked around. "Who discovered it?"

"Mike Sasso. He saw it when he was driving the sandboni up the beach. Jumped out and screamed like hell at us during our morning drills. Forgot to turn the sandboni off."

Holbrook crouched down on his haunches and studied the bulge in the deceased's right rear pocket. He unbuttoned the flap and pulled out a wallet soaked in seawater.

He cradled it in his left hand and gingerly opened it, revealing various cards packed into the small sleeves. Right above the credit cards was a driver's license. When Holbrook pulled it out and saw the name and picture, he dropped his head. "Aw, Christ."

"What is it?" asked Cochran.

"Morty Sandberg."

"That's Morty? What the hell was he doing out in the ocean?"

Holbrook stood up, folding the wallet closed. "That's one of many questions." He slipped the license into his shirt pocket for safe keeping and patted it. "Where's Mike?"

"He's still over by the sandboni," said Cochran. "He's pretty shaken up."

Holbrook nodded. "I don't blame him." He looked down the beach and saw the sandboni parked at an odd angle. They were usually driven parallel to the boardwalk. He walked over the sand against the early morning breeze and down to the sandboni, where he saw Mike Sasso leaning against it, fanning his baseball cap in front of his face.

When he saw Holbrook, he swallowed hard and managed, "Morning, Chief Holbrook." He was a portly man in his fifties with a farmer's tan. However, at the moment, his face was the shade of sea foam.

"Jesus, Mike. I heard you found the body."

Mike's face was drenched in sweat, and his eyes were hysterical. "Body? You call that a body? There was barely anything left."

"Mike, explain to me what happened."

"I was driving up the beach, and I saw a crumpled heap washed up on the sand, not too far from the water's edge. I can't drive over anything like that, so I got out to gather it up and throw it in the garbage."

"What happened then?"

"I smelt it, and then I saw fingers, and then a shoe. I realized it wasn't garbage, but a person. So, I called nine-one-one."

"Mike, I'm sorry."

"In all my years driving the 'boni, I ain't never seen nothin' like that. Ever."

"You gonna be okay?" asked Holbrook. "You want a paramedic to have a look at you?"

"I-I…" Mike's eyes drifted off for a moment, welling up.

"I'm going to have someone come look at you, make sure you're all right."

A white van up on the boardwalk caught Holbrook's attention. It was Dr. Hickey, the county medical examiner.

When Holbrook didn't receive an answer from Mike, he took it as his cue to leave, giving the man some space. He walked back to where Morty's remains lay as he saw Dr. Hickey walking onto the beach, kicking sand up. Hickey stopped in front of Holbrook and the remains.

"Morning, Chief."

"Morning, Doc. Seems we've had ourselves an attack."

Dr. Hickey looked down at the pile of chopped meat, and his eyes went wide. "Shark?" It was more of an expressed hope than a suggestion.

"I was hoping you could tell me, Doc."

Dr. Hickey squatted down, hovering over the heap of gore that was once Morty Sandberg. "Do you know him?"

"Morty Sandberg," said Holbrook.

"Don't know him." Dr. Hickey slipped on a pair of gloves.

Holbrook shook his head. "Retiree. Lives with his wife on Neptune St."

Dr. Hickey began to manipulate the remains, examining the bite marks. "Small bite radius. Maybe a juvenile bull shark."

Holbrook shook his head. "Not common in these waters. Possible, but not likely."

Dr. Hickey furrowed his brow. "You don't think…?"

"C'mon, Doc. You and I know those teeth marks are human."

Dr. Hickey sighed. "Only one way to find out." He knew what had to be done. Protocol Z. "I'll get this all wrapped up and meet you at the morgue."

Holbrook nodded. "Right-o." Then to Cochran, "Mac, I want the beaches closed until further notice."

Cochran shook his head. "The fourth is coming up."

Holbrook sucked his teeth. "Jesus Christ, Cochran, this isn't *Jaws*. It isn't the Fourth yet. We're still in the off season, so it shouldn't be a big hassle. I'm talking twenty-four hours. If the remains pass Protocol Z, the beaches can open right back up, you guys can throw up red flags to keep everyone out of the water, and we'll send up another shark copter."

Cochran put his hands on his hips. "If it fails?"

"Then we have a big problem on our hands."

21

Within minutes, the remains were carefully gathered, packed, and brought to the medical examiner's van, all before foot traffic began to pick up on the boardwalk.

*

Under the boardwalk, little April crouched in the midst of several feral cats, her brain foggy but her eyes alert. She watched the group of officials on the beach from the shadows, failing to register what was happening. The virus had already taken hold and was coursing through her veins like greased lightning, her young, healthy circulatory system helping it along.

She knew enough to stay hidden, at least until the official-looking men all left the beach. She placed a hand on her stomach as she wheezed, her stomach lurching from a primal hunger that she hadn't known before.

Soon, she would have to feed, and something in the primal recesses of her reptilian brain told her she needed to make more of her.

All viruses had their primary and secondary directives—sustain and reproduce.

* * *

Lenny stood at the edge of the motel pool next to the ghost of Billy, gazing down into the water. It wasn't really the ghost of Billy, but Lenny imagined his late friend as a ghost or imaginary friend of sorts for company, and mostly because he missed his friend. He forgave him for what he did to Officer Joann.

Although the surface was still, and the water clear, all Lenny could picture was his mother at the bottom, walking around, as he had heard his Aunt Patricia describe it once.

He missed Alice. He never referred to her as his mom or mother because he was not a kid, and only kids had moms. Moms told kids to brush their teeth and take a bath. He was an adult, had been for quite some time, and she had become his close friend. This was a common sentiment amongst those with Down Syndrome.

As he gazed into the water, he missed his friend. He even allowed the word 'mom' to pop ever so briefly into his mind before shooing it away.

Now his Aunt Patricia told him to brush his teeth and take a bath, but that was okay because she wasn't his mom. And he wasn't a kid. He was a grown-up.

"Lenny!" It was Mallory, one of his cousins. She was working at the motel for the summer to earn some money before returning to college.

Lenny smiled. He liked his cousin Mallory. She was pretty and nice to him.

"Lenny, Mom wants to talk to you in the front office."

He winced at the word, wondering why Mallory would use that word when she wasn't a kid. She went to college. Lenny knew that it was the school you went to after high school, but having never been, his concept of college was left to his imagination.

His mind's eye conjured up images of vast classrooms the size of ballrooms, lined with bookcases running from floor to ceiling, where students learned about all kinds of things like science and history, and there were vending machines containing every type of tasty treat he wasn't allowed to have...

"Lenny, did you hear me? Mom wants to see you."

He nodded and winked. "Okie-dokie."

Dressed in dark pants and a short-sleeved white button-down shirt for work (because Dr. Tara drilled into him the importance of being a professional), he marched over to and into the office. His aunt was examining the oak tag chart of the month's reservations.

Last year, a television show about helping hotel owners modernize and become more efficient had shot a segment at their hotel. Lenny remembered the mean man had made fun of his Aunt Patricia's oak tag system, and she had told him to go jump in a lake. Lenny had reminded her that there was either the ocean or the bay. The man left, and other than some cosmetic upgrades, operations had remained unchanged. His aunt said they made some money for doing the show, so it hadn't been a total waste.

"I'm here, Patricia." He didn't use her title of aunt when addressing her, because it made her like an adult and him like a kid. If he said 'Patricia,' it made them both adults.

She looked up from her large chart. "Lenny, did you remember to take out the garbage in the back building?" She already knew the answer. The question was more a prompt than an inquiry.

Lenny thought about it for a moment and snapped his fingers. "I will do it now."

Patricia smiled. "Great. Thanks, Lenny. You can go do that now."

Lenny gave her a thumbs up and whistled a jaunty tune as he stepped back out of the office. As it was late June and still off-season, the motel was mostly empty, except for a few guests and the annual Prescott family reunion. He greeted a few early risers cordially as they emerged from their rooms for breakfast.

Lenny's now imaginary friend Billy addressed them as well, tipping his baseball cap, as he wasn't dressed as Lava Man's sidekick Magma Boy at the moment. As they made their way across the grounds to the newer back building, Lenny snuck a brief conversation with Billy, something that Dr. Tara and his Aunt Patricia had both discouraged.

Lenny briefly discussed their plan to foil Doctor Industry, the evil mad scientist bent on destroying the environment. Lenny tied the nefarious doctor's activities to the appearance of the dead two years prior, figuring they were likely the twisted result of some horrific experiment.

When he reached the first garbage pail, he ceased all discussion as his other cousin, Lucy, was manning the back office. If she saw him talking to Billy, he'd get an earful from his Aunt Patricia about how there was no one there and how badly it looked that he was conversing with no one.

Dr. Tara had agreed that it was unprofessional, the flipside to his favorite catchword (other than 'Super'), 'professional.' So, most of the time, Lenny agreed to suspend all conversations with Billy until after work.

Lenny tore the lid off the one garbage can, and grabbed the edges of the plastic bag. There was the faint smell of garbage as he tied the bag off, noticing the new siding behind the pail. He didn't like the new siding because it didn't match the old siding exactly, but after the superstorm, the entire first floor of each building had to be redone. That meant new carpeting, new furniture, new sheet rock, and yes, new siding.

The smell reminded him of the dead. Not that they smelled like garbage, but they stunk of something else…death. Decay. His mind wandered back to that day the dead invaded Smuggler's Bay when he found all of those people and brought them to the second floor of the hotel.

*

Two Years Prior

Lenny paced back and forth in his room on the first floor, sloshing through the water as Dr. Tara and her boy Tyrell sat on his bed. He heard car horns, the screeching of tires, and police sirens outside. And shrieking. That awful screech the dead made.

"Lenny, we can't stay here." Tara looked terrified, and she was clutching her son. She was looking down at the rising water and then back at Lenny. She was looking to him for help. "Lenny, we need to get to a safer place."

Lenny stopped pacing and frowned as he thought. "I have a h-h-hiding place."

Tara leaned forward, loosening her grip on Tyrell. "Good. Where?"

Lenny pointed up at the ceiling. "Upstairs."

"Is it safe?"

He nodded without hesitation. "It is my s-s-secret spot."

"Anywhere's got to be better than here." She grabbed Tyrell by the shoulders and turned him to face her. She met his gaze. "Listen to me. We have to move. It's too dangerous here."

Tyrell looked less terrified than she estimated he should given the circumstances, but she was grateful for that. "I know, Mom."

Lenny placed an index finger up, signaling them to wait. He threw open the sliding door to his closet and reached towards the back, producing a Lava Man cape and cowl. He quickly tied the red plastic cape around his neck and slipped on the red cowl with a large 'M' on the forehead.

Tyrell smiled. "Cool."

Tara stepped forward, now grabbing Lenny by the shoulders. Lenny didn't like this. "Lenny, we have to go now." Then she said out loud to no one in particular, "We need something we can use as weapons."

Lenny and Tyrell simultaneously began to look around the room. Lenny reached back into the closet, bent at the waist, leaning so far inside that only his legs remained outside.

He heard Tyrell say, "Here, Mom!"

Then he heard Tara answer, "I suppose we can use it to put some distance between us and one of those things."

As if on cue, there was a loud screech not too far outside the room they were in.

Lenny pulled out a large, metal replica of a sword with a black and purple hilt, the blade polished and shiny. However, the edges were dull.

"Cooool," said Tyrell in admiration.

"From the m-m-movie D-Dracula!" Lenny announced proudly.

Tara shrugged her shoulders. "I suppose that could be used as a club...of sorts."

Lenny saw that Tyrell had a broom, and he gave him the 'A-Okay' sign.

Tara looked around and then at Lenny's closet. She pushed Lenny aside and dove right in.

Lenny and Tyrell exchanged looks and shrugged their shoulders.

Tara was yanking on something, lifting and pulling, grunting with exertion as she pulled the metal crossbar on which all of Lenny's hangers were hung. His clothes spilled to the ground as Tara hefted the metal pipe, holding it out in front of her to gauge its length and weight.

Lenny frowned at the mess she left in his closet. "You shouldn't have done that. S-s-someone is going to have t-t-to clean that up." The insinuation was that it wasn't going to be him.

Ignoring Lenny's rebuke, Tara took a couple of practice swings with the metal pipe. "Yeah, this'll do." She looked at Lenny. "Let's go."

They opened Lenny's door slowly, and Tara peeked out into the hotel parking lot. Guests were running back and forth, scurrying around as the dead chased after them.

She pulled her head inside as a guest ran past, clutching a bloody bite on his arm. Two doors down, the dead had forced their way into someone's room, and there were screams coming from inside. Human screams.

Tara looked back to Lenny and Tyrell. "Okay, we go now."

Lenny and Tyrell, hefting their respective sword and broom, nodded and bunched up behind Tara. Tara held her metal pipe in her right hand and grabbed Tyrell's hand with her left, and she yanked him outside behind her.

The three dashed out of the room, clinging to the side of the building, as they witnessed the mass carnage of the dead overrunning the hotel. There were people lying on the ground, their bodies twitching, as the dead tore chunks of flesh from their bodies in a ghastly feeding frenzy.

Tara yanked Tyrell close to her. "Look at me, sweetie! Don't look out there! Look at me!"

He nodded, terrified, but he had already seen more than he was able to handle.

Tara pulled him forward, Lenny following behind them. "Lead the way, Lenny!"

Lenny jumped in front and stalked over to the stairs, this time Tara and Tyrell in tow. Fortunately, none of the dead in the parking lot had noticed them.

Lenny rounded the corner when a pair of bloodied hands reached out for him and grabbed him by the neck. The zombie let out a screech and, eyes wide, snapped its jaws at him.

Tara and Tyrell both screamed as Lenny stumbled backwards, falling to the ground. The zombie, a middle-aged woman in a tattered, gore-stained sundress, landed on top of him, craning her neck to reach his face. Her teeth snapped millimeters from the tip of his nose as he cried out.

Tara shoved Tyrell up against the wall and lunged forward, swing her pipe at the zombie's head. It hit, and there was a dull thud of impact as the reverberations shook Tara's wrists, but the zombie kept snapping its teeth at Lenny.

Tara swung two more times, the third strike causing the zombie to go inert. Lenny pushed it off of him, grimacing in disgust as it lay next to him twitching.

"Mom!"

Tara turned around to find another zombie, a small boy, reaching out for her son. Tyrell was shoving it away with the bristled end of his broom as it swiped jagged fingernails at him.

Tara, ever the tiger mom, sprang at the child in all of her maternal fury, shoving it off of her son with her hand. It staggered backwards but maintained its footing. It let out a high-pitched howl, narrowed its wild eyes, and ran forward, hands outstretched as it chomped down on its own tongue in bloodlust.

Tara swung at it, connecting with its jaw, sending it into the wall of the building. It righted itself, undeterred and jaw dislocated, and lurched at Tara again. This time, she brought her metal pipe straight down on top of its head. Its small skull crunched under her strike, and the zombie boy fell to the ground, still.

She wheeled around, but neither Tyrell nor Lenny were there. Panicked and fearing the worst, Tara searched the parking lot. "Tyrell!"

A zombie woman shrieked back at her in response and started making a Bee Line for her through the melee.

"Mommy! Up here!"

Tara turned around and saw that Lenny and Tyrell were at the top of the stairs. A wave of relief washed over her but was quickly replaced with urgency. She dashed towards the staircase to the second floor of the back building as the woman zombie was closing the distance.

Tara took two stairs at a time, looking through the open slats of the staircase, as she saw a car popping the curb and hurtling towards the stairs. She reached out, and Lenny grabbed both of her hands as the car took out both the staircase beneath her feet and the zombie woman in one fell swoop. Lenny pulled her up and onto the second floor.

As Tara lay there, catching her breath, Tyrell looked down at her. "Are you okay, Mom?" He was standing next to Lenny's Dracula sword.

She smiled sweetly at him. "I'm okay, honey."

Lenny helped her to her feet. She hugged him, catching him off guard. He smiled and hugged her back, closing his eyes.

"Thank you, Lenny."

He opened his eyes. "I will protect you. The both of you."

They broke the embrace. All three of them looked down at the broken staircase and then over the railing on the other side.

Someone popped his head out of his room a few doors down. "Get out of here! You'll draw them here!"

Tara turned, as she controlled her flash of anger, and she mustered some of that clinical calm. She shook her head. "A car took out the staircase."

"Yeah? What about the other side?" asked the man.

Shit. She turned to Tyrell and Lenny. "He's right. We have to destroy the other staircase."

"How?" asked Tyrell.

Tara looked determined. "The same way. Lenny, take Tyrell to your hiding place. I'm going to drive a car into the other one."

"H-h-how will you get back up?" asked Lenny.

Tara thought for a minute. "Lenny, grab me a sheet. When I crash a car into the stairs, you need to lower the sheet like a rope and pull me back up."

Tyrell grabbed his mother. "No, Mommy. Don't go."

"I have to, sweetie, or they'll get up here and we're all dead."

"You're crazy, lady!" shouted the man poking his head out, and he pulled it back inside his room, slamming the door closed.

Lenny nodded. He knocked on the door closest to them. When there was no answer, he produced his skeleton key and opened it. They entered the room, and Tara pulled a sheet off the nearest bed. She handed it to Lenny. "Here. Lower this. I'll grab it, and you'll pull me up."

Lenny nodded, dubious about his strength to accomplish this important task. He weighed about as much as Tara. He'd have to put his back into it.

Billy appeared next to him in superhero sidekick uniform. "You can do it, Lava Man!"

Tara, not able to see Lenny's imaginary friend, turned to Tyrell. "I'm going to lock you in here. Don't come out for anyone."

"No, Mommy, don't!"

"I'm going to knock when I come back." She brushed the vertical blinds aside with a swipe of her right hand. "You peek out to make sure it's me, and only me. Then you open the door."

"Don't go, Mommy, please. Please!"

Tara knelt down and looked him in the eye. "I don't have time to argue. When I knock, you check to make sure it's me."

Tyrell nodded, but his eyes pleaded with her not to go.

Tara pulled Lenny outside of the room. She reached inside, turned the lock on the doorknob, and pulled the door shut, testing the door knob. It was locked.

Lenny looked past Tara and saw that two zombies had made it up the second staircase. He pointed at them. "Look!"

Tara turned and saw them as gunfire erupted below. The police were engaging the dead, but they were being overrun. "Stay close, Lenny!"

She hefted the pipe as the two walking corpses saw her and cried out in savage hunger.

She shook her head. "No good." She turned to Lenny. "Give me the Dracula sword. Hurry!"

Lenny held it out, and Tara snatched it from him, shoving her pipe into his hands. The two zombies were almost on her, but the common balcony was only wide enough for one of them, so they came at her in single file.

She hefted the sword, its weight emboldening her. "Yeah. Let's go."

She ran forward, pushing the long blade in front of her, its point finding purchase in the first zombie's chest. She shoved hard. The tip being dull, it only sank in about an inch. She pushed forward with all of her might, putting her back into it, and the first zombie fell backwards, taking the one behind it down with it.

Tara wasted no time. She stood over the first—a bald, older man—placing her foot on its neck as it glared up at her. It tried to screech, but Tara was crushing its windpipe. She brought the pointy end of the sword down into its mouth hard and twisted the wide blade, dislocating its jaw.

The second zombie, a teenage girl with blonde hair matted in blood, reached up for her with wild hands. She allowed it to grab her ankle. As it tried to pull itself up, it opened its mouth for a blood-curdling screech. However, Tara jammed the sword into its mouth and twisted, cutting its blood-thirsty battle cry short and dislocating its jaw like she did with the first zombie.

Tara stepped over it, shaking her right leg free of its grip as its jaw hung off to the side, unable to clamp down. "It's okay, Lenny. They can't bite you now. Follow me!"

Lenny stuttered, unable to voice his doubt about the neutralized threat and his reluctance to step over the two zombies, but Tara had already taken off and was down the other staircase.

He looked down at the dead with their dislocated jaws, scrambling around on the floor to regain their footing. They were more of a threat on their feet, so Lenny summoned his courage, seeing himself in his Lava Man costume in the reflection on the large window to his right. He puffed up his chest and decided to make a go of it.

He gingerly began to step over the first zombie. It reached out and grabbed his legs. Lenny whimpered as it mouthed his ankles, but it was unable to bite down. He kicked his leg free and began to negotiate the second zombie, which also grabbed him and attempted to bite down but was unable.

Lenny shook his legs free, one at a time, as he climbed over the heap, wincing at the wetness on his ankles as they salivated all over him. Just when he thought he was free, he made to dash down the lane when the second zombie grabbed his ankle, causing him to fall flat on his face. Tara's metal pipe clanged on the ground just in front of him.

He felt the two zombies crawling up his legs, pulling themselves over his prone body, gurgling and growling, dragging their limp jaws over his pant legs. He heard gagging and retching sounds. Lenny cried out as he felt wetness land on the backs of his thighs and then his back. He pushed himself off the ground with both hands as blood and bile pooled under him.

The rabid dead clung to him like barnacles as he began to crawl, a now stained sheet clutched in his right hand, dragging behind him and dripping with blood. Tears streamed down his face with terror, exertion, and an overwhelming feeling of helplessness as the dead clung on.

Lenny heard gun shots on the street below, screams of terror, and the shrieks of the dead as he commando crawled, succumbing to the weight of his unwanted passengers. Suddenly, the weight became inexplicably lighter, and he was able to push himself to his knees and then his feet.

As he looked over his shoulder, he saw two men dragging the two creatures away from him by their ankles. One of his saviors was that man who popped his head out his room and yelled at Tara.

He wanted to thank the men, who worked together in hoisting the monsters up and tossing them over the railing to the street below.

However, he was interrupted by a crash coming from the staircase on the other side. The impact jarred the whole building. A car horn blared, as if someone was leaning on it.

Lenny shambled over to the other end of the second floor as the car horn stopped, and he looked down at the ruined staircase. Tara stumbled out of the car, its front end smashed, clutching her forehead. When she pulled her hand away, her fingers were covered in blood.

She looked up at Lenny. "Lower the sheet!"

Lenny looked down at the blood and bile-stained sheet in his hands and snapped out of it. Holding the dry end in his hands (he didn't want to touch the pungent fluids), he lowered the other towards Tara.

"Tie it to the railing!" she directed from below as she looked around nervously. The car she commandeered blocked her off from the street, but her back was vulnerable to the parking lot.

Lenny tied his end of the sheet to the railing at the top of the demolished staircase. The sheet wasn't long enough to reach down to Tara, so she climbed onto the trunk of the car and stood on the roof.

The two men who tossed the zombies over the railing ran over to Lenny.

"What the hell are you doing?" asked the impatient one who yelled at Tara.

"He's trying to help her!" said the other, pointing down to Tara. "She took out the stairs!"

Tara grabbed her end of the sheet, tied it into a knot, and grabbed the knot. "Pull me up!"

Both men grabbed the sheet and began to pull. However, a few of the dead were now piling on top of the trunk of Tara's car, and one grabbed her ankle.

She felt her grip slide in all of the slimy muck on the sheet, and Lenny and the two men above almost lost their grip. Lenny, having been pulled forward, almost fell off the edge and right on top of Tara.

The impatient man shoved Lenny aside to safety, and both men began to pull. Lenny looked down as another zombie grabbed her other ankle, eager to enter into this game of tug of war, the prize being a hot lunch.

Tara screamed as her fingers clung to the knot she made, her legs dangling. She kicked and swung her feet every which way as the dead grabbing her began to lose their grip on her ankles.

All she could do was think of Tyrell, hiding in his room. She needed to be there to protect him. Failure was not an option.

She looked down as she saw one of the zombie's fingernails peel away, and it lost its grip. It fell sideways into the other one, causing it to lose its grip, and Tara was finally free.

Lenny looked on, his hands over his mouth in horror, as the two men hoisted her up. He was ashamed that he wasn't able to do what she instructed and help. "I'm s-s-so s-s-s-sorry," he repeated over and over.

Tara got to her feet, dusting herself off. She placed a hand on his shoulder. "Lenny, you did just fine."

This made him feel a bit better, and Tara thanked the other two men who saved her life.

"I'm sorry I yelled at you before," said the impatient man, now looking sheepish.

Tara smiled. "You saved my life, so now we're even." Then, as if suddenly remembering, "Tyrell!"

She pushed through Lenny and the other two men and dashed down to Tyrell's room. Lenny followed right behind her. She knocked three times on the door, and Tyrell's face appeared in the window. He looked relieved, until he saw the gash on her head.

He opened the door and hugged her hard, nearly causing her to lose her balance. "You came back!" he cried into her shirt, his tears wet and hot.

"You sound surprised," she quipped, smiling at him when he finally released her.

"I helped," added Lenny, who was standing in the doorway.

"You're hurt," Tyrell said, his relief turning to concern.

Tara walked over to the sink area and grabbed a clean towel, dabbing her gash and then applying pressure. "I'll be all right. I think we all will for the time being."

They returned outside, and more guests of the second floor had come out of their rooms to survey the situation. The two men who helped Tara were now standing with their wives and children as they explained to everyone how Tara had taken out both staircases.

Tara received looks of gratitude, and Lenny stood there with Tyrell, feeling ineffective and powerless. However, as time passed, the survivors on the second and third floors needed water. As bathrooms were used, toilets were clogged and people ran out of toilet paper.

While lacking in physical prowess and quick thinking in a crisis, Lenny found himself doing what he did best. Lenny did his job. He went into the supply closets, which were the hiding places he had referred to down in his room, and got extra plastic disposable cups out for the guests so that they could have water from the tap. He shared his secret stash of bags of chips and cookies with the children, staving off hunger for a while. He walked around with a plunger, unclogging toilets. As hours passed, he even made beds and brought fresh towels, anything to make the guests more comfortable as long as supplies lasted.

When the National Guard retook the town and found the camp of survivors on the second and third floors, the guests had related what Tara did to keep them safe. Additionally, and to Lenny's surprise, they spoke of how he kept them comfortable and took good care of them.

Lenny was a hero after all.

*

As Lenny slipped out of his private reverie, he felt heartened. Dr. Tara always told him that he had to focus on the positives about what happened that summer. He had to focus on how everyone pulled together and helped each other. Lenny understood this. The townspeople's goodness trumped the horror of the dead, and the town rebuilt.

His hotel continued to operate, and he still had a job. Dr. Tara said his mother would've been proud of him. Lenny smiled to himself and tackled the rest of the morning chores in earnest.

CHAPTER 3

Marie Russo smiled at Tyrell as he was folding T-shirts. "Your mom taught you well."

Tyrell pulled down the corner of his mouth. "Yeah, well, it's just me and Mom now, so I have to pitch in."

"Have you asked your mom about coming to the gun range yet?"

Tyrell paused for a moment, knowing the sermon that was to come. He continued folding again. It was the same sermon he got almost every day he worked at Ms. Russo's store. "Not yet."

Marie regarded him with sympathy and walked over to him, placing a hand on his shoulder. Her grip was firm, and her eyes intent. "I know she's not a big fan of guns, even after the attack two years ago."

Tyrell met her gaze. "Nothing's going to change her mind."

"She should learn how to defend herself, and you."

"My mom doesn't like guns. It's against her philosophy."

Against her philosophy? Spoken like the son of a head shrink. Marie felt her indignation well up in her chest. She didn't understand that mentality, particularly after what happened. Tara lost her husband to the dead. She almost lost her son.

She took a deep breath and let it out, reminding herself that she wasn't talking to Tara. She was talking to her son, and it wasn't his fault.

Tyrell sensed her exasperation and became totally absorbed in his task, avoiding eye contact.

Marie winked at him and smiled. "I'll talk to your mom when she picks you up later."

"She'll get mad at me," he said, still avoiding eye contact. His skin felt hot, and it wasn't entirely from the temperature. "She won't want me to come here anymore."

Marie smiled, and her grip on Tyrell's shoulder softened. "Nonsense. There's nowhere else for you to go. Plus, you do such an amazing job here."

Tyrell smiled at that, but in the back of his mind various scenarios where Marie broached the topic of going to the gun range played out, each iteration ending in his mother being pissed off.

He was in a difficult position. He, of course, sided with his mother. After all, she was his mom. But, he respected Marie. She was tough and strong. So was his mom, but in a different kind of way.

Marie decided to let it drop, and she disappeared into the back room. Salvatore came over and helped Tyrell with the folding. "She's right, you know. It can't hurt to know how to defend yourself."

Alessandra shot him a reproachful look. "Mom is being too pushy. It's none of her business."

"She only means well, Ali," snapped Salvatore.

Great, thought Tyrell. Now he was caught between Marie's two children arguing over guns. The whole topic just made him sick to his stomach. He thought about his dad, and how they used to fly kites on the beach. How they used to do homework together. How they used to wrestle in the living room. Then he thought of his father, dead, lunging at him like a rabid animal.

"We haven't seen any of…them in two years," said Alessandra.

Salvatore snickered. "That doesn't mean they're gone."

Alessandra pursed her lips. "The police are cooperating with the CDC and the military. I heard Mom talking about it with Mr. Guarnucci. They'll protect us."

"Yeah, right. Like they did before. The CDC doesn't know what they're doing. The government is inept."

Alessandra wagged a finger at her brother. "We'd be dead if it wasn't for Chief Holbrook and the National Guard. All of us."

Salvatore laughed at her faith in government. "They almost let the virus spread to the mainland."

"Yeah, but they didn't."

"Blind luck. If it ever happened again, God forbid, I don't think they're prepared or equipped to stop it again."

Alessandra threw her hands down at her sides, her palms slapping her legs, and turned on Salvatore. "Blind luck? What about Tyrell's dad? What about our dad? Do they feel lucky?"

Salvatore put up his hands defensively. "Hey, that's not what I meant."

Alessandra stared her brother down, undeterred. "What about the hundreds of people who lost their lives? Were they lucky? They were torn apart like fresh meat, eaten alive by the dead. Does that sound lucky to you?"

Marie, perhaps overhearing the contentious tones, re-emerged from the stock room. She looked at Tyrell, the expression on his face, and then her son. Alessandra looked pissed. "What's going on here? What are you guys arguing about?"

Tyrell dropped his gaze to the floor. "I have to get some fresh air. I don't feel so well."

Marie shot Salvatore a dirty look, to which he replied, "What? What did I do?"

Head hanging low, Tyrell shuffled out of the store and walked down the boardwalk to the nearest public restroom, avoiding the small washroom Marie had in the back.

"You need to leave him alone," said Alessandra. "The both of you."

Marie glared at her son, and then her expression softened. "She's right, Sal. No more talk about guns or the range. Got it?"

Salvatore nodded and then looked down at the ground. He had heard this debate many times before between residents of the Bay. He had heard it in his mother's store, out at restaurants, and on local television. He even heard it in school, where his classmates mirrored their parents' stance on the matter, regurgitating their reasoning.

New Jersey wasn't exactly a gun-friendly state. However, Smuggler's Bay wasn't typical New Jersey. The business owners in town were mostly Republican and were pro-gun, even more so after the attack. Many of them kept guns in their homes. Some had always done so, while others were new converts. Others in town, like Tara, were Democrats espousing gun control. To them, the attack had little to no impact on this belief. However, there were fewer and fewer of them over the last two years.

*

Down the boardwalk, Tyrell slipped into the closest public restroom and stood in front of the sink. He opened the faucet and splashed cool water on his face. He remembered the summer after the storm. The town hadn't fixed up the bathrooms yet. Instead, they had focused on repairing and replacing sections of damaged boardwalk.

His right hand trembled as it closed the faucet, cutting off the water. He decided right then and there that he was going to broach the subject with his mother, if only to put the topic to rest. He was getting tired of hearing about it at Marie's store. She would either consider it, or he wasn't going to go back to the store.

Emboldened by his conviction, he marched out of the bathroom and decided to apply for a job at whatever store or stand would have him. Not an official job, as he was too young, but maybe somewhere where he could help out.

He looked right and then left, and his eyes settled on Cantone's Pizzeria. Vinnie was a nice guy. Maybe he'd let Tyrell wipe down tables or something.

He walked up the boardwalk to the pizzeria and saw Vinnie wiping down the kitchen area. His father, Marco, was in the back fiddling with the ancient air conditioning unit.

As Tyrell approached the stand, Vinnie looked up. When he saw him, he smiled. "Hey, Tyrell. Wassup?"

Tyrell thrust his hands into his shorts pockets and leaned up against the glass counter. "Hey, Vinnie. How's it going?"

"It's going. What can I do for you? It's a little early for a slice."

"Yeah, I mean, no. I don't want a slice."

"Oh? What's going on?"

"Can I talk to you?"

Vinnie's smile faded, and he started to look concerned. "Sure. Everything okay?"

"Yeah, I just need to ask you a question."

Vinnie waved him inside. "C'mon. We'll grab a booth in the back. Step into my office."

Tyrell entered the store and joined Vinnie, who stepped from behind the counter. Vinnie called to his father, "Dad, I need to talk to Tyrell for a minute."

Marco looked up from his futile effort, looked at the expression on Tyrell's face, and threw his hands up. "This damned thing is hopeless. Why couldn't the storm take this damned antique? Then the insurance company could've gotten me a brand new one."

Vinnie shook his head in disapproval. "Dad, we're lucky we still have the shop."

Marco looked at Tyrell and softened. Here he is, complaining about air conditioning, and this poor kid lost his dad. "Yeah. Yeah, I guess you're right." He went up front by the registers and continued the chore of wiping everything down.

Vinnie went all the way to the back for privacy and slid into a booth. Tyrell slid in across from him, sitting with his hands folded.

"What's on your mind?" asked Vinnie.

"Maybe I could help out."

"Help out?"

"Yeah, you know, here."

"You mean you want a job?"

"Kinda."

Vinnie smiled, amused. "Aren't you working for Marie Russo, helping her out in her store?"

"Yeah. But, she's driving me crazy."

Vinnie gestured to his father up front, who was already preparing the dough. "Yeah, well he's no bargain to work with either. Besides, don't you want to be with your friends, Sal and Ali?"

Tyrell hesitated, knowing it was rude to badmouth other adults behind their backs, but he felt comfortable confiding in Vinnie. Vinnie was a kid, like him. Kind of. "Mrs. Russo is driving me nuts about guns."

Vinnie cracked another smile. "Yeah, she's become a real gun nut. She thinks she's Rambo."

Tyrell scrunched up his nose. "Who's Rambo?"

Vinnie shook his head. "Never mind. Continue."

"Well, she wants my mom to learn how to shoot. Me, too. She said she'd teach me how to shoot a rifle."

"That's pretty hardcore. What does your mom think about that?"

"She talked with my mom about guns once. My mom hates guns."

"Hmm. I'm surprised. Your mom was a bad ass when the attack happened. I heard she took out zombies with a replica sword."

Tyrell looked down at the table. "She killed my dad."

Vinnie leaned forward. "Hey, look at me." Tyrell met Vinnie's eyes. "Your mother had to do it to protect you. Besides, he wasn't your dad anymore." Vinnie thought of the pounding on the metal gates in the arcade and the moans of the dead. "He was a monster. Something evil that needed to be destroyed."

Tyrell frowned. "He was still my dad."

"Listen, if you want, I can talk to Marie for you. Get her off your back."

Tyrell's expression brightened. "You'd do that for me?"

Vinnie put out his fist. "Anything for you, bro."

Tyrell bumped it.

"Now you'd better get back to the store, or Marie will coming looking for you…guns blazing."

Tyrell looked stunned, as if Marie hunting him down toting guns might have been a real possibility.

"Tyrell, I was joking about that last part."

Tyrell exhaled in relief.

"Now scram."

Tyrell jumped up and darted out of the pizzeria. He passed through the air conditioning of the pizzeria and into the bright light of the boardwalk when someone collided with him.

"I'm sorry," Tyrell began to say, but his voice trailed off as he saw a little girl standing there with a devilish grin. It was an unnatural grin that contorted her face in a disconcerting way. It appeared that she had smeared lipstick or ketchup on her mouth. Her eyes were distant, yet alert, an unsettling contradiction.

The girl sounded like she was wheezing.

Tyrell took a step back. "Are you okay?"

The little girl didn't answer.

Tyrell looked around, and she appeared unaccompanied by any adults. Her clothing was damp and covered in sand.

"Where are your parents?"

Still no response. Just that unnerving grin and the gravelly sound her breathing made.

"Okay…" Tyrell backed away slowly and turned to walk back to Marie's store. After he took a few steps, he turned around, but the little girl was gone.

* * *

Chief Holbrook sat on a metal stool inside the morgue, watching Dr. Hickey lay out the remains of Morty Sandberg on the shiny metal table. Holbrook looked around. The whole room was metallic, except for the rubber hoses and glassware. It left him with a bad taste in his mouth.

"Okay," said Dr. Hickey, grabbing a digital voice recorder. "The remains are covered in bite marks, consistent with a human bite radius. There are bites about the face, arms, legs, torso, and buttocks." He shined a small flashlight at the head, illuminating the hole. "There is an open head injury; most of the brain tissue is missing."

He took a long metal probe and began poking inside the skull. "Most of the frontal cortex is missing, part of the cerebellum remains. The brain stem appears mostly intact."

He looked over at Holbrook, who was watching intently. "You okay, Chief?"

Holbrook's expression was all business. "Don't worry about me, Doc. Continue."

Dr. Hickey nodded. "Initiating Protocol Z. The time is currently 9:53am. The body was discovered at approximately 8:20am." He backed away from the table, sat on a metal stool, and watched the body like Holbrook.

The two watched the body together in silence, Holbrook with his hand on his gun. That was what Protocol Z was. Nothing fancy or high-tech. The Department of Health instructed town officials that if remains were found, they were to be taken back to the morgue, the trauma noted and catalogued, and observed for movement within four hours.

That was how long it took a deceased person to reanimate. Those bitten but still alive and otherwise healthy took twenty-four to seventy-two hours to reanimate. It took longer because first the person had to succumb to death first.

There would be a prodromal phase, during which there would be drastic personality changes and uncharacteristic behavior—irritability, verbal aggression, acting out, violence. Some would exhibit socially unacceptable bodily functions, others would consume their own tongues or digits, others would taunt others and engage in self-injurious behavior. Then, eventually, the body died. Within minutes, the body would reanimate.

"Doc, you've been to all the conferences."

Dr. Hickey clasped his hands in his lap and nodded. "DOH, FEMA, Department of Emergency Management."

"That's right. Are there any theories on where the Z virus came from?"

"Well, they traced patient zero back to the dementia ward of a nursing home."

"Sophia Russo."

"Yes, that's correct. The current thinking is that it's some kind of opportunistic infection that attacks compromised brain tissue."

Holbrook shook his head. "But it was transmitted to non-elderly, uncompromised brains."

"Yes, but that's not where it originated. The compromised brain riddled with the plaques that caused dementia was the first step, where it was allowed to incubate."

Holbrook still had his hand on his gun. "It mutated?"

"Possibly. The life cycle is rapid, only a matter of minutes as it reproduces. It's possible to have mutations between generations."

"I'm sensing an 'or'…"

Dr. Hickey sighed. "Or, it could have developed. Matured into what it became."

"So where did it come from?"

"If the government knows, they're not sharing it. Could be a naturally occurring pathogen, like Zica. It may even be a variant of Zica."

"But we haven't heard of Zica until recently."

"It doesn't mean it wasn't out there prior, in one form or another, Chief. Symptoms and cause of death are similar. Acute polyneuropathy, Guillain-Barré syndrome. Only the Z virus works much faster and is much more lethal."

"And it reanimates dead tissue," added Holbrook.

"Yes, there's that."

Four hours passed without incident. There was nothing as much as a twitch from the remains. Dr. Hickey took several digital photos of the body. Holbrook's stomach was grumbling.

"I'm calling it," said Dr. Hickey. "Half past noon. No positive indicators of reanimation."

Holbrook stood and stretched, his hand now away from his gun. "So, that's it? This wasn't a zombie attack?"

Dr. Hickey stood over the remains, thinking. "That's one possibility. The other is that there might not have been enough of the brain left to allow reanimation."

"So we could still have a zombie roaming around Smuggler's Bay."

"Or a few. Or several."

"Jesus, Doc."

"I'll call it in to the DOH and treat the remains." That meant sterilization.

Holbrook put his cap back on. "I'll need a few pics to show Morty's daughter. I've got the entire force searching for the missing granddaughter, April."

"Do you think she was…?"

"No evidence one way or the other yet. We'll have to wait and see."

"I'll load the pics up and send you a few," said Hickey. "You'll have it by the time you get to the Morty's house."

"Thanks, Doc." Holbrook left the sterile, metallic room and the morgue building. He slid into his car and turned the ignition. He paused for a moment.

He hated this part, informing people that their loved ones were deceased. After the attack, it became a full-time job for a month or so. What was worse was that the treatment of the remains after Protocol Z was sterilization and eventual cremation, so there was no closure for the individual's loved ones. No body to bury, no saying goodbye. Only a few digital pictures.

He put the car in gear and drove away. On his way, he jumped on the radio. "This is Chief Holbrook. We may have a possible Contagion Z Scenario, Phase One. I want everyone on high alert, Code Orange."

* * *

Nancy looked on as her ride operators filed into the gated pier, reporting to their stations after clocking in. They had received their assignments and took their stations, and the dormant rides sprung to life on Blackbeard's Pier.

Mike walked up next to her. "So, are you attending the town events committee meeting tonight?"

"Damned straight I am. I don't like the direction this town is going. It's bad enough that we turned into zombie central, but now they're talking about a rave. A damned rave."

"I don't know," Mike said with a shrug. "Maybe a rave isn't such a bad thing. It'll bring more youth to the Bay."

"Jesus, Mike! Do you hear yourself…Do you even know what a rave is?"

"I don't know. It sounds like a big party on the beach with music. Like a bigger version of the bonfire."

"It's nothing like the bonfire," Nancy snapped. "It's that weird electronic music and teenagers doing drugs and having sex. We don't want more teenagers. We want families."

"When did you become such a prude, Nance?"

"It'll be nothing but trouble for the Bay, and these teens won't be feeding any money into the businesses."

Mike put his hands on his hips. "Ah, and so we come to your real objection. You won't make any money off this event."

"That's beside the point," insisted Nancy. "That sort of thing is not us. It's not what the town is about."

"I don't know. It might not be so bad."

"Which is why you're managing the pier and I'm going to the meeting."

Mike pointed an admonishing finger. "Now you behave yourself, Nancy. Remember what happened at the last meeting?"

She pointed a finger back, stabbing Mike in the chest. "You don't tell me what to do, mister. And I was right about those drug addicts filling the motels." She stalked off in consternation, but not without shouting over her shoulder, "I'll see you at the bonfire. Make sure you put on a nice shirt."

Mike shrugged his shoulders. "I thought all my shirts were nice."

Nancy waved a dismissive hand and disappeared into the arcade.

Mike's attention was drawn towards a little girl crying, clutching her arm. She was being comforted by her mother, who was looking around, searching the crowd with an angry expression on her face.

* * *

Chief Holbrook pulled up to Morty's house in his cruiser and parked in front. He remembered something Morty told him a couple of days ago, about his daughter visiting from Bergen County. He stepped out, scanning the premises. There were lights on.

He drew a deep sigh and moseyed on up to the front door. He rang the doorbell and waited.

Marney opened the front door. She looked surprised to see him. "Chief Holbrook! What a surprise!"

"May I come in, Mrs. Traub?"

Her face fell. It wasn't just his failure to reciprocate her greeting. He called her Mrs. Traub. It sounded too official for her taste. "Something wrong, Chief?"

Holbrook looked up and down the block. "I think I need to come inside."

Marney backed away from the doorway, nearly tripping over her own feet. "Of course. Come in." She looked concerned.

He entered the house, and she stepped into the living room, gesturing to the sofa. "Please, have a seat."

Holbrook took his hat off but remained standing. "I'm afraid I have some terrible news."

Panic struck Marney's face. "Is it my dad? He's been gone all morning. He took my daughter April fishing."

Holbrook hated this part. "We found your father's body on the beach."

First Marney looked confused, then as if she wanted to speak, but her mouth opened and nothing came out. She began to tremble. "Body? You mean he's dead?"

"I'm afraid so."

Her eyes began to well up. She backed away, as if avoiding the news would somehow nullify it, stumbling over the arm of the love seat. She plopped down into it, tears streaming down her face. "Was it a heart attack?"

"No, ma'am. It appears he was attacked."

"Attacked?! Where's April? Is she all right?"

"We haven't found April yet, but I have every officer in the Bay looking for her as we speak."

"Who attacked him? Do you think she got away? Do you think she's all right?"

"We found bite marks all over your father's body. We haven't ruled out a shark attack or some kind of wild animal."

Marney looked incredulous, then angry. "Wild animal? Shark attack? He was fishing with April, not swimming in the ocean! What wild animal? What are you doing to find April?" She stood. "I need to go look for her."

Holbrook produced his cell phone and started calling up the pics of Morty's remains. "Like I said, Mrs. Traub, every officer in the Bay is looking for her. Since there was no body, we think she may have been frightened and ran away. She's probably somewhere on the boardwalk."

"Then that's where I'll be."

"I understand. I'll take you there myself. First, I need you to identify your father's remains." He offered her his cell.

She stared at it, reluctant to take it. "What about his body? Why are you showing me pictures?"

"We had to initiate Protocol Z, as a precaution."

"Protocol Z? Are you serious?" Her eyes narrowed. "I fucking knew it. I told Dad he should've moved after the attack. He didn't listen."

Holbrook placed the phone into her hand. "The results came back negative, but there was quite a bit of brain tissue missing. We're not completely ruling out a zombie attack."

Marney glanced down at the phone. She gasped and placed her other hand over her mouth when she saw her father. She shuddered as her brain struggled to register the information. She looked at the torn face. "That's my dad," she whispered.

"His remains are down at the morgue. According to state law, they will have to be cremated."

Marney stood, her mind racing, looking as if she didn't know what to do first. "Why wouldn't she run home? You would think she'd run home first, right? The boardwalk isn't that crowded. Why hasn't she been found? How come no one's seen her? I have to call my husband."

"That's a good idea."

Marney turned on Holbrook. "What are you doing here? Shouldn't you be looking for my April?"

"I was involved with handling your father's remains, as per Protocol Z. A senior law enforcement officer has to be present."

"According to state law." Her tone was bitter. "And how did state law prevent my father from being killed? How will state law prevent another attack?"

"Ma'am, we are doing everything we can to anticipate another attack and contain it, if this is the case. The important thing right now is that we find your daughter. Hopefully she's safe, and maybe she can tell us exactly what happened."

"So what are you doing standing here?"

"Mrs. Traub, I need you to send me a couple of recent pics of April, close-ups on her face."

Marney toggled through her photos on her phone. "I need your cell."

"Send it to my email." He gave her his email, and she sent two pics from a few days ago when they were on the boardwalk. He never gave out his cell. It was a small island, and he was harassed enough as it was. "What was she wearing this morning?"

"I don't know. They woke up before me…wait a minute! She set her clothes out on her desk in her room the night before. She knows my father starts out early, and she wanted to be ready." Marney thought for a moment, desperately trying to pull the memory from the back of her mind.

"Take your time."

She snapped her fingers. "Her pink shirt with dolphins, and her white shorts."

"That's good."

Her angry expression faded and was replaced with determination. "I have to call my husband. Then I'm combing the Bay myself."

"That's a good idea. Would you like me to be here while you call?"

Marney pulled out her cell and called up her husband's number. "No, that won't be necessary." She hit 'Send.'

Holbrook saw this as his exit. "I'll be in touch as soon as we find her." He didn't want to say 'if we find her.'

Marney turned her back on him as she spoke to her husband. Holbrook saw himself out.

* * *

It was midday, and the temperature had climbed to a hot eighty-eight degrees. Vinnie strolled up to the sunglass store. Dharma was behind the register, and her mother, Emily, was unpacking boxes. When Dharma saw him, she smiled. She stepped from behind the register, practically skipped over to Vinnie, and threw her arms around him. She kissed him sweetly on the mouth.

Vinnie blushed, and Emily did her best to ignore the public display of affection.

Dharma hooked her arm in his. "So, are you here to take me out to lunch?"

Vinnie, recovering from his embarrassment, looked over at Emily. "Hi, Mrs. Ross."

Emily glanced up. "Hello, Vincent." Then she continued to unpack boxes of faux designer sunglasses.

"So, where are we going?"

Vinnie was still pondering being called 'Vincent.' "Wherever you want. But first, I need you to help me with something."

"Mom, we're going to lunch!"

Emily kept at her work. "I heard."

Dharma grabbed Vinnie by the arm and pulled him out onto the boardwalk, where they walked arm-in-arm.

Vinnie frowned. "I don't think you mother likes me."

Dharma pulled him closer, squeezing his arm. "What are you talking about? She loves you!"

"I don't know. My mother calls me 'Vincent' whenever she's pissed at me."

Dharma shook her head. "My mother doesn't like the idea of losing me."

"Losing you? To what? I'm sure I'm not your first boyfriend."

Dharma arched an eyebrow. "Watch it, mister. You're treading on thin ice."

"That's not what I meant."

"I know. You are not my first boyfriend, but you're the first boyfriend I've kept this long."

"I'm honored."

"I think she knows it's serious, and it makes her a little nervous."

Vinnie smiled at this. He liked hearing Dharma refer to their relationship as serious. He didn't have many girlfriends prior, so this was special to him. He was glad Dharma felt the same way.

"So what was it that you needed my help for?"

Vinnie had nearly forgotten. "We need to speak to Marie Russo."

"You look serious. About what?"

"Tyrell came into the pizza shop earlier. You know he's been helping her at her store." Dharma nodded. "Well, she's been pressuring Tyrell to talk to his mom about learning how to shoot. She even offered to give him lessons."

"And I take it Tara isn't exactly gun-friendly."

"Right. I promised him I'd talk to Marie." Vinnie was a fellow survivor of the attack two years ago, and survivors in the Bay had a connection, a comradery. He hoped he was going to be able to talk to her sensibly about this.

"Marie lost her husband and her mother-in-law to the attack," said Dharma. "She was jailed while her children were out there in the chaos. She's been through a lot, and although I don't like guns, I can see that this is her way of taking control of a crazy situation."

"I get that," said Vinnie. "I totally do, but she's forcing it on Tara and her son, and that's not right. Tara had to kill her undead husband in front of her son. She's no bleeding heart."

Dharma nodded. "I guess what I'm trying to say is that Marie doesn't ever want to feel helpless again. She means well. I'm sure she wants Tara and Tyrell to feel as able as she in case…" Tara's voice trailed off.

"Go ahead," Vinnie insisted. "Say it. In case it happens again."

"That's unlikely."

"Why?" insisted Vinnie. "How do we know it won't happen again? That's like saying after 9/11 that there will never be another terrorist attack again."

"That's different."

"Is it? How? Wanting something not to happen again won't prevent it from happening again."

They passed a bunch of police officers on foot looking around and down at their cell phones.

"There's an awful lot of police presence for the end of June," said Dharma, momentarily changing the subject, but Vinnie didn't pay attention.

He was watching a bunch of children at the Shoot the Zombie Freaks booth. They were laughing as they popped off paintball rounds at a man dressed in a heavily padded outfit and a rubber zombie mask. He was pretending to lurch towards them. One small child squealed in delight as her father aimed the gun and she pulled the trigger.

Vinnie wondered how everyone made light of the devastation and carnage that occurred two years ago. He didn't just think it in poor taste. He found it completely sick and disrespectful. Two years ago, the Bay was at war with the dead. People died. Between the zombies and the superstorm, the town was nearly destroyed.

He knew what Dharma would say. It was the town's way of coming to grips with what happened. But, Vinnie wondered if it was a way of moving past it. Could they move past it when the threat of another attack loomed over them?

The popping of the paintball guns reminded him of the popping of the National Guard's rifles as they slaughtered the dead when Vinnie was up on top of the Blackbeard's Pier Arcade. Suddenly, Dharma, the boardwalk, and the shooting booth were no longer there as Vinnie succumbed to an unwelcome flashback…

*

Two Years Prior

Vinnie was last to climb down the ladder back into the arcade. Dharma, Mike, Nancy, Alessandra, Salvatore, and Holbrook were down there waiting for him. Vinnie heard the moans of the dead on the beach outside through the yawning chasm the storm created in between the staccato pops of rifle fire outside on the boardwalk.

An officer approached Chief Holbrook. "I'm Sergeant Miller of the Tenth Mountain Division. Are you all okay?"

Nancy answered for them. "Yes, thanks to you."

Holbrook stepped in, extending his hand. "I'm Chief Holbrook of the Bay Police."

Sergeant Miller shook it. "Glad to meet you. We've taken back the bay side of town. There's a perimeter on Neptune St., and we've set up a staging base in the Ocean's Gate Motel. We're in the process of taking back the ocean side and boardwalk."

"What can I do to help?" offered Holbrook.

"Nothing," replied Miller. He looked around the crumbling arcade. "This structure isn't safe. Once we've cleared a path, I'm having a squad take you to the Ocean's Gate."

Vinnie was relieved at having been rescued from the rooftop, but they weren't out of the woods yet. According to Sergeant Miller, they were in the thick of it. He kept using lingo like extraction, firing corridors, and safe zones. Chief Holbrook appeared to understand what he was saying.

Mike placed a hand on his shoulder. "Are you okay, Vin?"

"Fine," he answered a little too quickly, his tone almost defensive.

Mike smiled. "It's okay. I'm terrified, too."

Both of them startled when they heard a military chopper hover over the beach sideways behind the arcade. Bolts of light shot out from the side, pelting the dead below with bullets.

Sergeant Miller signaled for them to follow him. He was shouting something, but Vinnie couldn't hear what he was saying over the gunfire and chopper blades…

*

Vinnie's flashback faded back to the present, the sound of chopper blades lingering, but becoming more distant. He looked over at Dharma, who was shielding her eyes from the sun with her hand as she looked at the sky over the beach.

"That's weird," said Dharma.

"What's weird?" asked Vinnie.

"There's a copter."

"Yeah, so?"

Dharma put her hand down and saw more police walking in groups of three, scanning the crowd and consulting their cell phones.

Dharma's and Vinnie's cell phones chimed simultaneously. Dharma consulted her phone. "It's an Amber Alert. Someone's missing."

Vinnie was looking at his phone. "Amber Traub. Do we know her?"

Dharma shook her head. "I don't think so."

Vinnie squinted in the sunlight. "Already? We're not even in season yet."

"Speaking of which," said Dharma, her hands already on her hips. "You know I'm dragging you to the bonfire tonight."

"I don't know…"

"C'mon, Vin. It's solidarity with your fellow Bay residents."

The bonfire was started the first June after the superstorm by the mayor as a way for townies to kick off the summer and blow off some steam. It was comprised of a large pit of burning shipping palettes and a local folk singer playing acoustic guitar. It was tame, even by Vinnie's standards.

"The last thing we need is another townie tradition." Even Vinnie knew that it was a weak excuse when he said it.

Dharma leaned into him, pressing her lithe body against his. "You don't want me going by my lonesome, do you?" She batted her eyelashes for effect. When he hesitated, she gave him a shot in the arm. "C'mon, what else are you going to do?"

A smirk crept across Vinnie's face. "I dunno. I was thinking of a little Netflix and chill."

Dharma shot him an exaggerated demure look. "Why, Vincent, you animal. We can do that after the bonfire."

Vinnie's smirk fell into a frown. "The 'chill' would only work if my parents were at the bonfire and we were home alone."

Dharma's smile was sympathetic. "Aw, poor Vinnie. We'll just have to change our venue."

"No, not the sunglass store again," Vinnie protested.

Dharma feigned insult. "Why, what's wrong with the Hut?"

"It's weird in there."

She threw up her hands in exasperation. "What do you mean? It's all tiki'ed out. It'll be like we're in Hawaii. We'll lay a blanket down and everything."

The truth was, this had been their only option since the beginning of June. As Bay merchants, Vinnie's parents took vacations in the

Autumn and Spring. Summertime was prime time, so once June came, there was no more empty house.

Dharma started hula dancing, waving her hands rhythmically, humming Aloha-Oe. Vinnie's face cracked into a smile, mostly in reaction to how ridiculous she looked.

She grabbed him by the arm and pulled him close, smiling. "There's my Vin."

CHAPTER 4

As the morning passed, the warm sun crossing the sky, little April Traub crept around the Bay in a haze, careful to remain in between buildings and businesses, but she wasn't exactly sure why. Her normally racing child's mind had slowed, becoming dull with thoughts of hunger and violence.

She re-emerged for brief moments, tracking down unsuspecting passers-by, placing a bite on a dangling adult's hand and running away. Sometimes she bit a child lost in the lights and sounds of the boardwalk. When a parent yelled at her, her blood boiled with rage, and she threw such a tantrum, growling and screeching, that they immediately pulled their children close and backed away, cursing under their breath.

She couldn't explain it, but she was filled with rage and hate. It was a sensation she had never experienced before, even when denied something she wanted on impulse by her parents. It was exponentially worse that the resentment of being correct publicly by a teacher or her mother. Hell, it made the Terrible Twos seem like a vacation. She didn't know why, but she just wanted to watch the world burn.

She no longer thought about her parents, her grandpa, school, or television. She was becoming a murderous blank slate devoid of thought, morality, or self-control.

As pedestrians passed by on the boardwalk, she didn't see people. She saw walking meat bags of flesh and blood, and her mouth watered. Her teeth chattered from a combination of barely suppressed animal appetite and the drop in her body temperature as her body died, the virus coursing through her system, more rapidly than it would have two years ago, transforming her into something less than human.

Something wrong.

April's transformation to reanimated dead was quicker than it would've been two years prior. The virus was maturing, adapting to the need to spread rapidly, to outpace the slaughter by the living so that it might increase its numbers and eventually overwhelm any resistance.

* * *

Vinnie and Dharma walked over to Marie's clothing and apparel stand. They saw Alessandra arranging shorts on hangars. When she saw them, they exchanged smiles.

"Hey, Ali. Whatcha doin'?" asked Dharma.

"The usual." Alessandra shrugged. "Work, work, work." She was holding a pair of purple shorts that read 'Princess.'

"Nice shorts."

Alessandra looked at what she was absent-mindedly holding and shrugged again. "Not my style."

Dharma laughed. "No, I guess it's not."

"What are you guys doing here?"

"Is your mom around?" asked Vinnie.

"Sure, she's in the back by the register."

"Thanks."

"Where's your cute brother?" asked Dharma, her tone conspiratorial.

"He's out to lunch. I'll tell him you asked for him and said he was cute." She shot a nervous glance at Vinnie.

Dharma gave Vinnie a light shove. "Ah, don't worry about him. I have to keep him on his toes. A girl's gotta have options."

Vinnie shook his head and proceeded to the back. Dharma gave Alessandra a hug as she passed. Ever since Vinnie and Dharma watched over them during the attack, Marie's children had a special bond with them, and Marie was eternally grateful. Vinnie hoped to cash in on some of that good will to help Tyrell out.

They saw Tyrell unpacking boxes. He saw them and looked like he wanted to crawl in a hole and die somewhere. He knew why they were here. His guilty expression revealed all.

Vinnie and Dharma waved as they passed. Vinnie threw him a nod that Tyrell quickly returned, and then he went back to unpacking boxes.

"Hey, Vinnie and Dharma," called Marie from behind the register. "I'm back here."

They made their way to the back as Marie was finishing ringing a customer up. Marie placed the receipt in the bag, and the customer grabbed the bag and left.

"So, what brings you guys by?"

Vinnie looked down nervously at his shoe and then met Marie's gaze. "Can we talk in private for a sec?"

Marie looked a little taken off guard. "Sure." She called out to Tyrell and Alessandra, "Why don't you two go for a walk?"

Alessandra and Tyrell looked at each other and nodded. Tyrell kept his head down as he joined Alessandra, and they both left the store.

That's it. They were alone with Marie. Vinnie was glad he had Dharma with him. Marie was a friend, but she was intimidating. Ever since the attack, she had come out of her shell. She was brash and outspoken. She took shit from no one and wasn't afraid to dish it out.

Vinnie guessed that was what killing your zombie husband and mother-in-law with your bare hands did to a person. Marie was free from her overlords, and she wasn't going to bite her tongue ever again.

"What's up, guys?" Marie asked.

"Well," began Vinnie, "I had a visit from Tyrell today."

Marie was arranging the impulse buys on the counter as she listened. "Yeah, he really like's your pizza."

Vinnie laughed. "Yes, but that's not why he came today."

"Oh?"

"He told me you've been pushing him pretty hard on he and his mom learning to shoot."

This got Marie's attention. "I see." There was an edge to her tone. "What business is that of yours?"

Vinnie blushed and stammered, unsure of how to respond. Although he was now a college student, Marie had always been Mrs. Russo to him.

Dharma stepped in. "Tyrell's in a bit of a tough spot. He wants to keep his mom happy, yet he doesn't want to disappoint you. He looks up to the both of you."

Marie leaned on the counter with both hands. "Well, if he doesn't want to disappoint me, he should try it. It's for his own good."

"Listen," said Vinnie, "he knows you mean well, but don't you think that's up to his mother?"

Marie's eyes looked fierce. She looked as if she wanted to argue her point, but then she let out a long sigh. "Listen, Vinnie. She's a shrink. She's not into guns. She's one of them liberals."

"If you're insinuating that she's a bleeding heart, she kicked some ass of her own during the attack," said Dharma. "She's no slouch in the zombie-slaying department."

Marie snickered. "Yeah, well she could kill a lot more of them with a shotgun than she could a broomstick or a toy sword."

"She killed her own husband, just like you did," pressed Dharma. "You two have more in common than you think. Both of you will do whatever it takes to protect your kids."

"It's not a competition, Marie," said Vinnie. "You're looking after your kids."

"Damned right."

"And you wouldn't want anyone telling you otherwise?" added Vinnie.

"Heck no."

"Then why don't you let Tara look after her kid?"

Marie shook her head. "She doesn't know any better. Learning to shoot could save his life. Maybe even hers."

"He's just a kid," said Vinnie.

"My kids are learning. Alessandra's a better shot than her brother."

"They're older than Tyrell," said Dharma.

Marie looked as if she wanted to say something, but she cut it off. "Is he really *that* upset about this?"

Vinnie nodded. "He doesn't know what to do. He respects both you and his mom."

Marie waved a hand out in front of her. "Oh, all right. I'll drop it. But, Tara's gonna be sorry when they come back."

Dharma laughed. "What, the zombies? What makes you think they'll come back?"

"We didn't get them all," said Marie. "Lots of them got washed out to sea during the storm."

"It's been two years," said Vinnie, trying to be convincing in taking Dharma's side, when in truth he actually agreed with Marie.

"That's right," said Marie. "I'd say we're overdue. What, do you think they drowned out there? They're dead. *Dead.* They don't die. They're probably walking around on the ocean floor."

"Marie!" said Dharma, appalled. "Stop it."

"That's right," Marie continued, her eyes intense. "They'll be back, and I'm prepared. They ain't gonna get me."

"Please don't take this out on Tyrell," pleaded Dharma. "He just wants to help you at the store and have a good summer."

Marie smiled, her indignation fading fast. "I won't. He's a good kid. I care about him, just like I care about you two."

"We know," said Vinnie, pretending not to be daunted by her.

In that moment, there was an unspoken understanding that passed between the three survivors. Like many of the survivors in the Bay, they all looked out for each other. That was how they recovered.

Vinnie was eager to get while the gettin' was good. "Well, thanks for understanding, Marie."

"Don't mention it. You two, say hi to your parents."

"Will do," said Dharma.

Vinnie and Dharma walked back through the store and out onto the boardwalk as a couple of teenage girls passed them to look at the shorts display.

Vinnie exhaled deeply. "That went well."

Dharma laughed at him. "You were terrified of her!"

"Were?"

"Oh, come on. She's not that bad."

"She's terrifying," joked Vinnie. "I thought she was going to blow my head off right there."

They bumped into Tyrell and Alessandra.

"That was quick," said Tyrell, looking dubious. "How'd it go?"

Vinnie smiled. "You're off the hook, buddy."

Tyrell looked relieved. Alessandra put her arm around him.

"She just cares about you, that's all," said Dharma.

"I know," said Tyrell. He placed his fist out, and Vinnie and Dharma each bumped it with theirs. "Good looking out."

"Anytime," said Vinnie smiling.

"You two better get back," added Dharma. "Break's over."

Tyrell and Alessandra walked off back towards the store.

Dharma elbowed Vinnie. "Let's eat. I'm starving."

Vinnie smiled. "Me, too. Mexican?"

"Si, senor. Tengo mucha hombre."

* * *

Mike Brunello was waiting for Holbrook by the Whip ride. Children screeched in delight as their little rolling car was yanked around the sharp turn. However, Mike wasn't smiling. Lt. Becky Michaels was standing next to him.

Holbrook strode up to where they were standing. He tipped his cap in greeting. "Mike."

Mike nodded. "Chief."

"Tell him about the bites, Mike," prompted Becky.

Holbrook crossed his arms in preparation. "Yes, tell me about the bites."

"It was the damnedest thing," said Mike. "It started with one little girl screaming. It wasn't like the screaming you hear on rides. I saw the girl clutching her arm and her parents looking angry. When I asked them what happened, they said a little girl bit their daughter."

"Did they say what she looked like? How old?"

"The mother said a young girl. Maybe five or six years old. Mangy looking."

"Where are these people now?" pressed Holbrook, looking urgent.

Becky put up her hand. "Wait, Chief. There's more."

Holbrook sighed. "Great. What else?"

Becky gestured across the pier. "Well, this mangy little girl cut a path across the pier, because there was a trail of crying children and disgruntled parents."

Holbrook looked around, his expression barely contained panic. "Jesus, Becky, do we know where any of these folks are?"

"What's wrong?" asked Mike. "I don't like the expression on your face."

Holbrook ignored the remark. "Mike, how long ago would you say this all happened?"

Mike looked up into the air, thinking. "I dunno, maybe fifteen, twenty minutes ago."

Becky understood what Holbrook was driving at. "She can't be too far."

"I'm sure she's just lost and scared," said Mike, the meaning of their conversation lost on him.

Holbrook nodded to Becky. "Right. I want a sweep of the boardwalk from Harriman Street to Atlantic."

Becky nodded "Right." She dashed off, issuing instructions into her radio.

"What's this all about?" asked Mike. "She's just a lost little girl."

Holbrook called over three officers walking by. "Mike, I need you to identify whoever got bit. Can you do that for me now?"

Mike looked perplexed, but his confusion turned to horror as he read between the lines. "No," he said, stepping backwards and shaking his head. "You don't think…"

Holbrook placed his hands on Mike's shoulders and looked him in the eye. "Mike, I don't have time to explain right now, but I need you to help these officers find whoever got bit, and I need you to do it right now."

Mike kept shaking his head, unwilling to accept the notion Holbrook was floating. "No, not again. It's been two years."

Holbrook's tone was firm. "Mike, the last thing we need right now is panic. I need your help, and we don't have time to waste."

Mike swallowed the reality of the situation, and he nodded, his face now drained of color. "Right, Chief." He looked to the other officers, who were standing at the ready. "Follow me."

As they walked off, Mike scanning the crowd for the attacked families and the officers scanning for April Traub, Holbrook parted with Becky and began to walk the pier himself, glancing down at the pic of April from time to time. He was looking for the pink shirt and the white shorts. Becky did the same.

He scanned what was left of the pier, the crane looming behind the Tsunami ride, the back, left corner filled with workers laying down support beams across the newly installed pilings. As it was only late June, the pier was barely crowded, mostly townies, as the tourists hadn't arrived en masse yet.

Children rode pretend motorcycles, slamming the buzzers, while others sat in boats, ringing bells to get their parents' attention. There were cries of glee as the Bog Hopper bounced children up and down in sudden bursts.

"April!"

Holbrook heard that cry above all the others.

"April! Get over here!"

He turned in time to see Marney Traub dashing over to April, just standing there, in a daze. Jesus, he had just looked over there. How had he missed her?

Her clothes were filthy and torn, her hair clumped and matted. Then he saw her eyes. They were alert and filled with rage.

"Marney!" he called out, as he ran over to intercept them, but Marney had a head start. "Marney, no!"

Marney had already taken a knee and thrown her arms around April.

"Back away!" he shouted as he ran, hand on his gun.

April was limp in Marney's arms as her mother squeezed her, chastising her as relieved parents do to lost and found children. Marney heard the chief's voice and released her daughter.

Holbrook saw the whole thing as if it was happening in slow motion. Marney turned to see him running towards her. She scowled as she saw his one hand on his gun and the other gesturing wildly for her to get out of the way.

That was all the time April needed.

She lunged forward and sunk her teeth into her mother's neck with such force that Marney was almost knocked sideways off her knee. Her scowl turned to horror as the pain of the bite registered, and she reached up and pushed April's head away.

April's mouth pulled away from her mother's neck with a chunk of her mother's flesh between her teeth in a ghastly grin. Marney cried out and clutched her wound as blood spurt from between her fingers. Blood dripped down April's chin and stained her pink shirt.

Holbrook drew his firearm and took aim, but Marney, now angry, knelt in front of her daughter, obstructing his shot.

"Marney, out of the way!"

"What are you doing?" she cried out, not registering what was actually happening. But, why would she? She didn't live in the Bay. She was a visitor. An outsider. She didn't know what one of these monsters looked like up close and in the flesh.

Holbrook was just about there. "Get out of the way!"

April let out a blood-curdling shriek, and she ran back to the Creeping Dead haunted house ride.

Holbrook side-stepped Marney, still kneeling on the boardwalk with her hand on her neck, and took aim. However, there were too many by-standers behind April. If he missed, someone would get hurt or killed.

April growled like a bobcat, shoved her way past outraged children and parents in line, and tore past the attendant.

"Hey!" shouted the young girl manning the ride.

April leapt past a car filled with three children, pushed open the airbrushed faux castle doors, and disappeared into the ride.

"Goddammit!" Holbrook waved over two officers as he darted over to where Marney was crouched in tears and muttering to herself. Officer Becky arrived from the other direction.

"Keep an eye on her," Holbrook ordered the two officers. "She needs to be quarantined, Protocol Z."

"What happened?" Officer Becky was panting.

"I found April. She's turned. She ran into the haunted house."

Becky strode over to the attendant, who was trying to get her attention. "I need you to shut down the ride!"

"I can't," said the girl. "There are people in there."

Holbrook grabbed an officer and spoke in hushed tones so as not to cause a panic. "Quickly and quietly have the pier evacuated, and create a perimeter where it meets the boardwalk, by Palazzo's sausage stand and the Frog Bog. There are two other officers rounding up those who were bitten."

The officer nodded.

Holbrook joined Becky.

"She said she can't stop the ride with people in there," explained Becky.

Holbrook pointed an officious finger. "This is an emergency. Stop this ride now. Put on the emergency lights."

The attendant watched police officers in the background rounding up patrons and escorting them off the pier. "Okay," she said. She was about to press a red button with the palm of her hand, stopping the ride.

"Wait a minute," said Becky, grabbing the girl's hand before she could stop the ride.

"What's wrong?" asked Holbrook.

Becky turned to the ride attendant. "How many people are on the ride?"

"Only two cars. They're almost through."

"Let them finish," suggested Becky. "Then we'll shut down the ride."

"Right," said Holbrook. "If we stop the ride now, April might capitalize on their confusion." Then to the attendant, "As soon as the last riders are off, shut down the ride and turn up the lights."

"What are you going to do?" asked Becky.

"I'm going in after her."

"Not alone, you are."

Holbrook clamped a hand on her shoulder. "It's too tight in there for the two of us. Watch the exit. Make sure the last of the riders come out, and make sure she doesn't escape."

"What do I do if I see her?"

"Protocol Z, neutralize."

"You want me to shoot her? She's just a kid."

"Not anymore. Head shot. Double tap. Got it?"

Becky nodded dubiously. She had been in Atlantic City during the attack two years ago. She had transferred to the Bay to get away from the hookers, pimps, and drug dealers. "Got it."

The attendant tried to slip out of the way, but Becky grabbed her by the arm. "Wait, I need you in case we need to operate the ride."

"I don't want to stay here," said the girl.

"Don't worry. You'll be safe with me." Becky drew her firearm as riders began to push their way out of the exit. "Go ahead, Chief. I've got this."

Holbrook nodded and hopped the small metal fence delineating the waiting line. He navigated a few cars and hopped into the backseat of a car just before it pushed open the faux castle doors. He pulled out his flashlight, holding it under his gun, and flipped it on. He took a deep breath and disappeared into the haunted house.

* * *

Vinnie and Dharma were on their way to Caliente's when they saw a crowd blocking the boardwalk, gathered around the entrance to Blackbeard's Pier.

"Now what's going on?" asked Dharma.

"I don't know," said Vinnie, craning his neck to get a good look. "There're cops blocking off the pier."

"Do you think something happened? Maybe it has to do with the repairs."

"Let's have a look."

They pushed their way into the crowd and meandered their way towards the front, where an officer was ordering people to get back.

"What's going on?" shouted Dharma to the officer.

"Nothing you need to worry about," snapped the officer. "Move along."

Dharma frowned. "Well, that was rude."

"Maybe there's something wrong with the pier," offered Vinnie.

"I heard there's a little girl who freaked out by the haunted house," said a woman behind them talking to her girlfriend.

Her girlfriend shook her head. "Why are they blocking off the whole pier for a little girl?"

Dharma was looking between bodies, trying to get a good look. She tugged at Vinnie's sleeve. "Look, Vin, it's Mike."

Mike Brunello was standing on the other side of the blockade by a young female police officer, with his back turned to the crowd.

Vinnie cupped his hands over the sides of his mouth to amplify his voice. "Mike!"

Mike almost looked over his shoulder, but he was really preoccupied with whatever was happening on the pier.

Vinnie tried again, waving his hands in the air. "Mike! Mike Brunello!"

This time, Mike turned around. He was white as a ghost. He searched the crowd and saw Vinnie. "Vinnie! What are you doing here?"

Vinnie and Dharma squeezed their way to the front of the crowd, apologizing as they jostled other spectators.

"Mike, what's going on?" Vinnie asked.

Mike's aghast expression grew stern. "You shouldn't be here. The both of you, go home!"

This was not the reception Vinnie expected from his old friend. He and Dharma looked at each other, perplexed.

"What's wrong, Mike?" pressed Dharma.

Mike was now face-to-face with Vinnie, the officer behind him eying him suspiciously. "Vinnie, take Dharma and get out of here." Vinnie was about to say something, but Mike interrupted him. "There's a problem at the Creeping Dead."

At first, Vinnie wasn't sure what he was getting at.

"Vinnie, remember that horrible night on the carousel with Dharma, the kids, and Nancy?"

Mike's words summoned the mental image of hands reaching under the metal gates of Blackbeard's Arcade. He heard the moans of the dead.

"Vinnie, *the Creeping Dead*." He said the last part more slowly and with great emphasis.

The female officer pulled Mike away and stood between him and the crowd.

Vinnie was stupefied into silence.

Dharma pulled him close and spoke in low tones. "Jesus, Vin? Why would he say that?"

Vinnie snapped out of it and grabbed Dharma by the arm.

"Hey," she protested.

Vinnie spoke softly into her ear as they walked away and back in the direction from whence they came. "Dharma, he's talking about the fucking zombies."

"Why would he…?" Then it dawned on her. "You don't think…?"

"If he told us to get away, I'm listening."

"What about him? Why is he with that police officer?"

"Something's going on," said Vinnie. "I don't like it."

"But it's been two years. *Two years.*"

"I told you it wasn't over."

"We don't know…"

"That's right," interrupted Vinnie. "We don't know anything. We don't know that those things are back. We don't know if there are more of them."

Dharma looked back over her shoulder at the growing crowd at the opening to the pier. People had their cell phones out, taking pictures and videos. She remembered two years ago when people were being attacked on the boardwalk, and instead of people trying to help, they stood there taking videos for social media. She was overcome with revulsion and disgust, but as Mike's words replayed in her head, it quickly gave way to stark terror.

She prayed Vinnie was wrong.

CHAPTER 5

Chief Holbrook sat in the back of his car as it crawled through the haunted house, gun drawn, scanning the dark area in front of him. The car rode on a track, and the sweep of his flashlight revealed that there was quite a bit of room on either side of him.

Tinny, creepy music blared from speakers overhead, and a light illuminated a graveyard scene ahead. Fans blew warm, stale air around, simulating wind, as Holbrook considered his options. He holstered his weapon and instead produced his retractable baton, extending it. He couldn't fire inside the haunted house, at least not until the ride came to a stop, which meant all riders were off.

He also wondered what the optics would be of a police chief entering a ride and shooting a child passenger, all without the benefit of Protocol Z. There were enough police shootings in the news.

As his car approached the foam gravestones, two zombie figures popped up from behind them and screamed. Holbrook thought they looked and sounded nothing like the real thing. However, he tried not to focus on the effects. He was scanning for April.

The car turned and winded along the track, passing a medieval torture scene. A body lay on a table, shackled, as a rotund ghoulish figure stood over it with a butcher's knife. There were screams and pleading, much like Holbrook heard during the attack two years ago. The dead were unsympathetic to the cries of their victims as they were pulled apart and eaten alive.

Holbrook waved his baton back and forth, sweeping the area ahead with his flashlight in his other hand, not trusting his eyes in the darkness. Until all of the emergency lights went on, finding a zombie April would be like finding a needle in a haystack amongst the horror effects.

He passed into a narrow corridor lined with digital, illuminated portraits of figures from past eras. As he passed each one, triggering sensors, the figures changed, leaping out at him, looking ghastly and demonic.

He tried not to startle, but he did anyway. He was on edge, frantically scanning the darkness. A face lunged at him, but it wasn't from one of the portraits. April screeched as she reached forward, swatting his baton away, eyes hungry and furious.

Holbrook sat back in his seat as April climbed into the front seat of the car. He recovered and swatted at her, landing blows on her shoulders and her arms. If she were a live girl, the blows would've been painful as they broke her bones.

Their car passed another scene of torture, and a dragon's head the popped out from the right, breathing fire made from jagged orange and red fabric flapping in the breeze of a small fan.

April was unfazed. She raised her head and cried out in ferocity, projectile vomiting on Holbrook. He screamed and wriggled in his seat, turning his head away from the spewed gore.

She lunged forward, clawing at his outfit with broken fingernails, snapping her jaws. Holbrook placed his baton horizontally across his face, holding on to each end, as she bit down on it, shattering her teeth.

He pulled his knees to his chest, raised his feet, and kicked her in the chest as hard as he could, sending her flying out of the car and to the right. Behind her, a tall vampire loomed, cast in a strobe light as the sounds of thunder blasted over the speakers.

Holbrook rolled backwards out of the car and onto the track, the metal digging into his back. He cried out in pain and horror as the ride halted and the lights came on. The animatronics went silent. Holbrook crouched on the track, his gun drawn and trained at the car in front of him.

The emergency lights weren't as bright as he had hoped, but he was able to see that April was no longer in the car. He was also able to see that the tracks pitched upward ahead into a narrow corridor going to a second floor. He had dropped his flashlight when she had surprised him. He leaned over the back of the car, gun trained forward, and saw the flashlight lying on the floor.

He righted himself, swung a leg over, eyes vigilant and gun pointed forward, slid his butt over the back edge, and swung his other leg into the car. He reached down and grabbed it.

He nearly jumped out of his skin when his radio crackled. "The last passengers are off. You all right, Chief?" It was Becky.

He grabbed his radio. "Ten-four. She's a zombie all right. Nearly bit my face off." He looked down at his shirt. It was covered in chunks of gore. It was all the evidence he needed to satisfy Protocol Z, only that there wasn't a witness.

"Do you want me to come in?" asked Becky.

"Why, so we can shoot each other? Man the exit. I'll force her out to you. Head shots only."

His radio crackled. "Ten-four, Chief."

He reached down and grabbed his baton, retracted it, and slid it back into its holster on his belt. He climbed over the front of the car, looking down before planting his feet between the tracks, and began to creep up the incline.

He swept the dim corridor with his flashlight and gun, clearing it foot by foot. There were rattling sounds ahead, as if props were being jostled. As Holbrook reached the crest, he lowered himself towards the ground, peeking over the rise.

There was a witch rocking back and forth on its stand, as if something had just bumped it. He rose to his feet and entered the second level. The walls appeared as if they were closing in, creating a bottleneck. Fewer places for her to hide, but also less room for him to maneuver.

He flashed his light back and forth, scanning the narrow corridor. He crept up to the witch, taking small, measured steps, gun sweeping back and forth. He heard wheezing from behind the witch. April was hiding. Waiting.

"April, it's Chief Holbrook," he said out loud. "Why don't you come out? I want to help you."

There were grunts and growling from behind the witch. It sounded like a bobcat.

"Come on, April. I'm not going to hurt you." He crept closer. He put his flashlight down, produced his baton, and flicked his wrist to extend it. He reached out, poking the witch mannequin, pushing it aside with the baton.

The wheezing stopped.

April lunged out at Chief Holbrook, teeth bared. She was fast, too fast for him to react. She shoved his gun aside and tackled him to the ground, the metal tracks biting into his back once again.

Her face hovered over his as she laughed like a demonically possessed girl from some horror movie. Her eyes were white, and her grin wicked. She drooled on him. He turned his face to the side to avoid the spittle and prepare for the coming bite.

She raised her head up, screeched, and vomited all over him, covering him in blood, bile, and the contents of her stomach. Half-digested fingertips landed on his chest and neck as he wailed.

He looked up, his vision blurry from bodily fluids, and saw April's head jerk to the side, knocking her off of him.

Becky reached down and pulled him away. "Jesus, Chief! Are you okay?" Her other hand trained her gun on April. But when she looked up, the little girl was gone.

Holbrook struggled to his feet. "Quick, she's going back out the entrance!"

They were close to the exit, so they continued through the ride as Becky hit the radio. "Be advised, the subject is fleeing out the entrance of the ride. We have a positive for Protocol Z. Repeat, we have a positive for Protocol Z."

As they collided with the exit doors and burst out into the sunlight, their vision was momentarily whitewashed.

As Holbrook's vision cleared, he heard the other officers shouting at April to freeze. He rubbed his eyes and wiped the blood from his face as Becky pulled him out of the line of fire.

April stopped in her tracks, snarling at the officers, eyes wild. Covered in dirt and blood, her clothes torn, she looked like a feral child. She took a step forward, and the officers again issued commands for her to stop.

Marney Traub was being restrained by two officers as she cried out for April, but April didn't even regard her with a single glance.

A grotesque smile split her face, both impish and hateful, and she continued to advance towards the officers. Holbrook heard noises from the crowd behind the barrier at the other end of the pier.

One of the officers shot her with the taser, the barbs digging into her chest. The surge of electricity caused her to stagger for a moment.

Marney Traub struggled to free herself, shouting at the officer who shot the taser, "Don't you hurt her! Don't you hurt my baby!"

April, oblivious to her mother's pleading on her behalf, grabbed the wires dangling from her body and yanked them out, tearing her pink shirt and her own flesh. Black blood pooled underneath her shirt. She let out a wild howl and rushed the line of police.

This time, they opened fire. Bullets ripped at her neck and shoulders as the officers attempted a head shot. Being little and light, the shots knocked her backwards. April stumbled, shrieking and waving her arms, as if she could claw the bullets away.

With a sudden burst of explosive energy, April dashed sideways to the end of the pier. The officers ceased their fire as she passed in front of the haunted house operator, who cringed, fearful of April and being shot.

April darted between the haunted house and the Caterpillar Coaster. She slipped through the large gap between the horizontal rails of the wooden fence at the pier's edge. The officers opened fire on her. Blood spurt out of the side of her head, and she took a header into the ocean below.

Marney dropped to her knees, crying out in hysteria, "My baby! My baby!"

There were screams and cries from the crowd behind the barrier. Holbrook tried to take a step forward, but Becky held him back with a hand. When he looked at her, she had her gun trained on his head.

Another officer approached, tentative. "Becky, what are you doing?"

"He's had contact with the subject," she said, never looking away from Holbrook.

"That's the chief," another officer said, incredulous.

"No, she's right," said Holbrook. "I've had contact with bodily fluids. I have to be taken into custody and subject to Protocol Z."

"Chief, were you bitten?" asked Becky.

"No, thanks to you."

"Scratched?"

"I don't think so. But I'll submit to a full examination."

Becky turned to one of the officers. "See where that little girl went. I've got this." The officer ran to the edge of the pier to investigate. Becky turned to Holbrook and swallowed hard. These next words were difficult to say. "Chief, I need you to turn around, get down on your knees, cross your feet, and put your hands behind your head. Lace your fingers."

Chief Holbrook nodded. He knew she was doing her job, and doing her job meant following Protocol Z to the letter. He was no exception.

Holbrook turned around and knelt down on the boardwalk, his back still aching. He got down on both knees and crossed his legs. He placed his hands behind his head and laced his fingers.

"Cover him," he heard Becky say to the other officer. There was a pause while she waited for him to draw and train his weapon, and Holbrook felt her hand grab his right wrist. Her grip was firm but not rough. She slapped a cuff on his wrist, brought his right hand and then his left behind his back, and cuffed his left wrist.

She helped him to his feet. He groaned as his body ached. She turned him back around. "I'm sorry, Chief."

He winked at her. "Don't be. Inform Deputy Chief Olson of the situation. Then call my wife."

"I'm going to be the one who supervises your Protocol Z. I'm a lieutenant, so I meet the minimum rank."

"That's up to Olson. Notify the DOH, tell them I'm on my way to quarantine."

Becky nodded. "I'll meet you there after I speak to Lena."

"Tell her I love her."

The officer who checked the edge of the pier came running back, panting. "The little girl's gone."

*

"They shot her!"

"The police shot the little girl!"

"Did you see the blood all over her face and shirt?"

"Did you hear the screams?"

"She fell off the pier!"

The crowd of spectators behind him, Mike Brunello watched in horror as he saw Officer Becky cuff Chief Holbrook. An officer approached with a yoke, like a dog catcher would use. The officer lowered the yoke over Holbrook's head and pulled, decreasing the slack. Holbrook was then escorted off to the right as two other officers followed, guns drawn and trained on their chief.

Jesus, thought Mike. *Chief Holbrook must've been bit. The chief's been bit!* It couldn't be true. Mike willed it not to be true. If the dead were returning, the town would need Holbrook.

Nancy shoved her way through the crowd and through the police barrier. They parted, letting her through. "What in the hell is going on here? Why did the cops shut down the pier?"

She saw Mike's stunned expression, his face drained of all color. "Jesus Christ, Mike. Are you all right?"

Mike turned to look at her. Behind her, he saw people with their cell phones out, capturing videos of what had happened. "Nancy, it was the little girl."

"She...she was one of them?" asked Nancy.

"I-I don't understand. It's been two years."

Nancy put her hands on her hips. "We have to talk to the chief. He'll know what's going on."

Mike looked away, wearing a pained expression. "They took him away, cuffed and yoked like a stray dog."

"What in God's name are you babbling about?"

Mike looked her in the eye. "He went into the spook house to get her. I think the chief's been bit, Nancy."

Nancy's eyes went wide. She prided herself on not being easily surprised. This bit of news, however, took her off guard. "The chief? Goodness gracious, not the chief."

Mike pulled her in close and embraced her. "It's starting all over again," he whispered in her ear. "The dead have returned to Smuggler's Bay."

Nancy pulled away from him, her expression fierce. "There's no need to panic. One swallow doesn't make a summer. I'm sure it's just an isolated incident."

"Nance, this girl was going around biting people. The police are trying to round up those who were bitten for quarantine. The chief appears to be one of them."

This saddened Nancy. She liked Holbrook. He was a man of action. When the shit hit the fan two years ago, he took charge and kept them safe until the authorities arrived. She respected that.

Officer Becky ran over to them. "Nancy, you're going to have to close down the pier."

"Is the chief all right?" asked Nancy.

Becky knew what she was asking. "We're just taking the proper precautions."

"That's not what I asked," demanded Nancy.

Becky frowned. "I need you to close the pier. We need to send a hazmat team in. I need you to do that right now."

Nancy looked like she was ready for an argument, but Mike grabbed her by the arm and spoke softly but firmly. "Nance, we need to close the pier. Chief Holbrook needs us to close the pier."

Nancy shook her head and swallowed her protest. She knew he was right. There would be time for a formal inquisition later.

"Okay, let's back this crowd up," Becky instructed the other officers. "The pier is closed until further notice," she announced to the crowd of cell phones and tablets.

* * *

Marie overheard two customers talking in her shop.

"Did you hear that the police shot a little girl on Blackbeard's Pier?"

"I heard she was only six years old."

"These cops are too damned trigger happy."

"It's already on social media. There's a bunch of videos up. It's horrible. Absolutely horrible. She fell into the water, poor dear. They never found her body."

Marie walked around the counter and approached the two ladies. "Excuse me, but I couldn't help but overhear. You said a little girl was shot by the police?"

One of the women, a fifty-something clad in a loose-fitting sun dress, pulled off her sunglasses and shot a nervous glance over at Alessandra, and then at Salvatore, both managing the clothing racks. They had also heard the conversation and were watching. Marie nodded for them to leave the store.

Alessandra understood and grabbed Salvatore. "C'mon." She pulled him outside onto the boardwalk.

This satisfied the woman. "A six-year-old. Shot in cold blood."

"That's strange," said Marie.

"Well, she attacked the police," said the other woman, pursing her lips. She kept her shades on and gazed at Marie under the wide rim of a huge straw sunhat.

"She's *a small child*," reprimanded Sundress. "They didn't need to use deadly force."

"She was covered in blood, howling at them," insisted Sunhat.

Sundress gasped. "You don't think…"

"That was no little girl," said Marie.

Sunhat looked around, as if she was about to ask something controversial. "You don't think the little girl was one of those monsters…?"

"It's been two years," said Sundress, dismissing the idea. "Why would one reappear now?"

"Why would the police shoot a little girl?" insisted Marie. "Where's the body?"

"Chief Holbrook *was* cuffed and led off the pier at gunpoint," said Sunhat. "He had a yoke around his neck."

"Was he bitten?" asked Marie, her tone urgent. "Was the chief bitten?"

"No one knows," said Sundress. "The police are being real hush hush about it."

Marie snapped her fingers. "Christ Almighty! I knew it! I knew it wasn't over."

"I'm sure that if it was another attack, the police would've provided some instructions," said Sundress.

Marie shook her head. "No, not yet they would. First they have to notify the Department of Health."

The two women shot uncomfortable glances at each other.

Marie chortled. "What, you never went to the town meetings after the attack? There's a protocol that needs to be followed. They're not going to make an official announcement yet."

"Well, I think all of this talk about…*them* is a bit premature," said Sundress.

Apparently, the two women no longer felt comfortable continuing the conversation and excused themselves, leaving the store. Salvatore and Alessandra drifted back in.

"What's going on, Mom?" asked Alessandra.

"Remember what I told you? What I said would happen?"

"You don't know for sure..." began Salvatore, knowing where she was going.

Marie cut him off. "What else would it be? Chief Holbrook must've been bit. That's why he was taken away. Don't you see? He's going to quarantine." Marie's eyes were wild. She looked crazed, like a person who had been told she was delusional but had just been vindicated.

"Chief Holbrook?" asked Alessandra in disbelief.

Marie nodded. "That's right. I told you they'd be back. This time, we're ready. This time, we won't let them take our town.

"This time we fight back."

* * *

Nancy paced back and forth inside the Blackbeard's Pier Arcade, looking out the locked glass doors facing the pier, watching the Hazmat team sanitize everything. The arcade was crowded with spectators earlier, but it was now almost empty. "Goddammit. I can't believe this."

"Take it easy," said Mike, pacing as well, but for an entirely different reason than Nancy.

"How am I supposed to take it easy? It's the beginning of the season, and we're already off to a bad start."

Mike turned on Nancy, eyes fierce. "All you care about is money! Jesus, there are worse things going on here? The dead are back, and they're going to infest the Bay again!" He braced himself for a nasty retort.

However, Nancy's expression was that of disappointment. "You old fool. Is that what you think I'm worried about? Money?"

Mike threw up his hands. "Well, aren't you?"

Nancy took a few steps towards Mike and stopped, fists clenched at her sides. "For your information, mister, I actually care about this town. You prance about with all of your sentimentality, thinking Smuggler's Bay is all cotton candy and memories.

"The last two years have been rough. People have been getting by on insurance money and side businesses. Those who don't have any other revenue lost everything. They've closed up shop and left."

"What's your point, Nancy?"

"My point is, if there's another attack, this town is finished. No one will come here anymore. There won't be any more children riding the carousel, laughing, and having a good time with their families. After the attack, we're lucky anyone comes back at all. If it wasn't for other outbreaks along the coast two years ago, we would be singled out as Zombie Central."

Mike calmed down. "I think we've adopted that identity on our own. Look at all of the businesses who went zombie themed."

"That's exactly why I won't do it," said Nancy. "I want the Bay to continue to be known as a family destination. I love this town, which is why I've sunk every penny I have into this place when other business owners have run away with their tail between their legs.

"And you...you should know me better. I resent that you picture me as this Scrooge who only cares about her bottom line."

Mike was stunned. Never before had he heard Nancy express this. Not in this way, anyway. But, it was an indication of sentimentality, of sorts. He stepped towards her. "I'm so sorry, Nancy." He reached out to embrace her. He was relieved when she let him.

She kissed him. "We need to be strong, for each other. For the Bay. And being strong means staying in business."

"I have a confession to make," said Mike.

"Uh oh. What is it now? Do I need to get my baseball bat?"

Mike smiled. "I know you think I won't move out of the Bay and in with you because I'm dragging my feet with our relationship."

Nancy crossed her arms, her face stern. "Go on."

"I don't want to leave the Bay either. If I moved in with you, it would be as if I was giving up on it."

Nancy narrowed her eyes. "I thought it was because of Mary."

"It is, partially. She was part of my decision to move out of Brooklyn and come here. Coming here was one of the best decisions I've ever made."

"I see," said Nancy, her demeanor softening. "I had no idea it meant that to you."

Mike smiled. "See, we've both learned something about each other."

"I'll tell you what…I won't pressure you to move out just yet, and you don't balk at my business sense."

"Deal. Except for one thing."

"What now?"

Mike paused, unsure if he should even broach the subject. "Are you really going to protest the rave tonight at the town board meeting?"

Nancy huffed. "Why wouldn't I? You know how I feel about it."

"You said so yourself. We need to keep people coming here. This rave would be huge for the town."

"It would be a huge liability."

"It'll keep things going, at least for a bit," insisted Mike.

"Once again, families don't go to raves. Teens do. Teens who do drugs."

Mike waved a dismissive hand. "Oh, you don't know that."

"You're so out of touch. You don't know what you're talking about."

 "Teens play arcade games," reminded Mike. "They go on rides."

"What are you saying?"

"C'mon, Nancy. I think you know what I'm saying. Maybe, if this town is to survive, it needs to reinvent itself."

"I like Smuggler's Bay just the way it is."

"Now who thinks the Bay is all cotton candy and memories?" Mike walked away, leaving her with food for thought.

Nancy clenched her jaw. She hated it when he was right.

* * *

Chief Holbrook sat on a metal chair with his hands cuffed behind him and his feet shackled, quarantined in one of his own jail cells at the police station. Dr. Hickey sat in a chair outside the cell. Becky stood next to him, leaning against the wall, her hand resting casually on the handle of her gun. Becky had her phone hooked up to a portable speaker, playing hits from the eighties to ease the tension and pass the time. *Loving Every Minute of It* by Loverboy was playing in the background.

"How did Lena take the news?"

"She was upset," said Becky, "but she understood."

"Was Robbie there?"

"She asked him to go upstairs so we could talk privately."

Holbrook smiled. "Good."

"How do you feel?" asked Dr. Hickey.

Holbrook paused to take stock of himself. "Okay, I guess. No different, really."

"Your vitals indicate as much, thus far." As per Protocol Z, for a live subject suspected of being infected, vitals were taken every hour and recorded in an official log that was part of the subject's medical record.

Holbrook smirked at Becky. "I bet when you left AC, you didn't expect any of this."

Becky returned the smirk. "I don't think anyone expected any of this."

"Imagine my surprise when bodies started rising from my table," said Dr. Hickey.

They all shared a joyless laugh.

"Your sister was a good cop," said Holbrook.

Becky smiled, but it was a sad smile. "I know. She always spoke highly of you."

"Joann saved my life at the expense of her own."

"I'm surprised you put into a transfer into *this* town," said Dr. Hickey to Becky. "Even AC couldn't have been that bad."

"My sister cared about Smuggler's Bay. I guess I felt I was carrying on her legacy, or something."

Holbrook shook his head. "You know she wouldn't want you to be here."

"I can take care of myself."

"How does your husband feel about it?" asked Dr. Hickey.

Holbrook knew the answer to this.

"As long as we don't live in the Bay," replied Becky. "Greg didn't like it, but that was my compromise."

Hickey nodded. "You weren't worried about another attack?"

"The thought crossed my mind. The first attack took everyone by surprise, but I figured we'd be ready for it this time. It still took us by surprise."

"This was only one zombie," said Holbrook, "and we neutralized it and quarantined the bite victims."

"One that we know of," said Becky. "And we don't know if we got all of the bite victims."

"That's why we have increased patrols," said Holbrook. "We're on high alert."

"The DOH is getting involved," said Hickey.

"The mayor brought in State Troopers and County Police," added Becky. "I've been tasked with discussing rapid response at the town board meeting tonight with a rep from the DOH. There's even an acronym for it: R.E.C.—Recognize the symptoms, Evacuate to a safe distance, Call 911."

"Sounds about right," said Holbrook.

There was an uncomfortable silence.

"How long has it been?" asked Holbrook.

Dr. Hickey checked his watch. "Only a few hours."

"Jesus, if the Z Virus doesn't get me, I'll die from boredom. I wonder how the bite victims are faring."

Dr. Hickey frowned. "The DOH doesn't expect many of them to make it."

"If they've all been bitten, none of them should make it," said Becky.

Dr. Hickey shrugged. "The DOH never speaks in absolutes."

Holbrook smirked. "Fewer lawsuits."

"There's not a ton of information on rates of transmission and infection," said Dr. Hickey. "We don't know if there's a one-to-one relationship between being bitten and infection. Your case is even less certain."

"That's a good thing, isn't it, Doc?" said Holbrook.

Hickey nodded. "We don't know if the fluids you were exposed to were absorbed by the mucous membranes on your eyes or in your nose and mouth. So, we wait."

Holbrook turned to Becky, changing the subject. "Who's relieving you when you go to the meeting tonight?"

"Martinez."

"Good. If I turn, he'll definitely pull the trigger."

Becky chuckled. "What's that supposed to mean?"

"I don't think he likes me."

"What are you talking about? Everybody likes you."

"Do me a favor?"

"Sure, Chief."

"Check on Lena and Robbie for me."

"I will, and then I'm coming right back here."

Holbrook shook his head. "No, I'm feeling fine. Go to the bonfire. People need to see you there, especially since you're Joann's sister. If you're there, they'll feel better about things."

She shot him a dubious look.

"Don't worry about it," Holbrook insisted. "Martinez will take care of me, if it comes to that."

"So what do you think about the rave?" asked Becky. Now she was changing the subject.

"I think it's going to cause many problems," said Holbrook. "Drugs, date rape, property destruction. But, the town's going to go ahead with it anyway. It'll bring in much-needed revenue."

"The mayor will have to approve overtime for that," she said.

"We'll see. This might make zombies look tame by comparison."

"That's not funny, Chief."

"I know."

* * *

The day passed quickly, and Vinnie sat on a wooden bench waiting by the east end of the sky ride for Tara. He saw her strolling down the boardwalk. When she saw him, she smiled.

He stood up as she approached, not sure of what to do with his hands. He decided to extend his right hand, feeling awkward. "Thank you for meeting with me."

Tara shook his hand and laughed. "Why so formal, Vinnie?"

His face flushed. "Sorry. It's just that…"

"You've never been to see someone like me before."

"Right."

She gestured for him to sit back down. "Well, I assure you that I don't bite."

Vinnie sat as instructed, wincing at her choice of wording. "Did you have to put it that way?" His tone was more sardonic than rebuking.

Tara arched an eyebrow. "You know what I meant. I don't normally meet clients on the boardwalk. I have an office for this sort of thing on Poseidon Avenue, right above the bike rental place."

"Did you hear about the little girl on Blackbeard's Pier?"

"Yeah. So sad."

Vinnie swallowed hard. "Some say the girl was one of them. You know, a…zombie." He hesitated in uttering that word, as if saying it aloud would bring them back to Smuggler's Bay.

"If it was, it sounded like an isolated incident," said Tara. "We don't know anything definitive yet. No need to panic."

"You see Lenny on the boardwalk," said Vinnie, changing the topic.

Tara shook her head. "He's an exception. He only feels comfortable on the boardwalk."

Vinnie smiled, looking sheepish. "So do I. It doesn't feel like therapy this way."

"I'm not sure if this *is* therapy. As long as you don't mind the lack of privacy."

"That's just it," he said. "It's the only place I can be amongst everyone, yet be by myself. No one's looking at us or listening to what we have to say."

Tara looked around. The passersby went about their business walking, licking ice cream cones, laughing—none paying any mind to Tara and Vinnie on the bench. "What made you call me?"

Vinnie looked uncomfortable.

"Is this about the little girl?" asked Tara.

"No. I mean yes. Kind of. Ever since the attack, I've been having trouble sleeping."

"The attack was two years ago."

"Yes. At first, I was just going to bed later. Then it was becoming later and later. Then I was getting nightmares. Now I jump out of my skin every time I heard a loud noise."

Tara frowned. "Sounds uncomfortable. Even at school?"

"Yup. I'm always on edge, like I can never relax. It's like I'm always waiting…"

"For them to come back," offered Tara.

Vinnie knew who she meant. "Yeah."

"And this incident with the little girl has you worried?"

"We didn't get them all. Many were washed away in the storm."

"So?"

"So, they don't drown. They have to be roaming around out there, somewhere."

"I see," said Tara. "And that's what keeps you up at night."

"Exactly. My parents talked about possibly moving, but my dad says it's difficult starting over. He's got everything invested in the pizzeria."

"Vinnie, there's something we in psychology call an 'assumptive world.' Do you know what that is?"

Vinnie shook his head.

"It's the way we view our world around us. You got up out of bed this morning, right?"

Vinnie nodded, unsure of where she was going with this.

"Well, were you worried about slipping and breaking your neck?"

"No, of course not."

"Is it possible for that to happen?"

Vinnie thought for a moment. "Unlikely, but I guess it's possible."

"You left your house this morning."

Vinnie chuckled. "Obviously. I'm here."

"Were you worried about getting hit by a car or attacked by a dog, or mugged even?"

"No, I wasn't."

"Are these things possible?"

He laughed. "Yeah, I guess so. What's your point?"

"The point is, statistically there are lots of things that can happen, some more likely than others. Things that should keep us home under our covers in bed. But, we look past these things, assuming that these things won't happen. We operate on that premise."

Vinnie's expression grew serious. "I see what you're saying. But, the reality is that the zombie attack *did* happen. I saw it. Friends of mine died. Horribly."

Tara smiled. "Vinnie, people get into car accidents every day. In fact, statistically, you are way more likely to get into a car accident than attacked by a zombie."

He smirked again. "That probability has increased recently."

"But, it's still much less than getting into a car accident, or choking on food. Vinnie, you could drop dead right now from a brain aneurysm. A terrorist could blow us up where we sit. The world is a dangerous place."

"Jesus, Doc. This how you're trying to make me feel better?"

Tara sat up straight and leaned in towards Vinnie. "What I'm trying to say is you don't think of all these very possible things because they haven't just happened to you. You witnessed something terrible and traumatic. We all have."

Vinnie looked down for a moment, feeling awkward again.

Tara noticed. "What's wrong?"

"I feel strange talking about this with you."

"Why is that?"

"Here I am complaining, and you lost your husband during the attack. You almost lost Tyrell."

Tara paused. Although two years had passed, the wound wasn't fully healed. Wounds like this never did. They eventually became mental scars tucked away to the back of one's awareness, always lurking on the periphery, occasionally itching. It reared its ugly head at inopportune times—on quiet nights, lonely mornings, in the middle of the supermarket. "I killed what was once my husband with my bare hands. If I didn't, Tyrell and I wouldn't be here."

"Do you get nightmares?"

"Sometimes. Sometimes I dream that Marcus is coming after me in the house, chasing me from room to room, snapping his jaws at me. Other times I dream that we're all together on the boardwalk, walking, holding hands, Tyrell between us. Then I look over, and Marcus is one of those monsters, tugging Tyrell towards him."

Vinnie grimaced. "Jesus."

Tara nodded. "I try to pull Tyrell towards me, but Marcus' grip is too strong. I wake up just before he sinks his teeth into his neck."

"How do you go on, dealing with this?"

"I have to. Tyrell needs me to. I want him to have as normal a life he can after all that."

"Do you think it's possible?"

"People carried on after 9/11. There are floods, tornadoes, and wildfires that destroy homes and entire neighborhoods. People always rebuild."

"So, what should I do?"

"Try to live your life as best as you can. Don't let fear or pain hold you back. You survived a zombie attack *and* a superstorm. Your life is a gift. Don't squander it."

Vinnie grinned.

"Wow, I actually got you to smile," said Tara, pleasantly surprised.

"No, it's not you, Doc. It's Dharma. She's been bugging me to go to the bonfire tonight."

"You don't want to go?"

Vinnie shrugged. "I dunno. It seems kinda silly."

"After all we just talked about, do you still feel that way?"

He pondered this. "No, I guess I don't. I guess I should go."

Tara nodded. "This is your community, pulling together in solidarity after two natural disasters that nearly wiped the town out. I believe you should be there. And, for Christ's sake, have some fun. Tyrell loved it last year."

Vinnie smiled. "He's a brave kid."

Tara placed a hand on Vinnie's shoulder. "He told me what you did for him today."

Vinnie's face flushed in embarrassment. "I…uh…well, he was really upset. He didn't know what to do."

"Thank you, Vinnie." She sighed, pushing down her annoyance at the situation. "Marie means well. Different people react in different ways to crisis. Some reactions are healthier than others."

"Mrs. Russo said that she'd leave him alone," said Vinnie. "I believe her."

"I do, too. It's not like I don't appreciate everything she's done, watching Tyrell at her store. He enjoys working there. He loves Sal and Alessandra."

"Yeah, they're great."

"He looks up to you and Dharma, you know."

"Really?"

"Yeah. He kind of sees you as a big brother, and Dharma is like a big sister."

"Wow, I never realized that. That's pretty cool."

"Yes, it is. So, you gonna be okay?"

"Yeah, I think so. How much do I owe you?"

Tara stood and placed up a hand. "Don't worry about it. This really wasn't therapy, anyway. You are a friend to me and Tyrell. A good friend."

Vinnie smiled at that. Hearing her say so made him feel better about things. He hadn't realized that other people, people he would've never thought, actually needed him.

He stood as well. "Well, thanks again. I have a bonfire to get ready for."

ACT II
TIPPING POINT

CHAPTER 6

The small auditorium in town hall was overflowing with locals, the seats filled with various business owners and, in some cases, their families. There was much discussion and debate, and the meeting hadn't even been called to order yet.

Mayor Vitulli checked his watch and stepped up to the podium, adjusting the microphone, causing a bit of feedback. At the sound, the room began to settle, and the din died down.

Mayor Vitulli cleared his throat. "Thank you all for coming to this meeting of the town planning board. I would like to call this meeting to order."

He waited as the room fell quiet. A baby babbled out loud, and his mother cradled him, looking up at the mayor expectantly. "Thank you. Tonight's agenda is a busy one, so I appreciate your attention."

Nancy looked around, confused as to why the agenda would be so involved. As far as she knew, they were only going to discuss the proposal for the rave. She recognized the town's deputy mayor and event planner, the board all seated in folding chairs behind the podium, and Captain Larson and Lt. Becky Michaels of the police. She did not, however, recognize the rather officious-looking men, one a gray suit and the other in a black suit, seated next to Becky by the podium.

Vinnie and Dharma sat together, next to their parents. Vinnie looked around the room and caught Nancy's eye. He smiled and nodded. She returned the nod, but she didn't smile.

"First, I would like to introduce to you Dr. Klein from the New Jersey State Department of Health and Mr. Reinbeck from the Office of

Emergency Management." Mayor Vitulli stepped aside, and the man in the black suit stood first. He was tall and thin with thinning gray hair. There was whispering and murmuring in the crowd.

The man walked over to the podium and adjusted the microphone as he was taller than the mayor. The room fell silent. "Good evening. My name is Mr. Reinbeck, and I'm from the Ocean County Department of Emergency Management. As many of you have undoubtedly heard, there was an incident on Blackbeard's Pier earlier today."

The crowd stirred again. Nancy heard the words *dead, zombies,* and *attack* bandied about as the din rose again.

Reinbeck waited until the room settled. Although the room quieted, it didn't fall silent this time. He continued anyway. "There has been a confirmed incident of a six-year-old girl who tested positive for the Z Virus."

The din rose as people muttered and gasped, whispering in excitement.

"Unfortunately, she had to be neutralized, and her bite victims have been identified and quarantined."

"Neutralized!" Marney Traub's husband was standing, his right hand clenched in a fist and raised in front of him. "The police shot my daughter in cold blood! They murdered her!"

"Please, Mr. Traub, I ask that you reserve your comments for the question and answer period to come later." The crowd hummed with disapproval at the coldness of Reinbeck's remark.

Mr. Traub trembled with outrage. "My daughter was murdered by the police! What have you done to keep her safe? My wife is in quarantine. They won't even let me see her!"

Reinbeck remained stoic. "Mr. Traub, I understand your grief, but if you would allow me to continue, if you all would allow me to continue, I can provide an explanation as to how we plan to keep you safe."

He made to speak in retort, but a woman next to him—Marney's friend, Trisha Vance—placed a hand firmly on his arm. He looked down at her hand as if it was an unwanted spider that had landed on his arm, but he stayed his tongue. He reluctantly sat, glaring at the official up at the podium, as if he could burn a hole through his chest with his gaze.

"Thank you," said Reinbeck, putting in little effort to look sincere. "What happened to your family is terrible, but we are taking measures to make sure it doesn't happen to anyone else.

"The State Police and National Guard have been called in. They will be setting up a staging base in the abandoned King Arcade on the boardwalk tonight. There will be increased patrols of the beach and bay areas, as it is believed that the subject that infected the young girl and killed her grandfather came from the shoreline."

"She has a name!" blurted Mr. Traub. "Her name is April!"

"Yes, Mr. Traub. I know."

"I want to hear you *say* it," he insisted. This time, Trisha made no move to silence him.

"I want to hear you say *zombie*," said Nancy.

Everyone turned around and looked at Nancy, who was now standing, fists balled. No one dared place a hand on her arm for fear of losing it.

Reinbeck squinted his eyes. "Nancy Rizzuto, owner of Blackbeard's Pier." He knew her name because he dropped by the arcade to supervise the pier's sterilization.

"Yes, that's right," snapped Nancy. "You can say my name, but I noticed you bending over backwards not to say that this is the work of zombies."

"Ms. Rizzuto, that's not the proper terminology employed by myself, the Department of Health, or the Department of Emergency Management."

Nancy crossed her arms. "So, you bombard us with euphemisms, like 'young girl' and 'subject.' Why don't you call things what they are? Her name was April, and what infected her was a zombie." Mr. Traub nodded at Nancy from across the room in acknowledgement. "Now," Nancy continued, "I believe you were going to tell us about what you were going to do about the zombie problem."

"That's just it," interjected Mayor Vitulli, running up to the microphone. He leaned over Reinbeck, speaking into it. "It's not a zombie problem."

Reinbeck shot the mayor a look, and he withered. Reinbeck then cleared his throat. "What the mayor is trying to say is that we can only confirm the existence of one subject zero...or zombie...the one that infected April. We are taking measures to spot any further zombies so that they can be dealt with quickly and the spread of infection contained."

"What about this so-called Protocol Z?" asked Marco Cantone. "How will it be employed so that any more zombies will be taken out quickly?"

Reinbeck nodded. "There is a different Protocol Z for each phase of readiness. The one for Code Orange, which is a heightened state of alertness after a sighting, employs a more expedient protocol involving body language, much like Israeli airport security screening. In this case, we would look for unusual gait in the form of staggering, high-pitched screeching, and vomiting blood and digestive fluids.

"For confirmation, we have darts containing an enzyme that becomes luminescent when coming into contact with the Z Virus. Once infection is confirmed, we shoot on sight. Headshots only. A clean-up crew would then sweep in and place a second headshot at point-blank range to ensure complete neutralization."

The crowd stirred.

Reinbeck cleared his throat. The din fell to a low murmur. "Keep in mind that there has only been one infected person, and she has been neutralized. Any suspected of being bitten have been identified and are being quarantined and treated. There haven't been any other sightings since this morning."

"How can you be sure that you've caught all of those bitten?" asked Frank McCarthy, an ice cream shop owner.

"We cannot be one hundred percent certain," said Reinbeck. "Which is why we have representatives from the Department of Health and the Smuggler's Bay PD here to explain how we can facilitate rapid detection response to infection."

He stepped aside from the podium and waved Dr. Klein, Captain Larson, and Lt. Becky Michaels over. Dr. Klein took the lead. He nodded to Reinbeck, who stepped aside, and took his place at the podium. Captain Larson and Becky stood next to him.

Dr. Klein placed papers onto the podium, shuffling them around for a moment as he organized himself. He looked up. "Good evening." He adjusted the microphone to his smaller stature. He was a thin, beady-eyed, bespeckled man, looking like someone who worked in a lab. "My name is Dr. Klein from the Department of Health. I would like to thank Mayor Vitulli for having me here, and I commend his police department's speedy response to what could've been a much worse scenario without their efforts."

There was some limp applause that died out quickly. Mr. Traub sniffed audibly.

"An important question was just raised," continued Dr. Klein. "What if we didn't identify all those bitten? That is a very real concern, and although we expect those undetected to be at a minimum, the fact of the matter is that there may have been a few that were missed.

"So, what should you, as residents, do if you think someone is infected with the Z Virus? First, don't panic…" There were snickers and chortles coming from the seats. "…I want you to remember the following acronym: R-E-C—Recognize the symptoms, Evacuate to a safe distance, Call nine-one-one.

"What symptoms do you need to recognize? A pale, sickly pallor, dark discoloration under or around the eyes—we call it raccoon eyes. In the prodromal phase, before the virus manifests itself completely, the subject will exhibit strange, uncharacteristic behavior. Visual hallucinations—they will react to things that aren't there. They can become belligerent, crude, and even engage in self-injurious behavior, such as biting off one's own appendages…"

"We know the signs," shouted Marie Russo. "We've seen them first hand."

Dr. Klein appeared rattled by the interruption. "Yes, well, I understand that. However, I don't see the harm in reviewing…"

Marie stood, defiant, shaking her fist for emphasis as she spoke. "All I know is that I'm prepared, if the zombies were to return, as all of us should be. Last time, the police were quickly overwhelmed. I'm not waiting for their response this time."

Dr. Klein was stammering, looking down at his notes, shuffling papers around, not sure of how to respond. Captain Larson made to take the podium, but Becky whispered something into his ear, and he deferred to her.

Instead, she took the podium. "Ms. Russo, I know who you are, and I know that you've armed yourself in the event of another attack."

"Damned right," said Marie, her two children sitting next to her, holding her chin high. Salvatore smiled, proud of his mother. Alessandra looked like she wanted to die. "I know my Second Amendment Rights."

Becky nodded, keeping her composure. "While I agree with you and support your Second Amendment Rights, what we don't need is panic."

"Who's panicking?" retorted Marie.

Becky traded uncomfortable looks with Larson. "What I'm trying to say, Marie, is that if there are any further sightings, we need to clear a path for first responders, keeping lines of fire clear. We want to minimize friendly fire and accidents.

"No one is saying that you shouldn't protect yourself. Arm yourself, stand your ground. But let the police and National Guard get first licks. Keep your children back, out of harm's way. Then, if the zombies get to you, have at it."

Marie looked as if she wanted to respond, but Becky's appeal seemed to have registered with her. She nodded and remained silent.

"Which brings us to the E and C of R.E.C.," said Dr. Klein, stepping in. Becky let him retake his place at the podium. "Evacuate to a safe distance, as Lt. Michaels has just indicated. Keep your loved ones out of danger. Then Call 911. With increased manpower and patrols, we have ensured faster response time. You are our eyes and ears. If you see something, call us. Even if you are unsure."

"What about the proposed rave?" asked Nancy. "This town is going to be flooded with young people. Have you Googled what these ravers look like. They're going to be staggering around stoned, with stickers under their eyes, acting like a bunch of damned zombies. How will you tell the difference?"

Mayor Vitulli stood and rushed over to the podium. He adjusted the microphone. "Yes, regarding the proposed concert, the town council believes it wise to postpone the event until August, allowing time for our current situation to resolve."

"I don't know," said Melinda Scalli, owner of the Surf Bar and Grill. "Do we really think this town needs any more challenges? Don't we have enough to deal with before inviting in teens doing drugs and destroying property?"

"There's no direct connection between concerts and drug use or property destruction," insisted Mayor Vitulli. "We will have enough manpower to manage any difficulties that may arise."

"I don't think you know what a rave is," said Marie. "It's not just a 'concert.' There is drinking and drugging involved, and I don't want my kids exposed to that."

Mayor Vitulli's expression grew stern. "Listen up, folks. We need to bring in more tourism, or we're finished. We simply cannot afford another summer like last year. Our very livelihood depends on it.

"I know you all are used to doing things the same way. However, we can no longer survive solely as a family destination. We need to bring in more young people. Young people who don't necessarily care that there was a zombie outbreak here. Hell, some of them might even like it." He saw sour faces in the crowd, and there were sounds of disapproval.

"Oh, come off it. You all have embraced this identity. I walk down the boardwalk, and I see everything zombie-themed, and you're not just capitalizing on the popular cable show. You know that in order to survive as a town, we must own this thing.

"The local press got a whiff of what happened this morning and were reporting on it by midday. Probably right now, as I speak, the network news is covering it. Either we let this thing consume us, or we run with it.

"I promise you, that the concert will not go on until we have this current situation resolved."

*

The crowd slowly exited town hall all a-chatter.

"I don't know about all this," said Vinnie. "First we have a zombie sighting. Then we have the State Police and National Guard. Now they're talking about still having the rave."

"I hate to admit it," said his father, "but the mayor does have a point about bringing in more young people."

"Yeah, but it's unsafe," said Dharma.

"This town can't just stop and wait for things to be completely safe," said her mother, Emily. "We have to pay our mortgages and college tuition bills."

Dharma looked at her mother in disbelief. "I can't believe you, my mother, is actually encouraging the rave, and I'm actually against it."

Nancy strode up beside them as they walked. "I, for one, am more concerned with what's going on right now. There's been the first zombie sighting in two years, and nobody seems to know what they're doing."

Just then, two army trucks and an armored vehicle lumbered past them on their way to the staging base on the boardwalk.

"See?" said Marco. "The authorities are already here. If the zombies are coming back, we'll be ready for them this time."

"Are you all going to the bonfire?" asked Nancy.

They all nodded and answered yes.

"Good. I'm doing half-price rides tonight. Drop by the pier afterwards. It's been thoroughly sanitized, and the haunted house is closed."

"I dunno," said Vinnie. "I don't much feel like going on rides."

"Oh, please," snapped Nancy. "Tonight is about commemorating our survival. A zombie attack and a superstorm couldn't destroy this town, and do you know why? Because we carried on."

"I think what Nancy is trying to say is that it'll be good for the town to see you on the rides having fun," said Marlene, Vinnie's mother.

"What about the zombies?" asked Vinnie.

"There's tons of cops and military here now. If you hear anything funny, just head straight home and away from whatever it is," said Dharma's mother, Emily.

"You're not little kids anymore," reminded Vinnie's father, Marco.

"This is rich," said Dharma. "When we were in high school, they never wanted us to go out. Now that there's a zombie apocalypse, they're kicking us out the door."

"I'm going to be running the sunglass store," said Emily.

Vinnie did his best not to look deflated. So much for nookie. Dharma read his expression and squeezed his arm.

"And I'll be at the pizzeria," said Marco. "We all have to do our part."

"Then it's settled," said Nancy. "I expect to see you two later on tonight. Free ice cream for the both of you." Nancy walked ahead, wanting to drop by the pier to see if she was needed before heading to the bonfire.

"I scream, you scream, we all scream for ice cream," said Dharma.

"Or for zombies," said Vinnie.

"That's not funny," rebuked his mother.

Vinnie's father looked up at the darkening sky. "Why don't you two go on ahead to the bonfire? We'll catch up. We have to stop by the pizzeria first."

"And we have to check on the hut," said Dharma's father, Ira.

The parents crossed the street, parting ways from their children, heading towards their respective boardwalk shops. Vinnie and Dharma headed towards the very beginning of the boardwalk, where the bonfire would take place.

Dharma saw that Vinnie was stewing in his own juices. She nudged him with her elbow. "What's eating you?"

"I don't appreciate your wording."

"Oh, c'mon. We'll still have our little tawdry rendezvous. We just have to wait a little later, when the hut closes."

"It's not that," said Vinnie.

"Oh," said Dharma, the smile fading from her face. "The zombies."

"Yeah."

"Well, there haven't been any more sightings."

"Since this morning. What makes you think that's it?"

"You never told me how your session with Tara went," probed Dharma.

"It went okay. She said it wasn't really a session."

Dharma shot him an exasperated look. "What else did she say?"

"That it's an unsafe world."

"Go on…"

"That I could get hit by a car or drop dead of an aneurysm today, maybe even at this very moment."

"Jesus," gasped Dharma. "So I guess the threat of zombies isn't so bad."

"That was her point," said Vinnie. "If people stopped and really considered all of the dangers out there, no one would leave their house."

"You know," said Dharma, leaning in, "it sounds like neither of our parents are going to be home…"

God, she smells good. Vinnie shook his head. "We promised Nancy that we'd go to the pier. We can't just ditch her and run home to fool around. She'd notice we weren't there."

"What if we made a quick cameo at the bonfire, left early to go on some rides, and ran back to my house?" suggested Dharma.

"Don't forget about the ice cream."

"Right, and eat some ice cream."

"What time are your parents closing the hut?"

"Probably ten o'clock."

"That doesn't leave us much time."

"You don't need more than a few minutes," teased Dharma.

"Hey, watch it."

"Either way. If we're still out before they close the hut, I have spare keys. If we have time, we'll run home and have a quickie."

Vinnie thought about it a moment. "You know, this just might work."

Dharma grinned. "What could possibly go wrong?"

* * *

Chief Holbrook sat in his cell contemplating life when the door to the cell area opened and Officer Pacelli escorted a drunk man inside. The man, disheveled and filthy, was dragging his feet and being difficult.

Martinez looked over, and when he saw who it was, he shook his head.

Holbrook recognized the man immediately. "Jesus, Tim, again?"

Timothy O'Leary's head rolled on his shoulders, and he looked up at Holbrook. "How's it going, Chief?" He squinted. "Whatcha doin' in there?"

Holbrook sighed. "Long story, Tim. We'll have plenty of time to talk about it."

Tim O'Leary was one of the town drunks. The guy had mental problems, but he always refused care. He preferred to work at his father's restaurant during the day and spend his nights inside a bottle.

He chuckled, amused at the sight of seeing the police chief in a cell. "Looks like you an' me are gonna be housemates." He laughed raucously at his own joke as he was shoved into a cell. As Pacelli closed the cell door, Tim planted himself on the cot and stared listlessly at the black ink on his fingertips from being printed.

"You look like hammered shit, O'Leary," said Holbrook.

"I'm sorry, Chief," said Pacelli, as he and Martinez traded chuckles.

Holbrook waved a hand. "Don't worry. Now I can't complain I'm bored."

Pacelli tipped his hat to the chief, shot him a smirk, and went back upstairs.

Tim turned and faced Holbrook. "Whatcha in for, Chief?" His smile revealed a few missing teeth. Those that were left were badly stained by coffee and cigarettes.

"You didn't hear?" answered Holbrook.

"You know I don't watch the news, Chief. But ol' Bob Murphy does. At the pub he said you got bit by a little girlie on the pier in the spook house."

Holbrook and Martinez looked at each other.

"What else did ol' Bob Murphy say?"

"He said that the girl was one of them zombie things, and that they might be back."

"Jesus," said Holbrook to Martinez. "Word gets around fast."

"Hey, Chief, you're not going to bite my ass while I'm sleeping, are you?" He again laughed at his own joke. He stuck his arms out in front of him, "Brains! Braaaaaaains!"

"Pipe down," said Holbrook.

Tim O'Leary chuckled quietly to himself.

The door to the cell area opened again, but this time it was Holbrook's wife, Lena. He stood up immediately. "Honey, what are you doing here? Where's Robbie?"

Lena said hello to Martinez, who nodded and said, "Ma'am."

Holbrook gripped the bars of his cell. He wanted to see her so badly, but he didn't want her to see him like this.

Lena approached her husband's cell. "Robbie's upstairs with Pacelli. Jesus, Jim." She placed her hand on his, her eyes welling up. "I couldn't believe it when I heard it. Are you…all right?"

"I'm okay, but Martinez, here, has to babysit me until Protocol Z is over."

"Do you feel any different? Strange or sick?"

Holbrook shook his head. "Nope. In fact, I've been doing so well, the doc stopped taking my vitals. He said I'm stable, and if I was sick, my vitals would've gone south by now. The rest is just precaution."

"Hello there," said Tim O'Leary, flashing a lascivious grin at Lena. "Are you the chief's wife?"

"Pipe down, Tim," warned Holbrook.

Lena glanced at him, but she ignored the question.

Tim didn't care that he was being ignored. "Damn, Chief. I had no idea you were married to such a piece of tail."

This rubbed an old wound dealt by Billy Blake. "Goddammit, O'Leary. I said that's enough."

Tim chuckled to himself in his cell, muttering under his breath.

Holbrook shook his head.

Lena slipped her hand through the bars, touching her husband's chest. "Don't worry about it. He's drunk."

"And crazy," added Martinez.

Holbrook shook his head in disgust. "There's so much going on right now. So much that needs to be done. The State Police and the National Guard are here, setting up on the boardwalk. Then, after the town council meeting, I'm sure some folks are skipping town." He checked his wristwatch. "In fact, meeting's over already."

Lena nodded. "There're cops guiding traffic. It's not a mass evacuation, but some folks are leaving. You can't blame them."

Holbrook averted his gaze. "Maybe you should take Robbie to your parents, until things blow over here."

"Why, Jim? They said it was an isolated incident."

Tim O'Leary was now standing, leaning up against the bars of his cell. His right arm swung lazily in front of him. He looked like a drunk ape. "Hey, Mrs. Chief's wife. Are you coming to visit me, too? I could use a conjugal visit."

Holbrook wheeled around, pointing a finger at Tim. "I said can it, O'Leary. Last warning."

Lena frowned. "I want to be here with you. I don't like you sitting alone here in this cell. Especially with this character, here."

"I'm fine, Lena. Besides, if the shit hits the fan, I can't help you in here."

"I can help you, pretty lady," jeered Tim. "Why don't you come over here and gimme a big, wet kiss?"

Martinez jumped in this time. "The chief told you to knock it off!"

"Get out of my face," said Tim.

"Hey," said Martinez, stepping closer to the bars, looking Tim dead in the eyes. "Cool it."

Tim O'Leary exploded into violence, grabbing Officer Martinez through the bars. His raccoon eyes were fierce. "No, you cool it." He puked up blood all over Officer Martinez as the poor cop squirmed in his grip, turning his head away from the spray.

Lena Holbrook screamed.

"Jesus!" cried Holbrook.

Martinez wriggled out of Tim O'Leary's grip, tearing his uniform shirt in the process. He backed into the wall opposite the cell and frantically wiped his face with his sleeves and the backs of his hands, whimpering.

Tim O'Leary jumped up and down in his cell, bouncing off of the bars like an agitated chimp at the zoo. He grunted and wheezed, his laughter punctuated with short shrieks.

Holbrook grabbed Lena's hands through the bars. "Lena, listen to me!"

She gazed in horror at the monster in the cell and the cop covered in gore.

Holbrook pulled her close to the bars. "Lena!"

She looked at him, about to cry. "Not again. Please, not again."

Holbrook's eyes were intense with urgency. "Listen to me. Go get Pacelli. Tell him that Tim O'Leary is positive for Protocol Z. Then take Robbie and get out of here."

"Where will we go?"

"Get Pacelli, then wait for me at home. *Now,* Lena."

She nodded and practically tripped over her own feet leaving the cell area.

Holbrook called out to his officer. "Martinez! Martinez, are you all right!"

Martinez was slowly backing away from O'Leary's cell towards Holbrook. "I think so. Christ, it's everywhere."

"Don't let it touch your eyes or get in your mouth."

Tim O'Leary now had his penis out and was masturbating all over his cell, tugging away with fervor. "Now there will be three monkeys in a cage! Three little monkeys infected by the dead, one fell down and cracked his head, me an' Chief's wife are goin' to bed, one more monkey to give me head!"

CHAPTER 7

Vinnie and Dharma descended the wooden ramp to the beach. The fire marshal looked on as two lifeguards were arranging two wooden shipping palettes in the large, rusted metal basin. The area was cordoned off with yellow police tape wrapped around a red garbage pail at each corner. The musician was already tuning his guitar, preparing to belt out some tunes.

When they hit the sand at the base of the ramp, Dharma kicked off her sandals and carried them in her hands. She loved the feeling of sand between her toes. Vinnie, on the other hand, kept his sneakers on.

They meandered into the crowd of locals.

Vinnie scratched his head. "I'm surprised so many chose to stay for this, given what happened this morning."

"It was only one sighting," said Dharma, flashing warm smiles as she passed folks she knew. "Besides, after last summer, I don't think people can afford to pick up and stay in hotels elsewhere."

Vinnie hadn't thought of that. "There're always relatives."

"Yeah, but it's a major disruption of daily life. That would mean shops would have to close during the beginning of the season, the worst possible time. And how long would you have to stay with said relatives? A week? A month? When would it be 'safe' to come back?"

Vinnie frowned. "You sound like Tara."

Dharma's face lit up, and she pointed ahead of them. "Speaking of Tara, there she is with Tyrell and Lenny."

Lenny saw Dharma pointing at him. He smiled and waved her over. Dharma and Vinnie waved back. They passed Marie Russo and her kids sitting on a blanket. Marie waved and smiled, but Alessandra leapt to her feet and threw her arms around Dharma. "Hey, Dharma!"

Salvatore, playing it cool, offered his fist to Vinnie to bump. "Wassup?"

Vinnie bumped it. "Nothin' much, man. Ready to hear some old tunes?"

Salvatore rolled his eyes. "I'd rather be going on rides."

Dharma broke her embrace with Alessandra, reached out, and ruffled Salvatore's hair, causing him to blush. "As it ends up, we're going to Blackbeard's in a little bit. Nancy wants people on rides. She said it'd be good for people to see us having fun."

"Sounds like it'll be good for her pockets," quipped Marie.

"You should come with us," offered Vinnie.

Salvatore looked pleadingly at his mother. Alessandra, less subtle, jumped up and down chanting, "Please, Mom! Please, Mom!"

Marie smiled. "Okay, but you two have to stay with Vinnie and Dharma. I don't want you two wandering off."

"Yay!" cheered Alessandra.

Salvatore smiled, high-fiving Vinnie.

"We're going to go in a few minutes," said Dharma, consulting the time on her cell phone. "I just wanna say hi to Lenny and Tara."

"What about the music?" protested Marie. "I hear this guy's good! He's gonna sing some Bob Dylan, Bruce Springsteen, and Meatloaf!"

Salvatore grimaced. "Gross, Mom."

Marie shrugged. "What, you love my meatloaf?"

Salvatore rolled his eyes. "You need new jokes, Mom. Seriously."

"Well, you two be back by nine at the latest," warned Marie.

"We'll have them back with most of their fingers and toes," cracked Dharma. She placed her arm around Alessandra, and they walked towards Tara. Vinnie and Salvatore followed, shuffling through the sand.

The fire was underway and growing, as people gathered round in folding beach chairs and on blankets. The musician, a portly older man with long, straw-like hair and side burns, introduced himself as Pete Wendell, and he began to belt out "American Pie" by Don McLean.

"Hey, guys," Lenny said, beaming.

"Vinnie!" cried Tyrell, running over and slapping him five with the gusto only a seven-year-old could muster. Vinnie pretended to wave his hand in the air, as if it hurt. Tyrell then gave Dharma a hug.

Tara smiled at Vinnie. "I'm glad you made it."

"Thanks," said Vinnie, returning the smile. "A good friend told me I should be here."

"But we're not staying long," said Dharma. "We're all going to Blackbeard's to go on some rides. Nancy's orders."

Tyrell's head immediately whipped around to his mother.

Tara was already nodding her consent. "That sounds like fun. You can go with them, Ty, but you have to stay with Vinnie and Dharma at all times."

"Yay!" He jumped up and down in the sand.

"It appears we've formed a posse," said Vinnie.

"Let's hit the pier before it gets crowded," suggested Dharma.

"I don't think it'll be all that crowded," said Tara. "Some people have already left. The ones who don't work here in town. There's nothing keeping them here."

"Well, we'd better get going before it's too late," pressed Dharma, quickly changing the subject away from zombies.

"Can you drop him by here by around eight?" asked Tara, checking the time on her own cell.

"Aw, Mom. That's too early," protested Tyrell.

Tara put her hands on her hips. "You can always stay here with me…"

Tyrell realized he'd taken it too far. Some rides were better than none. "Eight o'clock is good, Mom."

Tara arched an eyebrow. "Thought so."

"Can I go, too?" asked Lenny, fearing he was going to be left out.

"As long as you stay with Vinnie and Tara at all times," said Tara. When she saw Lenny begin to grouse, she added, "and keep an eye on Tyrell. Make sure he stays out of trouble."

Lenny's expression softened. He smiled and gave Tara an enthusiastic thumbs up. "Okay!"

"Okay, gang," said Dharma, making a large sweeping gesture with her right hand. "Let's roll out!"

The small gang now negotiated their way back through the crowd and toward the boardwalk to the tune of "Keep on Rockin' in the Free World" by Neil Young.

They passed Officer Becky, in full uniform talking to Mr. MacDonald and his wife. She glanced at Vinnie and smiled. Vinnie blushed and smiled back, quickly averting his gaze.

Dharma noticed and punched him in the arm. "What the hell was that?"

"What?" Vinnie said, shrugging.

"You know what! I saw that."

"I have no idea what you're talking about."

"You're lucky we're surrounded by all these kids."

"I'm not a kid," complained Lenny. "I-I-I'm all g-grown up now."

"Yes, Lenny," assured Dharma. "I wasn't talking about you, silly."

This assuaged him, and he continued on, keeping a watchful hand on Tyrell's shoulder as per his charge.

As they took to the boardwalk, Dharma slipped her sandals back on, and she and Vinnie led the way. This was more than a group of friends. This was a group of survivors who went through hell together and emerged on the other side, which made them a kind of makeshift family.

They passed the heavy metal T-shirt shop. Incense wafted on the gentle breeze. Dharma inhaled deeply, savoring it. To her, it was the smell of summer. Lenny scrunched his nose up, not appreciating the potent odor.

They passed balloon dart games, smaller arcades, and ice cream parlors. Lenny tugged at Vinnie's sleeve, winking and nodding towards the ice cream. Tyrell eyed Vinnie expectantly, gauging his response.

"Maybe after the rides," prompted Vinnie. "You don't want to get sick."

Lenny nodded and gave Vinnie a thumbs up. Tyrell frowned, not wanting to delay gratification. His frustration quickly gave way to enthusiasm when he saw the Shoot the Zombie booth. "I wanna do that!" He pointed at the booth.

Now Vinnie's expression soured. "Really, Ty? C'mon. I thought you weren't into guns and shooting."

"I said *my mom* wasn't. Besides, those aren't real guns."

"He has a point," said Salvatore.

Alessandra elbowed him, shooting him a dirty look.

"Oh, why not?" offered Dharma. "Let's see if we can hit more targets than the boys."

Alessandra gripped Dharma's arm, and she grinned in wicked delight.

"You're on," chortled Salvatore. "You girls don't stand a chance."

"I don't know," hesitated Vinnie. "Don't you think this is in poor taste, especially after this morning?"

"Someone sounds chicken," said Dharma to Alessandra, and the two of them giggled conspiratorially.

"C'mon, man," pleaded Tyrell.

"Think of it as therapy," coaxed Dharma.

Vinnie smiled and pointed an accusatory finger at her. "No one calls us chicken! Right, boys?"

He, Salvatore, and Tyrell exchanged high fives, and they all approached the booth.

"How many of you?" asked the carnie behind the counter.

"Are you playing?" Vinnie asked Lenny.

Lenny put up both hands, palms facing out, and shook his head. "Nah, you guys p-p-play."

"Five," Vinnie told the carnie.

"Fifteen bucks."

"Jesus," muttered Vinnie, as he reached into his wallet. He slammed a ten and a five down on the counter top. He turned to the rest of the group. "You guys aren't cheap dates."

Vinnie kicked a milk crate over for Tyrell to stand on as Salvatore took his place by a paintball gun. Dharma and Alessandra were at their stations. Each of them picked up their paint guns, hefting them, as Lenny stood to the side and watched.

Inside the booth, multicolored lights flashed over a paint-stained room with wooden cutouts of zombies towards the back in various menacing poses. The carnie stepped aside, "Go ahead."

The girls immediately started firing. Dharma's shots were wild, but Alessandra's were controlled and disciplined. Even though shooting paintballs was akin to firing balls out of muskets, Alessandra managed to score some hits, mostly head and shoulder shots.

Tyrell's shots were wild like Dharma's, but Salvatore's were like his sister's, controlled and often hitting their marks. Vinnie stood there, weapon raised and sighted, but he didn't fire. Instead, he blinked and squinted as lights flashed and tinny moans emanated from cheap speakers mounted inside the booth.

He narrowed his gaze, focusing on the zombie targets, but to him they didn't appear to be wooden cutouts. He knew it was a trick of the lighting and his mind, but he could've sworn, for the life of him, that they were moving slowly, hands reaching out for him. His palms grew sweaty as the kids cheered around him.

When the others had expended their ammunition, Vinnie stood there, transfixed. Dharma's voice called out to him from off-stage in his mind's eye as the lights dimmed, "Vinnie, are you okay?"

Vinnie clenched his teeth as the ambling zombies gnashed theirs in feral hunger. He yanked on the trigger, firing one shot after another, actually making head shots here and there. He growled with each pull of the trigger, grunting every time a paintball found purchase. His growls synchronized with the zombies' moans as he sneered at them in contempt.

After a minute, he found himself pulling on the trigger, but no more paintballs were firing. There was only the sound of discharged CO2.

"You can stop now," said the carnie, also from off-stage in the darkness. "You're out of ammo."

The darkness in his periphery receded, and Vinnie shook his head, chasing away the moans and the illusion of staggering dead. He slowly lowered his paintball gun to the countertop. When he looked over at the rest of the gang, he saw them staring back at him, stunned.

Dharma looked concerned. Alessandra looked from Vinnie to Dharma, mirroring Dharma's concern, not exactly sure what had just happened. Salvatore looked away awkwardly, as if embarrassed for Vinnie.

Tyrell beamed, triumphant. "I think we hit more than the girls!"

Dharma put her arm around Vinnie. She whispered in his ear, "Are you okay?"

Vinnie, wiping sweat from his brow, his hand trembling, nodded silently.

Dharma wanted to move on past whatever just happened. "Okay, kids. Enough of this. Let's go on some rides!"

Everyone, including Lenny, cheered.

As they strolled down the boardwalk, they passed Mac's Pub. Inside there were hulking bikers huddled around the bar, arms around each other, belting out "Never Gonna Give You Up" with Rick Astley on the jukebox.

This shook Vinnie out of his funk. "Now, there's something you don't see every day.

They walked onto Blackbeard's Pier and were immediately inundated with the sounds and flashing lights of rides. There was the buzzing of the motorcycles, the bells of the boats, and the roar of the Pirate's Cove roller coaster. In the distance, there was the bass thumping of the Raging Rapids—a fast, circular ride that had its own DJ pumping out heavy dance beats.

"I wanna go on that," said Alessandra, pointing to the Raging Rapids.

Dharma looked at Salvatore, who nodded his approval.

"That looks too s-s-scary," said Lenny.

Tyrell looked on in awe, thankful he was too short to meet the height requirement.

"Why don't I take Lenny and Tyrell around while you guys go on that ride?" offered Vinnie.

"Good idea," said Dharma. "You guys find rides you can go on. We'll meet up later, right here."

Vinnie and the boys nodded, and they watched Dharma, Alessandra, and Salvatore head off to the Raging Rapids ride, which had already garnered a sizeable line. Due to the dance beats pumping out from a live DJ, the ride was always popular, particularly with the teens. It was currently blasting a remix of "Cool for the Summer" by Demi Lovato, laying on the bass thick.

Vinnie looked around the pier. "So, what do you guys wanna go on first?"

"I wanna go on the sky ride," blurted Tyrell.

Vinnie looked to Lenny. "Sound good?"

Lenny nodded and gave a thumbs up.

The three boys headed towards the sky ride. There was a short line. Vinnie produced a ten dollar bill as the line moved quickly to the ticket window. There was a cute blonde girl selling tickets.

"How many?"

"Three," said Vinnie, shoving the ten under the glass.

The girl rang up three and handed back two-fifty in change with three orange tickets. "Here you go."

"Thanks." Vinnie snatched up the change and shoved it into his right pocket. He palmed the tickets and headed inside the chain-link fence with Tyrell and Lenny. Lenny was rubbing his hands together in eager anticipation. He didn't like fast rides, but he didn't mind height, as long as it was slow. The sky ride afforded a nice view of the beach, which was a bonus. Tyrell extended a hand for his ticket.

"I'll hold the tickets," insisted Vinnie, correctly assuming that it was unsafe in unsure hands. He had babysat Tyrell on more than a few occasions. He didn't want them falling between the planks of the boardwalk. "Ty, you're riding with me. Lenny, you'll get your own chair. Okay?"

Lenny was looking around, excited. He grinned at Vinnie. "No problem." He didn't mind at all, because in his mind he wasn't alone. Billy Blake, in his superhero sidekick costume, was right beside him, currently checking out the ass of a teenage girl with her boyfriend in front of them. Some things never changed.

As they approached the turnstile, the attendant took the tickets from Vinnie. "Only two per chair."

"I know," said Vinnie, pulling Tyrell to his side. "He's with me."

She looked at Lenny and smiled, recognizing him. Everyone knew Lenny. He was the unofficial Mayor of Smuggler's Bay, especially after the attack two summers ago.

"Hi, Lenny." Her greeting had a flirty, singsong quality to it.

Lenny blushed, which seemed to please the girl.

Being a resident of the Bay from birth, Vinnie knew the drill. As she let him and Tyrell through the turnstile, she guided them to the psychedelic green footprints on the ground. He and Tyrell stood side-by-side, waiting. As the next chair swung around, the attendant swung the safety bar up, grabbed it, and slowed it down, her feet dragging slightly on the wooden planks.

"Hold on," said Vinnie.

Vinnie and Tyrell hopped up and sat in the chair, and the attendant swung the safety bar down. Vinnie's feet touched the footrests, but Tyrell's feet dangled. He was wearing sneakers, so it was all right.

As the chair took off on its gradual climb, Vinnie looked back at Lenny, who deftly hopped into his chair right behind them. The girl said something that made Lenny smile, and she lowered the safety bar.

Lenny saw Vinnie looking back. He smiled and waved.

When Vinnie turned back around, he saw Tyrell looking down at the boardwalk. His feet kicked in excitement, which made Vinnie smile. It was just as well. Vinnie wasn't crazy about those fast rides and their drops. No, the sky ride was just his speed.

Watching Tyrell reminded him of when he first went on the sky ride as a kid. His mother had taken him. Like Vinnie, she did not particularly like the fast rides. That was his father's cup of tea.

They were able to see the rooftops of the various arcades and storefronts, and the rest of the Bay behind it all. The Smuggler's Bay water tower, blending into the fabric of the night sky, was no longer visible. There were cars driving on the streets, but nowhere near the traffic during prime season.

Vinnie pointed ahead. "Look, you can see the bonfire at the other end."

Tyrell looked, trying to make out the people. However, they were too far away. They'd be there soon enough. Vinnie had purchased round trip tickets, so they'd swing right through the station on the other side and return to the pier.

Tyrell scrunched up his face and narrowed his gaze. He pointed off in the distance, towards the water. "What's that?'

Vinnie looked in the direction he was pointing. At first, he didn't see it. "What are you talking about?"

"Those glowing things," insisted Tyrell. "They look like animal eyes."

Vinnie laughed. "They're probably a horde of feral cats. We've had a ton of them since the superstorm."

The wind was picking up, as the ride had reached its apex. Vinnie felt goosebumps on his arms. There was a low moan to the wind, a disconcerting sound that reminded him of something.

Then he saw it.

Vinnie screwed his eyes to try and make it out. It looked like pairs of glowing eyes, like cats' eyes, off by the water, a short distance from the bonfire. They were moving slowly in the dark. Vinnie heard the sound of the waves crashing, but the waves were concealed by the darkness.

"No."

"What?" asked Tyrell, unsure of why Vinnie's expression suddenly became grave.

"It can't be," demanded Vinnie, now leaning forward in his chair.

"What?" pressed Tyrell, now looking off in the distance at the glowing eyes.

"Those aren't cats," declared Vinnie.

"What are they?"

Vinnie reached for his phone. He pulled it out of his pocket and dialed 911. "Hello. This is going to sound weird, but I'm calling from the sky ride on the boardwalk, and I think I've spotted a large group of zombies on the beach! They're headed right for the bonfire!"

Tyrell's eyes grew wide. His body became rigid, and a chill ran through his little frame that had nothing to do with the cool ocean breeze.

"No," argued Vinnie, "I know this isn't funny. This isn't a prank. There is a group of zombies on the beach heading right for the bonfire."

Tyrell saw the glowing eyes advancing slowly towards the bonfire. Towards his mother.

"Please, get someone to check it out!"

Tyrell grabbed Vinnie's arm. "My mom's down there."

"Okay, okay. Just make it quick. People are going to get hurt." Vinnie hung up the phone.

"Vinnie, my mom."

"I know, Ty. I just got off the phone with the police. They have someone down there."

"She needs to get out of there!" Tyrell was nearly hysterical. "We need to get her out of there!"

"Calm down," said Vinnie, placing his arm around Tyrell. "We're going to warn them."

"Are you sure it's zombies? Are you sure it's them, Vinnie?"

As the sky ride crept closer, they passed alongside the glowing eyes and were closing in on the bonfire celebration. Vinnie began to wave his arms and shout down at the people below. Mellow folk music bellowed out of the speakers on the beach.

There was no way they would hear him.

"What are we going to do?" asked Tyrell.

Vinnie was leaning forward in his seat, ready to jump out. He looked determined. "We're getting off on this end."

At last, their chair was approaching the landing platform. Vinnie flipped up the safety bar and looked back as the attendant scolded him for doing it himself and too early. He saw the glowing eyes floating in the darkness, flickering in the reflected firelight and the light of the moon.

The attendant grabbed the chair to slow it down, and Vinnie jumped off, pulling Tyrell with him.

"Hey!" the girl protested, but Vinnie didn't stick around to argue.

Tyrell's feet were dragging on the boardwalk. "Wait up!"

Vinnie paused for a second, allowing Tyrell to get his footing. "C'mon! You want to help your mom, don't you?"

They only had to wait a moment for Lenny's chair to reach the landing platform. Vinnie was already shouting at him, "Lenny, you have to go home!"

The attendant, frowning at Vinnie's apparent mean outburst, raised the safety bar and slowed the chair so Lenny could hop off.

Lenny stepped to the side, and Vinnie grabbed him. "Lenny, go home! You have to hide!"

"Hey, leave him alone," said the attendant.

Vinnie turned on her. "The dead are back! They're on the beach!"

"What?" asked the girl.

Vinnie realized that she probably wasn't here for the first attack, so he didn't waste time explaining to her. She wouldn't get it.

"Noooo." Lenny shook his head in denial of what was unfolding. It couldn't be happening. Not again. The good guys won last time.

"Lenny, go!" Vinnie insisted. "I'll meet you later."

That last part seemed to soften the order. "You and me?"

"Yes, Lenny, you and me. Go!"

Lenny nodded and began to hobble his way off the landing platform. Vinnie and Tyrell followed right behind him, Vinnie pushing him through the turn style. Vinnie picked Tyrell up and carried him as he passed through.

Vinnie pointed with his whole arm off the boardwalk. "Lenny, go to headquarters. Put on your cape and mask and hide. This is a job for Lava Man! Wait for me."

Lenny looked over at Billy, who shrugged. Excited by the opportunity to don his superhero outfit and be a savior once more, Lenny gave two thumbs off and walked off the boardwalk in earnest.

*

Lenny walked as fast as his legs would take him, breezing past people walking onto the boardwalk. His walking wasn't the best, so he kept his hands out, balancing and bracing himself in case he fell, like his physical therapist taught him.

He looked to his right, where Billy Blake kept up with him. "We have to save the day again."

Billy winked and gave him a thumbs up. "I'm with you all the way, Lenny. Let's kick some ass!"

The families Lenny practically knocked down as he rushed in the other direction looked back and squinted as they saw a special person talking to thin air.

*

Vinnie turned to Tyrell. "We've got to warn everyone."

Tyrell nodded, and they dashed down the wooden ramp to the beach. People were standing around as the musician was belting out "Dream A Little Dream of Me" by the Mamas and Papas.

Vinnie looked around frantically, searching the crowd.

"There's my mom!" cried Tyrell, pointing.

"I see Officer Becky," said Vinnie. "You go get your mom. Tell her what we saw."

Tyrell nodded obediently and dashed off. Tara smiled at first, checking her watch and wondering why they were back so soon. When she saw Tyrell's expression, hers turned to concern.

Vinnie wasted no time. He bee-lined over to Becky, who was standing with one of the National Guard officers. "Officer Becky, am I glad to see you." He was catching his breath.

She saw the expression on his face. "I was just chatting with Captain McBride, here. What's wrong, Vinnie?"

"Good…I'm glad…he's here, too."

McBride frowned. "Catch your breath, kid."

"There're zombies on the beach, and they're headed right this way!"

There were murmurs and concerned looks from other bonfire goers. Becky grabbed Vinnie by the arm and pulled him aside. She leaned in close and spoke through gritted teeth. "What do you think you're doing? You're making a scene."

"No, really! I saw them from the sky ride. There's a whole bunch of them heading this way from the water."

Becky put her hands on her hips. "This isn't funny, Vinnie."

Captain McBride was looking towards the blackness, listening to the waves crashing. "I don't see anything."

"There must be a hundred of them." Vinnie pointed to the pitch black. "There!"

Becky looked and saw nothing but full dark. "Vinnie, you're scaring everyone." Her tone was reprimanding, but there was also fear in her voice.

Vinnie grabbed her by the shoulders and looked her in the eye. "You have to do something. They're here. Please!"

Vinnie was a good kid. Plus, he was one of the heroes of the first attack two years ago. If anyone knew what those things looked like, it'd be him. Becky nodded. "Okay. We'll have a look." She nodded to Captain McBride, who got on his radio.

"Send down a squad, and bring some lights," he said.

Tara shuffled through the sand towards where they were standing and accosted Vinnie. "What in the hell is going on here? You have my son scared half to death, talking about seeing zombies on the beach."

"I saw them," insisted Vinnie. "I swear it. We need to get out of here. All of us. Now."

"I thought we had an understanding, to move past all this zombie stuff," scolded Tara.

"I'm not lying, and I'm not crazy," insisted Vinnie.

"Now hold on just a second," said Captain McBride. "No need to create a panic until we've had a look."

Six guardsmen strolled across the sand towards them. They were carrying lights. Three had odd-looking rifles. They looked like flare guns.

"What's up, Marty?" asked one of the soldiers.

"Captain McBride," McBride insisted. "This boy, here, said he saw something advancing up the beach towards us from the sky ride."

"They were zombies," explained Vinnie. "I know what I saw."

"Let's get some lights on this beach," said Captain McBride.

The three men with powerful LED lamps spread out. The musician kept playing, but the crowd's eyes were on the National Guardsmen.

They flicked on the lights, and the pitch darkness by the water lit up with numerous pairs of reflections, like cats eyes.

"See!" cried Vinnie. "That's them!"

"What in the hell...?" Captain McBride strained his eyes, trying to make it out.

"We've had a big feral cat problem," offered Officer Becky. "There're probably tons of them out there."

There was murmuring in the crowd. The musician had stopped playing, and everyone was backing away from the beach.

McBride waved at his men holding the rifles. "Fire bioluminescent rounds."

The other three men stepped forward and fired a round each. There were pops, and a green spray scattered in the air. The spray illuminated and appeared to stay suspended in the air, never reaching the ground.

"Signal flare," McBride ordered.

A soldier brought him a small box. Captain McBride opened it, removed a small pistol, loaded it with a flare, and took aim above the suspended bioluminated green dots. He fired above the middle of them.

At first, there was a bright red light that bounced around and blurred everyone's vision. Within seconds, everyone saw an illuminated horde of dead standing there, waiting silently.

"Evacuate the beach!" shouted McBride, and everyone began to run and scream. Like the predators they were, the dead screeched and took off after their terrified prey.

McBride was on his radio, and Officer Becky had her weapon drawn. The townsfolk swarmed past them and towards the ramp. They stormed the wooden ramp, pushing and shoving to get back onto the boardwalk.

When the crowd cleared, Tara was standing there, shouting for Tyrell. An older woman was face down in the sand, and an old man was sitting in the sand, stunned, knocked over by the wave of fleeing people.

Vinnie was still beside Officer Becky.

"What are you still doing here?" she asked.

Vinnie snapped out of his hysteria. "I'll get Tyrell! You and the captain get the other two."

As Vinnie took off to run, Tara was right beside him. As they closed the gap with Tyrell, the tsunami of dead were closing in on them. Unarmed, Captain McBride went for the lady who was lying face down in the sand. Apparently, she had been trampled by the panicked exodus. Becky placed her hands under the old man's arms and hoisted him up with a grunt.

Soldiers took to the beach, taking aim at the advancing dead swarm. Some remained on the boardwalk in an elevated position.

"Fire at will!" commanded Captain McBride into his radio. He hoisted the unconscious woman onto his shoulder and began to plod his way through the sand back towards the boardwalk.

The soldiers on the beach created firing lines, and the ones on the boardwalk began shooting at the dead.

Vinnie snatched Tyrell up in his arms. "I'll be faster," he told Tara. She nodded, and they ran back up the beach towards the ramps, ducking their heads. The hungry dead were right on their heels. However, they were slower in the shifting sand, which bought Vinnie, Tara, and Tyrell some time.

The soldiers on the beach in front of them held their fire, allowing them passage. Vinnie, carrying Tyrell, and Tara rushed past them.

Becky had one hand under the old man's armpit, helping him along, and the other held her weapon. She trained it at the closest zombies, watching them as she shoved the old man towards the boardwalk. Fortunately, they struggled as they staggered through the sand after them. Unfortunately, so did the old man.

When they all had passed the soldiers on the beach, clearing the lines of fire, the soldiers opened up on the screeching dead. They dropped several of the dead with headshots, but missed others, striking some in the center mass. The dead were too close, and they quickly overwhelmed the guardsmen. There were screams of terror as soldiers were engulfed in a tide of snapping jaws and teeth.

"Don't look back!" shouted Tara, as she and Vinnie dashed up the ramp. Tyrell, facing backwards, saw it all over Vinnie's shoulder. He saw soldiers fighting hand-to-hand, being tackled, spurts of crimson gushing from their uniforms where teeth found purchase. He saw the dead pulling out intestines and fumbling them like they were Slinkies, their wild eyes glowing in the firelight.

Becky and McBride had made it up the ramp and joined the others on the boardwalk.

"What are we going to do?" asked Becky.

McBride's eyes were sharp. "The State Police have been alerted. Reinforcements are on their way. The Army's been called in, too."

They looked at the beach. The wave of dead was currently being held back by the firing line up on the boardwalk. Many were also preoccupied with their fallen prey, biting and dismembering in frenzy.

Vinnie placed Tyrell back on the boardwalk. The boy almost collapsed, his legs like wet noodles, but Tara caught him.

"Get him out of here!" said Vinnie, shouting over the volleys of gunfire.

"What about you?"

"Dharma and Marie Russo's kids are on the pier!"

Tara understood. "You be careful!"

Vinnie nodded, and Tara dashed off, ushered off the boardwalk and into the town by police.

Vinnie turned to run when someone grabbed his arm. He wheeled around and saw Marie Russo. She looked fierce. "Where're the kids?"

"With Dharma on the pier!"

"Let's go!"

As they ran, Vinnie took out his phone and dialed Dharma. The phone rang, but she didn't answer. They navigated their way through the bedlam of first responders and National Guard, heading left down the boardwalk as everyone else was headed off.

* * *

Dharma, Salvatore, and Alessandra were all on line, their chests thumping to the bass being kicked out by the DJ. In fact, the whole boardwalk shook from the Raging Rapids ride, which is why none of them heard or felt their cell phones going off in their pockets.

They were only three people away from getting on, and the current ride was slowing to a stop.

"AS THE RAGING RAPIDS SLOW AND EVENTUALLY COME TO A STOP, PLEASE KEEP ALL HANDS, FEET, AND BODILTY APPENDAGES INSIDE YOUR CAR," instructed the DJ, a young black guy dressed in a white T-shirt and black shorts, from his booth.

The wide cars came to a halt, and the safety bars lifted. Teens of all stripes exited with smiles on their faces, still bobbing their heads to the DJ's sick beat.

"THANKS AGAIN FOR RIDING THE RAGING RAPIDS! I HOPE YOU HAD A GREAT TIME, AND DO COME BACK NOW..."

As the current batch of riders filed out the exit, Dharma and the kids waited patiently. When the last rider had exited, the attendant opened the entry gate. Alessandra nodded enthusiastically to Dharma. Salvatore did his best to look bored, but he was excited, too. Dharma could tell.

They entered the ride, climbing the curved slope alongside the cars. The first two people, a teenage couple, took the first available car. The third, a teenage boy, grabbed the second. Dharma and Alessandra grabbed the third, and Salvatore grabbed the fourth.

The rest of the riders went around, grabbing the next available car until the attendant closed the entry gate. It took another moment for the remaining riders to occupy all of the cars, and the DJ took the opportunity to introduce himself.

"WELCOME, LADIES AND GERMS, TO THE RAGING RAPIDS RIDE! YOU ARE OBVIOUSLY BRAVE SOULS WHO AREN'T AFRAID OF DANGER!"

Dharma knew this DJ. His name was Chris Washington, a student at Ocean County Community College. Nice kid. She waved to him inside the DJ booth, a small box made out of metal and Plexiglas with a single door. He saw her and winked.

WHILE THE LOVELY CLARISSA GOES AROUND LOWERING YOUR SAFETY BARS, I ASK THAT, FOR YOUR

SAFETY, YOU KEEP YOUR HANDS, FEET, AND ALL OTHER BODY PARTS INSIDE THE CAR THROUGHOUT THE RIDE.

"NOW THAT WE'VE TAKEN CARE OF BUSINESS, I HAVE JUST ONE QUESTION FOR YOU…ARE YOU READY TO PAAAAR-TEEEEEEY?"

There was a decent cheer that came from the occupied cars. However, the young DJ wasn't satisfied.

"C'MON, Y'ALL, YOU'RE ABOUT TO RIDE THE RAGING RAPIDS, SO I ASK YOU, ARE YOU READY TO PAAAAAR-TEEEEY?"

This time, the riders erupted into a collective roar of excitement and enthusiasm.

"THAT'S MORE LIKE IT. OKAY, FOLKS. HANG ON TIGHT AS THE RIDE STARTS, SIT BACK, AND ENJOY AS I SPIN THIS SAVAGE BEAT!"

Clarissa pressed the green button, activating the ride, and Alessandra reflexively grabbed the safety bar. Her body was tense with excitement. Dharma saw Salvatore in the car ahead of them, looking cool as a cucumber. He did, however, glance back at them once.

The ride lurched out of inertia and began to slowly rotate around its center, and DJ Chris crossfaded the current backbeat into a remix of a popular dance song.

The ride picked up speed, throwing Alessandra (seated on the inside) up against Dharma. They both smiled and laughed at the rising tickle in their stomachs. Within seconds, the ride was off at full speed, and they flew around and around as DJ Chris injected all kinds of sound effects into the song, periodically shouting cheers into the microphone.

As they flew round and round, Dharma caught quick glimpses of the pier, then the DJ booth, and the pier again. The breeze felt good on her face and neck, but as she passed the pier, she saw people running away from the ride. As they passed around again, she saw everyone on the pier running en masse, as if in panic.

What the hell?

Alessandra hadn't seen any of it yet. She was tipping her head back, enjoying the centripetal force and soaking in the music.

Dharma's skin went cold and chills shot down her back when she saw it.

Dozens of dead were shambling on the pier, grabbing fleeing people and biting down. Children…children were being snatched from their parents' arms as they cried out in horror.

Dharma sat forward in her seat, terror-stricken. Alessandra didn't notice. Dharma didn't know what to do first. Then she decided.

She had to signal Chris to stop the ride.

As she swung past the DJ booth, she waved her arms at Chris, shouting that he had to stop the ride. On the second pass, he saw her and waved back, flashing her his trademark smirk.

"REMEMBER, KIDDIES, ALL HANDS AND ARMS MUST REMAIN INSIDE THE CAR WHEN THE RIDE IS IN MOTION."

Alessandra noticed Dharma frantically trying to get the DJ's attention. "What's wrong?" she shouted into Dharma's ear. But when she was thrown up against her and caught a glimpse of the pier over Dharma's shoulder, she saw what Dharma was reacting to.

Now the both of them were waving their arms at the ride attendant, who mostly ignored them, playing on her cell phone. On the second pass, she managed a smile.

The ride began to slow down. *Didn't anyone else see what was happening?* Dharma and Alessandra waved their arms and shouted, but DJ Chris spoke over them.

"AND NOW WE PREPARE TO GO BACK IN TIME, SO HOLD ON TIGHT…"

The dead were approaching the ride. They must've been attracted to the sounds. They pushed at the entry gate, swiping cold, dead hands at Clarissa, who was watching the control panel.

"WITH ALL YOUR MIGHT…"

The dead pressed up against the gate. It was buckling, the half-engaged latch giving way.

"IT'LL BE ALL RIGHT…"

The ride momentarily came to a complete stop. Dharma and Alessandra looked on as the dead began to lean over the gate and fence in front of the ride. The flimsy metal fence was beginning to topple over.

"AND HERE WE GO…BACK TO THE FUTURE!"

The riders cheered. A couple of them were staring at the crowd of dead pouring over the flimsy fence and stumbling towards them.

Clarissa looked up from her texting and pressed a button, and the ride lurched backwards. The music grew even louder, the thumping bass matching the pulse in Dharma's ears. Riders began to scream, some from the sensation of going backwards, others from the zombies crawling up the side of the ride, reaching their hands out for the riders. A few managed to grab onto a car, snapping their jaws at the poor riders.

Clarissa finally looked up from her cell phone, but it was too late. She was quickly overwhelmed, tackled to the hard metal platform as teeth and fingers tore into her flesh. Her screams of terror and pain were drowned out by the music as muscle was torn from bone. She choked as she drowned in her own blood.

As the ride picked up speed, the zombies clinging on to a couple of cars were thrown. One hit the DJ booth.

"WHAT THE FUCK?"

The riders were now racing backwards at full speed. Dharma and Alessandra screamed, and dead hands reached out for them as they whirled around. Some of the dead even threw themselves at the ride, only to be flung away by the force of the ride's motion.

DJ Chris cut the music abruptly. "CLARISSA, STOP THE RIDE."

It was a strange feeling, hurtling through space backwards to no music while being attacked by the dead. Dharma leaned inward, crushing Alessandra against the other side of the car, as dead hands swept past her. One zombie threw herself at their car, holding on for a moment before being thrown.

Dharma saw that DJ Chris' booth was surrounded by zombies, screeching at the hot lunch hiding inside and pressing bloody hands up against the Plexiglas.

"HELP! SOMEBODY, HELP! OH, SHIT!"

* * *

Max Doogan leaned on the green carpeting of his booth's counter, lazily watching a couple of kids take pot shots at the stationary zombie targets with the paintball guns. It was still off season, so the live target (his buddy Carl dressed in a padded zombie suit) wouldn't be utilized until after July 4th.

It was a slow night, but the two brats popping off paintballs were having a grand ol' time. They were two brothers, and the older had made it a competition. Neither was a good shot, not that one could really be a good shot with paintball guns anyway.

Max straightened up as he saw two more rubes approaching his booth. "Shoot the zombie, here! Five dollars for twenty shots!"

From the looks of them, they looked drunk the way they stumbled over. Both reached out for the boys, so Max figured they were the boys' parents. However, one grabbed the older boy, leaned forward, and sunk his teeth right into his neck.

At first, Max thought the guy was making a joke, being that this was the Shoot the Zombie booth and all. But when the kid screamed and the guy pulled away with a chunk of the kid's flesh in his mouth, blood spurting everywhere, he realized that this wasn't the kid's parent, and it wasn't a joke.

Of course, it took the second zombie, a woman, tearing into the younger brother for this realization to fully sink in.

"Oh, shit!"

Max grabbed a paintball gun and began shooting at the zombies as they feasted on the poor brats. "Hey! Get the fuck off them!"

He saw another one approach from the left, another woman. Her clothes were torn, and her breasts were exposed. Her skin was green, and her right breast looked as if it had been gnawed on by a wild animal. Terrified, he raised a paintball gun and started shooting at its head.

It shrieked at him and projectile vomited blood, splattering Max's face. He cried out, wiping the blood out of his eyes with his right hand, still holding the gun in his left.

The woman was at his booth now. She reached out, gripped the inner edge of the counter, and pulled herself over.

Max stumbled backwards, dropping the paintball gun, and he began to make his way through the small, paint-covered wooden set to the back door.

Behind him, the dead woman fell to the floor with a thud. She slowly pushed herself up. He went to unlock the back door to the street, but he made the error of taking a glance at his pursuer.

She screamed again and gore hit his face, blinding him. It felt hot and sticky. He gagged, letting go of the doorknob, and fell against the door. The knob dug into his back. He let out a yelp that was a combination of pain and revulsion as he screwed his fingers into his eyes.

As he wiped the bodily fluids away, he felt probing fingers sink into his abdomen with unnatural strength, his skin yielding like butter to a hot knife. He felt his insides being pulled out of his body, and he looked down and saw the woman shoving them inside her mouth, his digestive fluids dripping down her face.

He slid against the door, down to the ground. Terror became disbelief, disbelief yielded to resignation, and the world rushed away from Max Doogan to the sounds of wet, ravenous chomping.

CHAPTER 8

Holbrook saw Pacelli burst into the jail area, thankfully without Lena. The man's face was white as a sheet.

Pacelli saw Chief Holbrook standing against the bars, clutching them with his hands, a desperate look on his face. He turned his head to the right and saw Martinez slumped against the wall, watching Tim O'Leary, who was shrieking at him like a caged animal. "Jesus tap-dancing Christ."

Holbrook reached out through the bars. "Pacelli, get me out of here."

Pacelli looked hesitant.

"For shit's sake, I'm okay! But O'Leary's seen better days, and Martinez needs to take my place."

Pacelli looked at Martinez, who nodded in agreement. He fished out his keys and opened Holbrook's cell.

Holbrook stepped out and grabbed Pacelli's gun from its holster. "Where's Lena?"

Pacelli looked surprised, but he let Holbrook take his weapon. "Upstairs. Listen, Chief, all hell's breaking loose on the beach and boardwalk. Dozens of dead. It's a real mess."

Holbrook nodded, walked over to O'Leary's cell, stepped over Martinez, and took aim at the creature howling at him.

O'Leary ran up to the bars, pressed his head up against them, and snapped his jaws at Holbrook. His eyes were white. Holbrook raised Pacelli's gun, pressed the barrel up against his forehead, and pulled the trigger, blowing his brains out the back of his head. O'Leary's body crumpled to the ground, inert.

Holbrook handed Pacelli back his gun. "I always wanted to do that."

"Are you sure you're okay, Chief?" asked Pacelli, thankful to have his weapon back.

"I'm fine. Help me get Martinez into this cell."

Each man hooked a hand under Martinez's armpit and hoisted him up. Dazed, Martinez allowed himself to be walked into the cell. Holbrook and Pacelli placed him on the cot.

Holbrook relieved Martinez of his weapon. "Get him some medical attention. We begin Protocol Z for him now."

Pacelli gave Holbrook an apologetic look. "The medics are busy at the moment."

"Get Martinez looked at, *now*, Sergeant."

"Yes, Chief."

Pacelli raced out of the cell area. Holbrook paused, looking at Martinez. "You gonna be all right?"

Martinez nodded. "I'm sorry, Chief."

Holbrook looked mildly amused. "For what?"

"I let my guard down."

"It's not your fault. You did your best. No one expected this. Not even me."

"Thanks, Chief."

Holbrook nodded. "Someone'll be down here shortly."

He walked through the police station, up to the bullpen. He saw Lena standing in his office, pacing back and forth and chewing on her fingernails. When she saw him, she stopped pacing, but she continued to bite her nails.

As Holbrook crossed the bullpen, officers approached him about the bedlam on the boardwalk.

"Chief, the beach's overrun."

"Chief, the dead have taken the boardwalk."

"We have people trapped on Blackbeard's Pier. I just got a call from the DJ on the Raging Rapids ride."

Holbrook stopped just outside his office. "I want roadblocks up and down Neptune Blvd. We have to contain them as much as we can. Call SWAT. What about the State Police and National Guard?"

"They're on the boardwalk, but they're being overrun."

"Jesus. Get the damned Army in here, pronto. We've got a war zone here."

"Yes, Chief."

He entered his office alone, but he left the door open.

Lena crossed the room and hugged him. She kissed him softly. "Are you all right?"

"I'm fine, but I've got to get you out of here." He unbuttoned his shirt, pulling it off and tossing it to the floor in a corner of the room.

She frowned, looking almost offended at his statement. "Where am I going to go?"

He pulled a spare uniform shirt off a hanger dangling from a coat hook on the wall and slipped it on. "You and Robbie need to get out of here." He paused buttoning up. "Wait a minute…where's Robbie?"

"He's all right. He was with Mrs. Holly at the bonfire."

"Holy shit almighty."

"I called her. They made it out."

Holbrook let out a deep sigh of relief. He finished buttoning up his shirt and tucking it into his pants. "Where are they now?"

"They're at her house."

"I'm going to go get them."

"What about me?"

"You're going to wait here until I get back."

"I want to come, too."

"It's not safe."

"He's my son, too," she snapped.

Holbrook hugged her.

"I'm sorry," she said into his ear. "I just can't believe it."

He broke the embrace. "I'll be back in a flash." He grabbed his Kevlar vest and slipped it on. His unlocked his right drawer in his desk, pulled out his weapon, and slid it into his holster, snapping it shut.

Lena looked terrified. "Be careful."

"I always am."

* * *

Marie Russo ran out in front of Vinnie, dodging panicked people, garbage pails, and overwhelmed police and national guardsmen. She stopped abruptly in front of her shop and grabbed Vinnie by the collar of his shirt, pulling him to the side. She yanked him so hard, he almost lost his footing and fell.

He struggled to maintain his balance. "What are you doing?"

She pulled him alongside and back to the street. She fished for her keys and opened the back door. She threw it open and pulled Vinnie inside.

"I thought we were going to get Dharma and the kids," he said, confused.

"Not unarmed, we are."

She disappeared into her supply room and re-emerged with a pistol and a shotgun. She shoved the shotgun into Vinnie's hands. He held it loosely, away from his body, as if she just handed him a live grenade. "What's this?"

"What's it look like?" She shoved ammo clips into her purse.

"I don't know how to shoot this!" That wasn't exactly true. He had been to the range once or twice with Mike Brunello, who owned a shotgun. Mike had taught him how to shoot it. He wasn't very experienced with shooting it, but he basically knew how to.

Marie disappeared back into the office and reappeared moments later with her hands cupped together, holding shotgun shells. She practically threw them at Vinnie. Some landed in his arms, and some of the red cartridges spilled onto the floor.

"Scattershot?"

Marie gave him a wry grin. "Don't know how to use it, huh? My ass."

Vinnie shoved the cartridges into his shorts' pockets. Then he stooped down on his haunches and picked the rest up. When he stood up, Marie holstered her pistol and snatched a couple of red cartridges out of his hand. She grabbed the shotgun, loaded them, and cocked it. "Now you just have to point and shoot."

"Scattershot won't do anything but slow them down," insisted Vinnie.

"They're right here, on the boardwalk. Point it at their rotten teeth and squeeze the trigger. You'll take their whole head off."

Vinnie's skin went white. He hadn't fully appreciated that they were about to be dashing straight into the heat of battle, amongst the dead.

"Let's go." Marie dashed outside.

Vinnie followed. As she locked up, police cars were pulling up and parking oblong, creating a roadblock between the boardwalk and the town.

"Come on." Marie unholstered her weapon and grabbed Vinnie by the arm, pulling him back to the boardwalk.

The boardwalk was complete bedlam. People were running to and fro, shoving past each other, dashing towards the ramps leading to town. The police were doing their best to direct the evacuation while holding the zombies at bay. They didn't open fire, as there were too many people around and too few clean shots. As Vinnie followed Marie into the crowd, pushing and shoving their away against the tide, he felt like a salmon swimming upstream.

When they passed the fleeing people, Vinnie saw the dead lumbering up the ramps from the beach. There were two cops at the edge firing into the advancing swarm, but their efforts were futile.

Within minutes, they were grappling with the dead hand-to-hand. Vinnie watched as they were overrun, falling to the boardwalk. The dead piled on top of them, sinking their teeth in. He was reminded of the cats snatching the seagull.

The cops begged and pleaded as they cried out. They writhed around as flesh was torn away from their body, like antelopes frenzied by lions in a nature show. They had those same blank looks of helplessness as they were eaten. Like the seagull from before, they went limp, powerless to fight back. Vinnie wanted to help them.

Marie saw him looking. "We can't help them. Let's go."

Vinnie nodded and followed her. There were a few zombies on the boardwalk, but Marie circumvented them, careful to conserve her ammunition. She'd need it on Blackbeard's Pier.

Dead hands reached out for Vinnie from both sides, grabbing his arms and shoulders. He shoved them back and struck them with the stock of his shotgun. He ran to keep up with Marie. Damn she was fast.

One, a woman with bloated skin and seaweed hanging from her tattered outfit, grabbed him and wrapped its fingers so tight around his upper arm that he wasn't able to shake it free. Its one intact breast swung free from its torn blouse. The other was missing, the wound glistening.

As he struggled with this zombie, Marie was getting away from him. He called out to her, but either she didn't hear him, or she didn't care. He twisted and turned to wriggled out of the woman's grip as it lunged its head forward, snapping its jaws at him. He felt its cold, putrid breath on his face.

The dead woman embraced him as Dharma had many times, pulling him close. He fought the wave of panic that would immobilize him. Instead, he turned his shotgun, bringing it up between them and pointing the barrel right under its chin. He pushed with all his might, creating a bit of distance between them using the gun as a lever. He turned his head away and pulled the trigger.

There was a loud boom, wetness splattered the side of his head, and the dead fingers loosened their grip. As he pulled himself free, ears ringing, he tripped over something and fell backwards onto the boardwalk.

He crunched his stomach to look at what he stumbled over and saw a small zombie child chewing on the face of a fallen adult. The body was a mess of gore, and the flesh around its right eye had been eaten away, making it look as if the eyeball was bulging out of its head. The victim's mouth was contorted, blood dripping out of the side.

The zombie child, its hair matted in blood, clad in tattered shorts and a T-shirt, was chewing on the poor bastard's tongue when it saw Vinnie. It dropped the chewy morsel and began to crawl towards him.

Vinnie shrieked, trying to find his footing, but the creature was fast. It scurried over to him, eyes clouded but wild, and screeched at him, spraying his face with its spittle.

He kicked at it, but it pulled its way up his legs in a commando crawl. That's when he felt its limp legs dragging across his own. They had been broken.

Marie ran up to Vinnie and wound her leg up. She gave the zombie child a swift kick in the head, sending it flying backwards. It landed just over the body it was feeding on, its neck broken. Its head flopped around like a wrecked jack-in-the-box as it whimpered and wheezed.

Marie pulled Vinnie to his feet.

"I thought you left me," he said, shocked and embarrassed all at once.

"Never," she said with an edge of anger in her voice. A dead man reached out for her. She lifted her pistol and shot it point blank in the head. It dropped to its knees and sat on its haunches, limp arms dangling behind it, its lights turned out.

She grabbed Vinnie's wrist and pulled him through the crowd. She jerked him to the left and to the right, dodging attacks, dragging him like a ragdoll.

As Vinnie was pulled, he looked up to the left, just above the beach, and saw a zombie hanging from the sky ride, gripping the chair's foot bar as two riders—a teenage couple—kicked their feet at it. The girl was screaming. A few chairs back, a man wrestled with a zombie until they both rolled out of the chair and onto the beach below. Out of the frying pan and into the fire.

On the right, Vinnie and Marie passed Mac's Pub. It was no longer filled with bikers. It looked abandoned, chairs and stools strewn about the place. There were large, matted bloodstains on the felt of one of the pool tables. There was a zombie leaning over Mac on the floor in front of the bar. It was pulling his intestines out of his pot belly. Mac's eyes were wide, staring up at the ceiling, and his mouth was moving, as if conversing with his attacker. Hell, maybe he was praying.

Vinnie shook his head and forced back hot tears as he and Marie saw Blackbeard's Pier coming up on their left.

* * *

It had all happened so quickly. One minute, Nancy was handing out complimentary cotton candy to the children, and the next people ran through the arcade screaming. Then she heard the other screams, the dead kind, and she ducked behind the prize counter as zombies came pouring in.

She saw Mike stunned as the dead ambled inside. Being opportunistic predators, the dead went for the children first, grabbing them and pulling them down to the floor. Some parents ran away, others tried to rescue their children. Some got away with bites taken of their arms, others weren't so lucky. Either way, they were all dead. Some just didn't realize it yet.

Like lions, the dead surrounded the poor families, herding them together. The people huddled together, crying and screaming, as if they felt an instinctive strength in numbers.

In the end, the zombies had more.

*

Mike stopped the carousel. He hopped up while it still moved, falling and hurting his right knee, as the child riders cried for their parents. He reached out and grabbed the wooden extended leg of a horse, named Lucky as evidenced by the red scriptive lettering on its cream-colored saddle. He pulled himself up, groaning.

He began to limp to each child, pain shooting up his leg like lightning, unstrapping them and helping them down. As each child ran off towards his or her parent, Mike moved on to the next child, and then to the next.

As he looked over his shoulder, he saw that the dead had already overrun the parents waiting in front. So, when the next child made to run off, he pulled him the other direction. "No, this way!"

He made his way around the carousel, collecting children, and they followed him like the tail of a comet. The dead reached over and through the metal fence, their collective moans and shrieks drowning out the calliope music.

When he had all of the riders, he led them to the back of the carousel, but there more dead waited for them. Surrounded, he brought the screaming, terrified children back onto the ride. They crossed the ride to its center, and he arranged them along the center hub, placing them with their backs up against the mirrors.

He limped back over the ride and down to his control panel. He pressed the green button, restarting the ride, as undead fingertips brushed his right shoulder and back, clawing at his shirt. One of the dead shrieked and projectile vomited blood on him, splattering the right side of his face and body with bile and plasma.

*

Nancy peeked over the glass counter, and she saw Mike turn the carousel back on. He hopped back on as it began to turn, and he made his way towards the center, dripping in blood. A pang of horror racked her body as she thought he was injured, but he only limped from his leg injury. Relief momentarily washed over her as she guessed…hoped the blood wasn't his.

She had to help him, but she didn't know what to do.

Attracted by the sudden movement and the sound of screaming children in the center, the dead began to converge on the carousel, pulling down the flimsy metal fence with the weight of their numbers.

Stumbling over the fence, the dead lunged at the ride, the rotation pulling them off their feet. Hope welled up inside Nancy as she watched the advancing dead struggle with navigating the moving ride. They shrieked and swept wild hands at the bobbing horses, their projectile vomit dousing them in red and brown, their broken fingernails deflecting off the lacquered wood.

Through the chaos, Nancy saw Mike looking at her, and her hopes were dashed. His look was that of futility and resignation. There was nowhere for him to go. His look told her all of this in an instant. It also told her to run.

Nancy stood, shaking her head in defiance. *No, you crazy old fool. Don't give up. It's not over.*

As the dead stumbled their way onto the spinning carousel, they crawled towards the center, hands reaching for Mike and the children huddling together in the center. The children were screaming and crying. Mike held a couple of them close. The look on his face was indescribable.

Nancy had to do something. She heard gunfire outside. There were police.

All of the dead were focused on the carousel. She ran to the door, right behind the undead pile-on, and shouted, "Help! Police! Help!"

She saw the police doing their best to contain the onslaught of dead, but the dead were winning. *Jesus Christ, there are so many of them. Where are they coming from?*

She waved her arms frantically, shouting into the confusion, trying to get someone's attention. Anyone's attention.

She looked over her shoulder and saw that the dead had made it to the center of the carousel. Hot tears streamed down her face as she no longer saw Mike or the children. They had disappeared under a heap of hungry monsters. Blood spattered the mirrors as the calliope music played on and the dead frenzied over their hot meals.

Bastards! You'll pay. I'll make you pay. Every single fucking one of you.

Nancy, in typical Nancy fashion, rolled up her sleeves and marched over to the carousel. Not knowing what else to say or do, she began hurling curses at the ravenous abominations.

* * *

Tara was two blocks away from the pandemonium of the boardwalk, practically dragging Tyrell at her side.

"What about Vinnie?" protested Tyrell.

"He'll be fine. He's going to help Dharma and Marie's kids."

"Slow down, Mom." His feet were dragging as he tried to regain his footing.

Tara slowed for a moment, as he was slowing them down. Once he found his footing, she pulled him down the block again. She was doing her best to keep her composure. She wanted to scream. She asked herself how this could happen again. However, such indulgences in panic would do nothing for Tyrell. No, she had to keep calm.

"Where are we going, Mom?"

"We're getting out of Smuggler's Bay."

Just ahead, she saw a police car pull up to a house. Chief Holbrook got out.

"Chief! Chief! Over here!"

He looked down the block and saw Tara.

She ran over to him, pulling Tyrell with her.

Tyrell was grateful when she stopped, as it gave him a moment to catch his breath. The pops of gunfire in the distance were getting closer.

"Chief, the dead are back! They're on the boardwalk!"

"I know," he said, still walking towards the house. "Get in your car and get out of here!"

He knocked on the door and ignored her. An older woman answered. Chief Holbrook shoved his way inside.

"What's he doing, Mom?"

"I don't know, but he's right. We're getting the hell out of here."

*

Holbrook entered the house, relieved that Mrs. Holly was home. "Where's Robbie?"

"He's in the kitchen drinking some water. Poor thing's in shock. We just got here a moment ago."

Robbie stepped out of the kitchen. "Dad!" He ran over to his father and threw his arms around him.

Holbrook got down on one knee and embraced his son as the both of them cried tears of relief. After a moment, Holbrook broke the embrace and stood up, wiping his eyes. "Thank you so much."

"I'm glad we got out of there," said Mrs. Holly. "We almost didn't. Fortunately, I was taking him to the bathroom on the boardwalk, so we weren't on the beach when…when *they* attacked everyone."

"You have to leave," said Holbrook, grabbing Robbie by the arm. "I'm taking you to the police station. Lena's waiting. You need to get out of Smuggler's Bay."

"Oh dear," was all Mrs. Holly could manage.

Holbrook ushered them outside. Mrs. Holly made as if to lock her front door, but he wouldn't let her. He grabbed her arm firmly.

"Ow!"

"There's no time."

They looked down the street all the way to the boardwalk and saw a tsunami of dead creeping in their direction. The police barricade had been overrun, the flashing lights on their roofs barely visible as the dead crawled over them like a plague of rats.

That was all Mrs. Holly needed. She rushed over to Holbrook's squad car and pulled the passenger door open. Holbrook opened the back door.

"Get in," he told Robbie.

Robbie hopped in the back, and Holbrook closed the door behind him. He rounded the car and hopped into the front seat. The car was already running. He threw it in drive and took off towards the police station. He gave one last look at the surge of dead in his rearview mirror, and it reminded him of the surging tide during the superstorm two years ago.

He took a left turn a little too fast. The car skidded on the pavement. Mrs. Holly grabbed the door and dashboard, steadying herself. Robbie slid to the right in the back seat, holding his arm out to brace himself from slamming into the door.

"Where's Mom?" asked Robbie.

"She's at the station. We're going to pick her up and get you guys out of here."

"You're leaving, too?" asked Mrs. Holly with obvious disapproval.

"I'm giving you this car, and you all are leaving. I'm staying."

"Oh," said Mrs. Holly, satisfied with his explanation. After all, it wouldn't do for the police chief to skip town in the middle of a crisis.

Holbrook squinted his eyes as he saw a man wandering in the middle of the street. The way he walked, he looked either drunk or injured. Or he was one of the creeping dead.

"Hold on." He swerved around the hobbling figure, and he let out a sigh of relief when he saw who it was.

Robbie was looking out the side and then the back window as they passed. "Dad, it's Lenny Krueger."

Holbrook hit the brakes and stepped out of the car. "Lenny, get in the car!"

Lenny looked up, startled, as he had been in the middle of a conversation with a non-existent person. "Chief Holbrook," he said, smiling.

"Lenny, get in! Hurry!"

Lenny nodded and staggered over to the car. Holbrook opened the rear driver's side door, and Lenny got in. Holbrook slammed the door shut and got back into the driver's seat. He took off and continued down the avenue. They were now only a few blocks from the station.

"Lenny, what were you doing wandering alone out there?"

"V-V-Vinnie t-told me to g-go home and wait."

"Vinnie Cantone?"

"Yes, sir." His voice was a little too cheerful given the situation.

"Where did Vinnie go?" Holbrook knew the answer. If he told Lenny to go home, that meant he was still on the boardwalk.

"He went to s-s-save Dharma and the k-kids."

"Whose kids?"

"Marie R-R-Russo."

Holbrook didn't say anything further on the matter. He pulled up to the police station, stopping right in front. "Wait here. I'll be back in a flash."

"Are you all right?" asked Robbie from the backseat, watching his father disappear into the station.

"Oh dear," was all Mr. Holly said. She appeared overwhelmed. As a senior citizen, this was a bit too much excitement for her. She barely got through the first attack two years ago.

"We are going to be all right," declared Lenny, nodding in emphasis, a big smile on his face. It was all he knew to say at the moment. It always made him feel better when people told him that, even if he didn't believe it.

"Oh dear."

Lenny looked to his left, and a cramped Billy Blake gave him the thumbs up.

CHAPTER 9

Vinnie and Marie barged into the entrance of the Blackbeard's Pier Arcade. Vinnie skidded to a halt, grabbing Marie by the arm, before they both ran headlong into a mess of zombies around the carousel. Vinnie dropped his shotgun on the ground.

Marie looked at the carousel, and then at a woman standing in front of it, fists clenched at her side and hurling obscenities at the dead. "Nancy?"

Nancy turned to look at Marie. Her teeth were clenched, and she had raccoon eyes.

Marie realized that Nancy's mascara had run from her tears. If she hadn't been cursing, Marie would've thought she was one of the dead.

"They got Mike and the kids!" Nancy cried out.

Vinnie picked his shotgun up off the ground and straightened up. "What?!"

Marie ran up to Nancy, pointing her pistol. She fired a shot right over her shoulder, hitting a zombie coming up behind her. "Jesus, Nancy. Where are my kids?"

"I-I-I don't know."

A woman in a tattered outfit, bloated and green, rushed Vinnie, arms outstretched, jaws snapping. Vinnie raised his shotgun and pointed it right to her temple. She let out a blood-curdling shriek, but it was drowned out when Vinnie pulled the trigger and fired right into a dead woman's face. Her face imploded, blood and brains splattering behind her. She dropped to the ground.

The zombies on the carousel began to shriek as if in response, and the frenzied mass began to stumble off of the carousel.

Marie grabbed Nancy by the arm, her grip firm, and pulled her past the prizes counter and towards the exit to the pier. "Come on, Vinnie. Time to go."

Vinnie, stunned by the news of Mike's death, paused a moment. However, as the dead climbed back over the flimsy metal fence surrounding the ride, he snapped out of it and ran to follow Marie and Nancy onto the pier.

When they spilled out into the night air, they gawked in amazement at the scene unfolding before them. The dead were everywhere, and there were very few of the living left. Many of the cannibalistic monsters perched over their fallen victims—men, women, and children. None were spared a gruesome death by being eaten alive.

Across the pier, a small boy was up on the obstacle course ride. He was at the top of the spiral slide that led down to the exit, where several dead were waiting for him. He stood at the top, frozen in fear as more of the dead began to slowly meander through the beginning of the course. They toppled through the spinning barrel, climbed up the shifting staircase on their hands and knees, and were lumbering through the gauntlet of sandbags. It was only a matter of minutes before they reached him. The boy was dead meat.

"There're so many of them. Where'd they all come from?" gasped Vinnie, staggered by the sight.

"Dharma and the kids!" Marie said it as if she were reminding Vinnie why they were there.

"Right!"

They began to fan out, Nancy sticking with Marie. They dodged the dead who lunged at them, side stepping and calling out for their loved ones. Nancy, numb, allowed herself to be led like a child.

"Dharma!"

"Alessandra! Sal!"

"Dharma!"

"Salvatore! Alessandra!"

Vinnie looked over his shoulder at the kid on the obstacle course. He was no longer standing at the top of the slide. He was clinging on at the middle as the dead approached from the top and bottom. The kid was crying out for help, sobbing.

Vinnie turned away before he saw the dead from the top reach the kid first. There was nothing he could do for the boy.

"Dharma!"

"Sal!"

"Alessandra!"

They were frantic in their search. All of the rides, although lit, appeared empty. Some were still moving, while a few had stopped. On the boat ride, a bell rung as a zombie clung onto the boat, feasting on a pile of gored meat that was once a child. Its foot kept hitting the bell as it leaned over its meat.

The Raging Rapids caught Vinnie's eye. There were zombies being thrown from it, landing on the wooden planks of the pier. The throws appeared to take something out of them, as they struggled to get up.

"There!" said Marie, seeing the same thing.

They converged, walking towards the ride. As they drew closer, they heard screams of terror. The DJ booth was surrounded by dead clawing at the Plexiglas. They were vomiting on it and pushing the window in.

"Holy shit!" Vinnie looked at the ride and tried to make out Dharma and the kids. He saw them. "There!"

They all ducked into the exit of the Buccaneer Adventure ride. Marie and Vinnie peeked out at the Raging Rapids right next door.

Marie nodded. "I see them."

"We have to turn off the ride," said Vinnie.

Marie shook her head. "If we do, the zombies will forget about the DJ and come after Dharma and the kids."

"What'll we do? We can't get them off the ride without stopping it."

Marie was deep in thought, weighing their options, desperate to find an approach that was feasible. "We need to get them away from that ride."

"I'll do it," said Vinnie.

"How?" Marie almost sounded annoyed.

"I'll lure them away, and then you stop the ride and get them off."

"Lead them where, Vinnie?"

"I'm fast. I'll lead them to one of the other rides. I can turn one on to distract them."

"That's ridiculous," said Marie.

"No, it isn't," said Nancy.

Marie and Vinnie were startled by Nancy's sober interjection.

"I'll go with him," said Nancy. "I know how to operate every ride here."

Marie looked around the pier. "Which ride?"

Vinnie and Nancy scanned the pier for options.

Vinnie's eyes lit up. "I've got it!"

"What?" asked Marie and Nancy in unison.

Vinnie pointed off to the right. "The swinging Pirate Ship ride! It's perfect. We can lure them over and then use the ride to crush them. Kill two birds with one stone."

Marie smiled. "And a hell of a lot of zombies."

"I can get the ride started," said Nancy. "You'll just have to make a ruckus to attract them."

"What about you?" Marie asked Nancy.

"I'll be fine," said Nancy. "If Vinnie makes enough noise, they won't notice me."

Vinnie was already having second thoughts. "Are you sure?"

Nancy pursed her lips in consternation. "Positive. Now let's go before I lose my nerve."

Marie shoved her pistol into Nancy's hands. "Here. Take this just in case. Do you know how to use it?"

Nancy chambered a round. "You don't think I've been to the range since the last attack?"

"Okay, okay," said Vinnie, exasperated. "You're both badasses. Can we get this plan in motion?"

Nancy and Marie nodded.

"I'll go first, get the ride ready," said Nancy. "When I give the signal, you get their attention and bring them over."

Vinnie nodded. "Got it."

* * *

Lt. Becky Michaels ran for her life as the dead pursued her. The barricade was toast, and she had expended her ammo. She needed to find a place to hide. She tumbled over a low metal gate and onto the

Nautilus Motel grounds, scraping her elbows on the cement path. She got to her feet just as the dead came barreling through after her.

She tried to run over to the motel office, but in her haste, she was tripping over her own feet. She stumbled to the right. The dead reached out for her, pushing her into the deep end of the hotel pool. They followed her like lemmings, dropping like stones into the cool water.

Chlorine burned her eyes and nostrils as Becky rolled around under water. She kicked her legs, struggling to reach the surface. When she breached, she gasped for air and swam over to the diving board at the end of the pool.

As she kicked her legs, she felt hands reaching out for her ankles under the water. She fought against their groping, doing her best to stay horizontal on the surface, reaching out for the diving board as murderous fingers sought to drag her down.

Her fingertips reached the tip of the board, and she grabbed on tight, pulling herself up as dead hands pulled her down. She cried out in fear as she struggled for her life, but her cries were only answered by the screeches of the dead.

The dead outside the pool converged on the diving board, clumsily stumbling onto it and falling into the water. Hands reached out for her on both sides as she lifted her legs and held herself parallel under the board, caught between the reaching fingers above and below, as she clung on for dear life.

Her arms and body were growing tired from the exertion, but she dared not let go. Her radio crackled over the moans of the dead.

* * *

"Becky, come in." Holbrook attempted to raise his lieutenant, but with no success. He prayed that she was still alive.

He leaned into the police car and looked Mrs. Holly in the eye. "I'll be right back out with Lena. Lock the doors. If you are in trouble, hit the siren."

Mrs. Holly nodded, and Lenny cheered in the backseat at all of the excitement. Robbie's eyes pleaded for him to hurry back.

Holbrook closed the car door and stalked his way up the cement path to the entrance. As he entered the station, he was approached by whoever was left bombarding him with status reports. But he already knew. He saw it with his own eyes on Mrs. Holly's block.

Lena burst out of his office, her face looking hopeful but anxious. "Did you find him?"

Holbrook nodded. She embraced him, her body shuddering with sobs of relief. He gently pushed her away. "There's no time." He handed her the keys to this cruiser. "You have to go. Robbie, Mrs. Holly, and Lenny Krueger are all in the car."

"What about you?"

"I have to stay. You know that."

She nodded, resigned to the fact. She knew he had his job to do. She didn't like it, but she had to come to terms with it.

"Chief!" called Pacelli. "They're going to close the bridge. No one in or out."

"What?! Who's *they*?"

"The Army, Chief."

"Lena, you have to go. Now!"

Lena nodded. She took the keys and left out the front door. Holbrook was right behind her, and Pacelli was right behind him. Holbrook saw the street was clear and watched Lena get into his squad car. She pulled away, heading for the bridge off the barrier island.

"They can't do that!" continued Holbrook. "We have people who still need to be evacuated."

Pacelli shrugged. He had no answer.

*

Lena Holbrook put her foot down on the accelerator, picking up speed. "Everyone okay?"

Mrs. Holly nodded, and Lenny gave the thumbs up.

"Mom, where's Dad?"

Lena saw Robbie's disappointment in the rearview mirror. "He has to stay, honey. He has to help everyone. But we're getting out of here."

Lenny leaned forward, speaking through the cage. "Can we t-t-turn on the lights, Mrs. Chief?" That was what he always called her. That was because he knew her husband as Chief, so that made her Mrs. Chief.

She smiled at the innocence of the request that was completely incongruent with their situation. "Sure, Lenny." She flipped on the lights and siren. It couldn't hurt, and if it kept Lenny and Robbie calm, all the better.

She made her way down the main boulevard in the direction of the Bay Bridge, turned right by old man McNally's hardware store, and straight to the approach. Several cars that were also heading off the island made way, and she raced right by them. She felt guilty, using the lights and sirens to jump to the front of the evacuation line.

She saw the Bay and its docks. The approach was shockingly free of traffic. She had indeed jumped to the front of the line.

This made sense. Everything happened so quickly, very few likely got a chance to evacuate. Poor people at the bonfire. She wondered how many died at the hands and teeth of the dead.

As she made her away up the incline of the bridge, her heart sank when she heard the sound of the warning bells. As she crested the bridge, there were a few cars stopped. She saw the drawbridge slowly rising. "Dammit. No."

She hit the siren, making it emit those short, funny tweets. Nothing.

"Oh, dear," was all Mrs. Holly could say.

"Mom, how are we going to leave if the bridge is up?"

Lenny bounced up and down in his seat, momentarily forgetting their predicament, excited about seeing the drawbridge rise.

Lena looked out the windshield and saw people standing outside of their cars. She saw Tara Bigelow.

Lena turned around. "Wait here, guys. I see Tara. I'm going to find out what's going on."

"Mom, don't leave," pleaded Robbie.

"I'll be right back. There are no zombies on the bridge, so you'll be okay for a moment. Right, Mrs. Holly?"

Mrs. Holly sat there stunned. "Oh dear."

Lenny gave Tara the thumbs up. "We're g-g-going to be a-ok-k-kay."

Tara couldn't help but smile. Lenny's reaction made Robbie smile, too. In that moment, she was glad her husband stopped to pick Lenny up. "See, Lenny's not scared."

"I'm a superhero," announced Lenny. "I'll p-p-protect all of you."

Lena pointed at Tara's car. "I'll be right over there with Tara." She closed the door, leaving the engine running just in case, and walked over to Tara.

Tara was looking at the other side of the drawbridge, where there were military stationed. There were three tanks on the other side, facing the other direction.

"Hey, Tara. What's the hold up?"

Tara whirled around. When she saw it was Lena Holbrook, she smiled, but it was not a pleasant smile. It was more the nervous kind. "They won't let us across."

"What do you mean? Why wouldn't they let us across?"

"They're not answering me," said Tara.

Lena saw Tyrell look out the side window of their parked car, its engine also running. "They must not understand our situation."

Through the metal grating of the raised bridge, they saw one soldier exit the control room to the drawbridge and return to the group.

"You're welcome to try and talk to them," said Tara.

Lena nodded, and she stepped forward, cupping her hands around her mouth to amplify her voice. "Excuse me! I'm the police chief's wife! Sir!"

The soldier turned around to look at her. She couldn't read his expression through the metal grating of the raised bridge. She swept a hand towards her husband's squad car. It's lights were still on, so she was certain he'd see it. "See, that's Chief Jim Holbrook's car! He wanted us to evacuate! We have to leave!"

The soldier cupped his hands around his mouth. "I cannot allow that, ma'am!"

Lena was incredulous. "Why not?!"

"It's not safe, ma'am!"

"Not safe?" Lena muttered to herself.

Tara crossed her arms. "Does he understand that the island is being overrun with zombies? How is keeping us here keeping us safe?"

"I'll tell him," said Tara. She cupped her hands around her mouth again. "It's not safe here! There are zombies all over the island!"

The soldier heard her, but he turned his back on her and walked back towards the group.

"Son of a bitch," said Lena to Tara.

"I guess it's not safe for them to let us over," offered Tara. "I think we're being involuntarily quarantined."

"This won't stand," said Lena. "I'm going to radio Jim. He can talk to them." She turned around and started to walk back to the squad car, but she stopped when they heard popping sounds off in the distance on the other side of the drawbridge. The side the soldiers were on.

She turned around.

Tara was craning her neck. "Come check this out."

Lena rejoined Tara just in time to see the soldiers on the other side scrambling into some kind of position. There was a grinding sound as the tanks raised their guns.

"What's happening?" called Tara through the grating.

Preoccupied, the soldiers didn't answer.

"Something's got them scrambling," said Tara.

Before Lena could comment any further, there was a loud boom as one of the tanks fired its gun.

"What the fuck?" shouted Tara, but it was drowned out by the blast of one of the other tanks.

Lena turned to look at the squad car. Robbie was out of the back seat calling out to her.

"Get back in the car!" But her instruction was drowned out by more artillery fire.

Lena began to walk towards the car, waving Robbie back inside, but he didn't listen. Lenny stepped out of the car, placing his fingers inside his ears. He didn't like loud noises.

Lena shouted for them to get back inside the car. When she reached Robbie, she shoved him back into the back seat. Then she pushed Lenny back inside. He went, but he didn't like being shoved.

"Mom, what's that noise?"

Lena bent at her waist and stuck her head inside the car. "It's the Army, honey."

Mrs. Holly looked at Lena with astonishment. "Oh dear."

Robbie crinkled his nose. "Who are they shooting at?"

"That's a good question." Then her face suddenly drained of all its color. It dawned on her that the army raised the bridge, not for their own safety but for *their* safety. Hers and Tara's, and anyone else's on the bridge.

The dead were attacking on the mainland.

Lena straightened up. She was going to run over to Tara to tell her what she thought was happening—what must be happening—but she froze when she saw a throng of the dead advancing up the bridge from town towards them. "Shit."

She slammed the back door of the car and made her way around to the driver's seat. She opened the door and got in. Her mind was racing. She had to warn Tara.

Lena reached down, grabbed the radio, and flipped on the intercom. "Tara!"

Tara, startled, whipped her head around.

"Tara, there are zombies on the bridge. We gotta go."

From the look on Tara's face, Lena was certain that she saw them. Tara ran back to her car and began to make a three-point U-turn.

Lena put down the radio and put the squad car in reverse. She cut the wheel and backed up until the back bumper hit the cement barrier. Then she threw it in drive, cut the wheel the other way, and drove forward, cutting across the second lane and straightening the car. She hit the brakes and looked ahead, weighing her options.

Tara pulled up in the other lane alongside the cruiser. She rolled down her passenger window.

Lena rolled down her driver side window.

"What'll we do?" asked Tara.

Lena thought it was funny *she* was asking *her* what to do. Tara was the badass who lived through the first attack. Lena figured it must've been the squad car. It was a cue for authority, and now she was it.

Lena looked ahead at the steadily advancing band of dead. There were about a dozen of them. She squeezed the steering wheel and steeled herself. "I say we plow right through them."

Tara looked ahead, and then she looked back at Lena, nodding her confirmation. "Let's do it."

Robbie leaned forward in the back seat. "Can you turn on the siren, Mom?"

Lena nodded. "Fuck it. Why not?"

Robbie cheered in the back seat. Lenny winced at the profanity, particularly coming from Mrs. Chief. Mrs. Holly opened her mouth, but she thought better of it and shut it without saying a word.

146

Lena was thankful for that. She didn't know if she could stand another 'Oh dear.'

Lena turned to Tara. "We go together. Side by side. Plow right through them."

Tara nodded. There were the pops of gunfire closer behind them and the occasional boom of artillery fire.

As they each rolled up the windows, Lena flipped on the siren. She was now able to make out the pallid faces of the approaching dead closing the distance.

She hit the gas, and the car lurched forward. Tara's car lurched forward next to her. The whole thing reminded her of a drag race, like one of those video games on the boardwalk that Robbie liked to play. Robbie and Lenny cheered in the backseat.

Lena and Tara closed the distance quickly and were running out of pavement. Lena braced herself for impact as the dead mindlessly reached out for them, oblivious to the four tons of Detroit steel barreling towards them.

* * *

Nancy left the dubious safety of the Buccaneer Adventure ride's exit and began to march her way over to the swinging Pirate Ship ride. Most of the dead were focused on the Raging Rapids ride. The rest were feasting on their inert prey, hunched over their meat, eyes down. They didn't notice her as she made her way to the back of the pier.

Seeing that she had a clear run to the ride, Nancy's walk morphed into a jog. She nearly jumped out of her skin as the public address from the Raging Rapids switched on. Chris Washington must've been leaning on the switch. When Nancy turned to look over her shoulder, she saw the dead pushing into the DJ booth, caving in the Plexiglas with their collective weight.

The sounds were terrifying. Screams turned to gurgling, and gurgling gave way to wet sounds, and the switch went off.

Nancy turned back around to see if the noise garnered the attention of the feasting dead, and she tripped on something. She reached out in front with her free hand to break her fall as she landed hard onto the wooden planks of Blackbeard's Pier. The impact of the fall caused the gun to pop out of her right hand and slide out in front of her.

Nancy felt pain all over her body. She was able to protect her face, but the side of her head had hit the wood, and she was dazed. Her back sent shockwaves of pain as she rolled over onto it. She craned her neck, which hurt even worse, and looked over her feet to see what she stumbled on.

It was a half-eaten body of a woman, her blouse and long skirt clinging wet to her bloody body, her flesh torn. Her face was half-eaten, exposing her cheekbone, her eye dangling from its socket. Her jaw bone and teeth were exposed on one side, making it look like a ghastly smirk.

Nancy recognized the body. It was Maddy Woods, and her one eye began to roll in its socket. It focused on her. The mangled jaw began to move.

"Poor soul." Nancy rolled back onto her stomach and reached out for the gun that lay a few feet in front of her. She also saw that several of the dead, formerly preoccupied with their meal, now noticed her.

They must've looked up when they heard the screaming from the DJ booth. They slowly rose and began to amble towards her, snarling and screeching like howler monkeys.

"Shit," she mumbled under her breath, cursing her clumsiness.

She propped herself up on her elbow and raised her gun out in front of her, training it on the closest zombie. She closed her nondominant eye to help her focus.

Something grabbed her from behind. She rolled on her back and took aim.

"Nancy!"

It was Vinnie.

She took her finger off the trigger. "I almost blew your head off. Get me up."

Vinnie hoisted her up quite easily. He was young and strong, and she was light. "We'll go to the ride together."

"Forget the ride."

"We can make it," he insisted.

"Well then let's get a move on already," she snapped.

He half-carried her to the Pirate Ship ride. He leaned her up against the metal fence surrounding the ride and opened the gate. They squeezed through and walked over to the control panel. He propped her up in front of it. She fished for her keys to activate the controls.

"You wait here," said Vinnie. "Get it ready. I'm going to get those zombies away from the Raging Rapids."

Nancy nodded and unlocked the control panel. "Hurry up."

*

Vinnie darted back through the gate and to the right towards the Raging Rapids. The dead that were closing in on the Pirate Ship saw him and followed in pursuit, forgetting about Nancy.

Vinnie ran up to the raging rapids and started yelling at the dead climbing all over the torn down DJ booth. "Over here! Fresh meat! Come and get it!" He jumped up and down and waved his arms as he shouted.

Having slayed the prey inside the little booth, the dead closet to the booth feasted. Those in the back of the crowd, however, now turned their attention to Vinnie. Slowly, they began to turn around and make their way back down the ride and to the pier where he stood.

"That's right, you dead, ugly motherfuckers! Come and get me!"

A few got too close to the spinning ride and were caught up and thrown off to the right of the ride. One had its right arm ripped off at the shoulder socket. It looked down where its arm should've been and grunted, unfazed. The rest filed through the gate, screeching and snarling, snapping their jaws.

Vinnie let them get close enough—within ten feet or so—and then he turned heel and darted off towards the ride. Careful not to run into the dead following him from the other side of the pier, he gave them a wide berth. The dead from the Raging Rapids absorbed them, and together they followed Vinnie in unison.

He found it kind of humorous. Here he was, the Pied Piper of the zombie apocalypse. "Come on, you bastards! Come and get me!"

They moaned and shrieked in response, shuffling as fast as they could to oblige him.

"Start the ride!" he called out to Nancy.

He saw her press a button, and the ride sprung to life. The massive seated gondola began to slowly rock back and forth, building up momentum.

As Vinnie reached the Pirate Ship, his cellphone began to ring. He pulled it out of his right shorts' pocket as he slid through the gate. "Hello."

"Vin, it's Dad. What in the hell is going on? Are you all right?" Cantone's Pizzeria was up the boardwalk, past Blackbeard's Pier. Maybe the dead hadn't reached it yet.

Vinnie stood next to Nancy.

Nancy sucked her teeth. "You damned kids. Always on your phones."

Vinnie rolled his eyes. "I can't talk right now, Dad. The dead are on the boardwalk. You have to get out of there."

"I know, one tried to climb over the counter to get me. I wacked it on the head with a peel and shoved it back over."

"There's a space behind the gondola," said Nancy. "We can wait there."

Vinnie nodded and helped her up towards the platform. The gondola was picking up momentum now. He timed it, as it whooshed by, waiting for it to swing all the way up to the left. He grabbed Nancy and shuttled her across the platform, smashing face first into the wall behind as it passed back down past their backs. He felt the breeze from its pass on his back and neck.

They quickly turned around, backs against the metal wall behind the ride. It was airbrushed with carnival art, depicting a pirate captain with eye patch, hook hand, and peg leg, waving his sword. Around him were his mates, wearing bandanas, earrings, and baggy black pants in various battle poses, wielding swords and holding daggers in between clenched teeth. They were fighting dead pirates that were boarding the ship. Right above Vinnie loomed a depiction of a zombie pirate, jaws gaping open, that familiar look of hunger in its eyes.

The massive swinging gondola whooshed by.

"Dad, you need to get out of there."

"I can't. We're surrounded. We pulled down the security gate."

The gondola swooshed by again. The dead were now pushing the gate to the ride open and pushing into the ride.

"Is Mom there with you?"

"Yeah, she's okay."

"Is he okay?" Vinnie heard her say in the background.

"Is Dharma okay?"

"I'm working on that as we speak."

"Where are you now?"

The gondola swept past again.

"That's kinda complicated, Dad."

"Can you get to the pizzeria?"

The dead were up by the control panel. They saw Vinnie and Nancy, and they doubled their efforts, teeth bared, eyes wild, none of them paying any mind to the massive swinging gondola.

"Dad, I gotta go. I'm okay. I'll call you when I can."

"Vin, please be careful."

Vinnie terminated the call. Nancy held the gun down at her side. There wasn't any room to extend her arm when the gondola swung down. If she was going to shoot, she had to time it right and make it count.

The dead began to reach the platform. As they got closer to their prey, they appeared to move faster. Reaching out and moaning with insatiable hunger, they began to cross the platform.

The gondola was on the upswing, but as the platform began to fill with hungry dead, and Vinnie and Nancy pressed their backs to the airbrushed metal wall behind them, the gondola rushed back down, clearing away the dead on the platform in one fell swoop.

They went flying onto the spinning dragon egg ride next door, the whirling eggs tearing them apart, rending limbs from joints, sending heads rolling like marbles.

As the gondola swung up in the other direction, the dead, oblivious to what happened to those before them, replaced the prior group on the platform. The timing was a little off, as the gondola was still reaching its apex on the pendulum.

Nancy reached out, training her gun on the closest zombie. It snarled at her in defiance. She squeezed the trigger, as she had so many times on the range, and put its lights out. It stood there long enough, delaying the dead behind it a second or two as they pressed up against it.

Nancy pulled her gun hand back and flush against the wall behind her as the gondola rushed down and swept away the second batch of dead.

*

When the dead filed away from the Raging Rapids ride and followed Vinnie to the Pirate Ship, Marie Russo, now unarmed, came out of hiding and ran over to the Raging Rapids ride. The ride, still spinning, was now clear of all zombies, except for several feeding inside the broken DJ booth.

It was as clear as it was going to get.

She ran up to the control panel, keeping a nervous eye on the caved-in, bloodied DJ booth. The dead hunched over their meal like animals, tearing flesh off the poor kid's body and juggling his entrails like Slinkys. She saw a red button. Guessing it was the emergency stop, she pushed it. The ride began to slow down.

Marie looked over at the Pirate Ship just as the gondola swept off a batch of dead. She saw Vinnie and Nancy pressed against the back wall.

As the Raging Rapids ride slowed to a stop, Marie started yelling at the passengers. "Everyone out! Now!"

The riders looked a bit dazed from being spun around for who knows how long. Marie first saw Dharma and Alessandra. As she ran over to them, she saw Salvatore in the chair behind them.

Dharma shook her head, looking stunned, and pushed the safety bar forward. Marie grabbed Alessandra and pulled her out of the ride over Dharma's lap.

"Mom?" Alessandra's face looked green. She vomited onto her mother's blouse.

Marie hugged her tight. "I've got you, honey."

Salvatore stumbled out of his chair and wobbled over to his mother and sister. "I feel like I'm gonna throw up."

The dead had apparently finished their meal and turned their attention to Marie and the riders exiting their cars.

"Everyone out!" shouted Marie. "Hurry!"

The dead tripped over the torn down panels of the DJ booth as they tried to exit in pursuit. It bought everyone a few precious seconds.

Dharma struggled to get up. Marie grabbed her hands and helped her out of the ride. "Are you all right?"

"Yeah, I think so. What happened? I thought I saw…"

Marie nodded. "The dead are back. Vinnie and Nancy led them away from the ride so I can get you."

At the mention of Vinnie's name, Dharma perked up. "Vinnie? Where is he? Is he okay?"

Marie pointed at the swinging Pirate Ship ride. "He's there."

They watched as the gondola took out the last of the zombies on the ride.

"It was Vinnie's idea," added Marie.

Dharma shook her head and smirked. "Yup. That's Vinnie, all right."

Marie saw the zombies crawl out of the DJ booth. "We have to get out of here!"

They joined the exodus of dizzy riders as they all pushed and shoved their way off the ride and onto the pier. There were screams and tears when they saw dead bodies, many half-eaten, littering the pier.

"We have to get out of here," said Dharma.

Vinnie and Nancy were making their way back to the Raging Rapids. Dharma, Marie, and the children dashed across the pier and met them halfway.

Vinnie was putting away his cell phone. "We can all go to my dad's pizzeria. He's got the security gates down in front, and he's got plenty of food."

Dharma ran over to him and threw her arms around him. Tears streamed down her cheeks. "I didn't know what happened. I thought you might have been…"

The normally cantankerous Nancy melted at the reunion, if only for a moment.

When Dharma broke the embrace, she hugged Nancy.

"Oh, sweetie," was all Nancy could manage.

They pulled apart, and Dharma frowned. "Where's Mike?"

Nancy, her eyes now watering, just shook her head.

Dharma looked at Vinnie, whose lip was twitching as he tried not to cry. She placed a hand over her mouth to stifle a scream.

The crowd of riders had begun to dissipate. They spread out over the pier, inspecting the remains of loved ones. Some were making their way back to the boardwalk.

"We have to get out of here," pressed Marie.

Nancy handed her back the gun. "You're a better shot than me."

Dharma's eye bulged. "My mom and dad! They're at the sunglass store! We have to see if they're okay."

"It's on the way," said Vinnie.

Two young girls—one about fourteen, the other about ten—were standing there looking nervous.

"Where are your parents?" asked Nancy.

"They were at the bonfire," said the older girl.

Vinnie and Marie traded knowing looks. There was a good chance that her parents were dead.

Salvatore stepped up, doing his best to look cool. "You can come with us. We'll keep you safe until this blows over."

The two girls looked at each other and nodded.

Marie looked stunned at her son's bold reassurance. She knew it was for the older girl's benefit. He was showing off. She smiled, amused. "That's right. You can stay with us."

Vinnie eyed the boardwalk nervously. "What's the plan?"

"The boardwalk will be crawling with the dead," said Nancy.

Vinnie looked back at the Raging Rapids. The DJ booth zombies were staggering across the pier towards them, but their advance was slow. "The pier is still crawling with dead. We can't stay here."

"Maybe not," said Marie. "Or at least maybe not as many as before. Some will have spread into the town, thinning out their numbers."

"Either way, we're sitting ducks on this pier," said Vinnie. "We have to get somewhere, and soon."

Dharma pointed at some of the other riders from the Raging Rapids ride leaving the pier. "Look, they're leaving."

Marie hefted her pistol, pointing it up at the sky. "Stay close behind me. We're going to creep very quietly up to the back of those stands, and I'm going to take a peek at the boardwalk. If the coast is clear, we'll make a run for the pizzeria." She saw Dharma's expression. "Checking on your parents along the way," she added.

Everyone nodded.

"What if it is overrun?" asked Alessandra.

"We'll cross that bridge when we get to it, hun. Remember. Quietly."

ACT III
RESISTANCE

CHAPTER 10

Becky clung to the diving board, caught between the dead above and below. As she looked around, fighting back the panic, surveying her situation, she saw that there were no zombies on the far side of the pool.

She just had to make a diagonal towards the other side, careful not to get snagged by the dead under her. There were only several in the deep end. She would have to swim completely horizontal, or as much as possible.

She looked down and saw the dead under the water wandering around aimlessly, waving their arms. The water was cloudy, which she figured would be to her advantage. Fingers clawed at her shirt sleeves from above the diving board, but they weren't able to grab onto her yet. She didn't have much time.

She pulled her body up out of the water, parallel to the diving board, pressing her feet up against the side wall of the pool. Greedy fingers reached for her ankles, but they slid off her wet pant legs.

She gave a kick and extended her body out as far away from the diving board as possible. She heard screeches from above as her body hit the surface of the water. She swam in a diagonal line towards the far end of the pool.

Hands reached up from below. One grabbed her ankle, but she kicked free, clawing at the water with her hands, straining her arms. She reached the other side and quickly hoisted herself up out of the pool.

She ran to the fence as the dead circumvented the pool in pursuit. She hopped the fence as they reached it, throwing their bodies against the chain-link fence.

She threw herself over the fence with such force that she staggered and collided with one of the maroon room doors. She stood with her back against the door, catching her breath and surveying a path for escape.

The door opened behind her, and arms reached out and embraced her. Before she knew what was happening, she was pulled inside the room.

She screamed and twisted in her assailant's grip, and whatever held her let go. She went crashing down onto the hard tile.

A middle-aged man stood above her. He slammed the front door shut and locked it. "Help me barricade the door."

Becky got up. The man was standing behind one of the dressers, knees bent. He started to shove it towards the door. She stood next to him, bent her knees, and pushed with him until the dresser was sideways and flush up against the front door.

The man rounded the dresser and peeked out between the drawn vertical blinds. "That was a close one."

Becky hugged herself, partially because she was cold and wet, and partially because she was terrified. "Yes, it was. Thank you for helping me."

The man didn't answer. He only peeked out between the vertical blinds. He was tall, thin, and shabbily dressed. His clothes were loose and threadbare. His hair was a greying rat's nest on his head. His weary face had stubble.

After the superstorm two years ago, with reduced tourism, many of the motel owners on the Jersey Shore resorted to taking in ex-cons, recovering drug addicts, even sex offenders to stay afloat. They struck an arrangement with the New Jersey Department of Social Services to house year-round tenants, as a bird in the hand was worth two in the bush. It was a sore topic in the Bay, as many didn't like these sorts of folks (particularly the sex offenders) living in a family resort in the proximity of children.

However, their living situation was predicated on their relative absence from public view. Subjected to a list of strict rules by the motel owners, many of these tenants complained that they felt like prisoners. Then again, some realized beggars couldn't be choosers. Plus, the Bay PD was hyper vigilant. Truthfully, the incidents each year were minimal. Last year, Becky ended up arresting a few of these tenants for drug possession, and one for attempting to rape a tourist.

Becky wondered what this man's situation was. "What's your name?"

He finally looked away from the window. "They know you're in here, but I think we'll be okay for now. My name is Sam."

"Sam what?"

"Sam Hodges."

"Well, thank you, Sam Hodges."

"What's your name, officer?"

"Lt. Michaels." She wanted to keep it formal. Most in the Bay knew her as 'Officer Becky.' However, she didn't want to get chummy with Sam. She never did with the welfare tenants. It was better for everyone if they saw her as an authority figure. Plus, she was out of ammunition.

He smiled. "Well, great to meet you, Lt. Michaels."

"I don't know you. Are you new?"

He shrugged. "I've only been here for a month or so. Social services relocated me from Paterson."

"If you don't mind my asking, what's your situation?" She looked around the room. It looked neat, but not clean. There were old clothes draped over the backs of chairs, pants and shirts. The room had the faint odor of BO. She figured him for a recovering drug addict.

He placed his hands up, defensively. "Whoa, I save you from a bunch of zombies and you give me the third degree?"

Okay. Paranoia. She figured he might be a section eight psych case. Most of them were harmless, but paranoia made some of them aggressive, particularly if they felt threatened. And if they were off their meds.

Becky quickly switched gears. "I didn't mean it like that. It's just I don't know you, is all."

"Well, if this is the end of days, Lt. Michaels, then it really doesn't matter who I am or what I did."

"Come on, it's not the end of days. We've been through this before."

He shook his head stubbornly. "No, this time it is the end of days. It's all over the news. It's not just here."

Okay, he's definitely a psych case.

He walked across the room and turned on the old cathode ray tube relic of a television set. It was on CNN. Sure enough, the banner at the bottom of the screen read: 'Zombie Outbreaks Along the Eastern Seaboard.'

She allowed herself a quick listen, then she quickly turned down the volume. "We don't want to attract any more attention to our presence here."

"Now do you believe me, Lt. Michaels?"

"Okay, okay. So, this is more than a little outbreak."

The man smiled, apparently delighted at her admission. "See. The world is coming undone."

Becky shook her head. "The military will retake the town. It'll be a bigger cleanup than before."

"I saw the military arrive earlier. Now the town's overrun. The entire eastern seaboard is overrun. It's going to spread inland."

Becky frowned. This man seemed to take delight in the fall of civilization, which made her uncomfortable. He was a couple of sandwiches short of a picnic. Although she was grateful for his help, all things being equal, she wished she was back outside.

She walked over to the window and peeked out through the vertical blinds. The zombies were milling about, as if they had forgotten where she went. Thank goodness for short attention spans.

"I've made you uncomfortable."

Becky turned and saw the man grinning again. Always that grin that didn't match the situation or context. "I need to get back to the station."

She was suddenly reminded of her radio. In all of the excitement, she had forgotten all about it. She reached for her shoulder, but there was only a dangling wire. It had been ripped off in the pool by one of the dead.

Great. Now she was cut off. "Do you think you could help me get back to the station, Sam?"

Sam's grin widened. He was practically giddy over the notion of helping her. "It would be my pleasure, Lt. Michaels."

"I need a clear path of escape." She looked around. This motel didn't have a back door.

"Maybe if you wait them out, they'll go away."

"I don't know. There's an awful lot of them. I just need less of them. They're slow and clumsy. I can run around them."

Sam looked like he was pondering something. "Do you have a car?"

"No, my car was part of the barricade just off the boardwalk."

"Even if you get out, how are you going to make it back to the station? On foot's a bit dangerous."

"You don't have a car?"

Sam shook his head. "Do I look like I can afford a car? I moved here because it's a small town. Everything's in walking distance."

"What about the other guests? One of them must have a car."

Sam shook his head again. "There only two others, and they're both like me. The rest of the motel is empty."

Becky paced back and forth, her mind racing to find options. She suddenly stopped. "Have you seen or heard from any of these other residents? Are they okay?"

Sam shrugged. "I hear sounds next door, as if someone's there. He's a man, a bit older than me. Really scraggly looking. He always is wearing stuff from the Army-Navy surplus store. The other is a girl, young, like early twenties. She's across the way, on the other side of the pool. I haven't seen anything of her." He stepped back to the window and peeked out, careful not to disturb the vertical blinds. "Her light's been off the whole time. She's a recovered drug addict, or so she says."

"You don't think she's clean?" asked Becky.

"She leaves her room even less than I do. Once in a while, a man drops by to pay her a visit, but the landlord spoke to her about that. We're not really allowed visitors."

"Well, we need to get to a safer place. You can come to the station with me."

"This, here, seems pretty safe," explained Sam. "So far, they haven't gotten in."

Becky shook her head. "They will eventually. Even with your barricade, that door is real flimsy. Plus, there's the large window. If enough of them press up against it, it'll break."

"If they don't know we're in here, we'll be fine. I have plenty of peanut butter for the both of us. I have a big bag of Doritos, too. Party sized. I've got some soda in the fridge."

Becky approached him, placing a hand on his shoulder. "I appreciate your hospitality, Sam. I really do. I know you don't have much, and I'm touched you would share with me. But, you were right. This is much bigger than two years ago. If this is a major attack…"

"An invasion!"

"…yes, an invasion, then we need to make more long-term plans. Peanut butter and chips won't last us. We're going to need to get to some help, whether it's police or military. It'll be safest there."

Sam listened to her well-reasoned argument. "I see. You're right." He walked over to the window and looked out. "We need to wait till some of them move on. Then we can go."

"So, you'll come with me?"

"Yes. I will. You're right. It won't be safe here for long."

"What about the other two? The man next door and the girl across the way."

This suggestion seemed to upset him. "No. No. The girl across the way may not even be there. Or she may be lying dead on the floor with a needle in her arm."

Becky placed her hand on his shoulder again. "We have to check, Sam. I'm a cop. I protect people."

Now Sam was pacing. Becky wondered what had him so perturbed. "Sam, did you have an argument or a fight with either of the other residents?"

Sam stopped pacing a looked at her. As a cop, she knew a guilty expression when she saw one. "No, why would you ask that?"

"Sam, you seem upset when I brought them up. Whatever happened between you and them, you have to let it go. It's now the dead versus the living. We have to pull together, or we're all going to die."

Sam sat down on his bed, shoulders slumped, like a pouting child. "Well, there's no way for us to contact them. We can't exactly go out and start knocking on doors."

"Well, we've got to do something. Strength in numbers, know what I mean?"

Sam smiled, but it was a pensive smile. "Funny how the apocalypse is the great equalizer."

Beck was pacing back and forth, pondering a way for them to get the others and get out. "I'm not sure I know what you mean, Sam."

"Look, if things were normal, you and I wouldn't be in the same room together. Now that all hell's breaking loose, we're stuck together in the same predicament. We have to rely on each other to survive."

"If you say so, Sam."

He smiled wider, encouraged. "It's like our pasts, everything we've done up until this point, don't matter. The slate is wiped clean. We are all reborn into this very moment, together."

Becky didn't like where he was going with this line of conversation. Apparently, he had a past he wanted to forget. Or he wanted others to forget. She wasn't thrilled about him placing the two of them on the same level.

She snapped her fingers, as if a sudden revelation had just dawned on her. "These walls are paper thin. We can bang on the wall to get the guy next door's attention."

Sam perked up. "The zombies will hear it. They'll come crashing in."

Becky thought. *Past. Army-Navy.* "Okay, so I won't bang. I'll tap. Maybe it'll get his attention, and he'll come to the wall." She wished she had her retractable baton, but she had dropped it in the scuffle at the barricade when they were overrun.

She looked around the room. She saw a dingy metal fork lying on top of a small table next to a box of cereal. She walked over to it.

"There's no more cereal." Sam looked sheepish. "I ate it all before you got here."

Becky pushed the empty box aside and grabbed the fork.

Sam looked perplexed. "What are you going to do with that?"

Becky placed the fork flush against the sheetrock. She pressed down on the curved prongs, popping the handle off the surface of the wall. With her other hand, she began to press the handle against the sheet rock, tapping hard so that it would likely be heard on the other side.

"What are you doing?"

"Morse code," said Becky.

"What if he doesn't know Morse Code?"

"I'm hoping he does. You said so yourself, he's always dressing like a soldier. Maybe he's a vet. At the very least, it will get his attention."

There was tapping on the other side of the wall. It was definitely Morse Code.

"He's answering."

"What's he saying?" asked Sam.

"Shhh. I'm trying to listen."

Sam backed off and began pacing back and forth, biting his fingernails.

Becky listened carefully. Then the tapping stopped. "Something about dangerous." She tapped a reply.

Sam frowned. "Duh. Captain Obvious over there."

"Shhh. I'm trying to concentrate."

Sam threw his hands up in exasperation. "Okay. Okay. Jesus Christ."

She tapped back, 'Safe for the moment.'

When she finished, she waited a moment. There was a brief pause, then the tapping on the other side started again.

'You...are...not...safe...'

Sam was silent behind her as she concentrated on deciphering the message. She didn't relay this one to Sam, and he didn't ask. She shot him a glance. He was still pacing and chewing his fingernails.

She tapped a reply. 'Why...not...?"

After a brief pause, the tapping continued. 'Sam...dangerous...rapist...'

* * *

Lena and Tara collided with the crowd of dead, who reached out for them, unafraid. Tara's car jerked as zombies crunched under its wheels. The front right tire slipped in the gore, causing the car to veer to the left and right into the cement divide as Lena raced forward in her police cruiser.

Tara felt the car partially climb the divider and then slam down hard, the right wheel catching on the bodies of the dead. The car flipped on its side.

Metal scraping on pavement, the car skidded to a stop and rolled over onto its roof. The whole thing had happened so fast, that all she could get out was, "Ty, hold on!"

Upside down, she shook her head, and shards of safety glass from the shattered driver's side window shook out of her hair. "Ty! Ty, are you all right?"

She heard moaning from the back seat. "Mommy."

Tyrell, no longer considering himself to be a little kid, usually called her 'mom.' He only used 'mommy' when he was really upset. Or scared.

"Ty, honey, are you hurt?" She tried to turn around at look at the back seat, but she wasn't able to. She unbuckled herself, and she fell to the car ceiling, raining more safety glass down with her.

She looked at Tyrell, who was upside down, the side of his face cut from his passenger window being shattered. An icy chill shot down her spine. She saw two zombies, their legs crushed from the weight of her car, dragging themselves on the pavement towards the car. They were only twenty or so feet away.

She quickly looked the other direction and saw Lena's squad car slow down at the bottom of the approach to Smuggler's Bay.

Tyrell saw the look of concern on her face and tried to turn around to look. There were growls and snarls in the near distance. "Mommy, what's wrong?"

"Look at me, honey! Don't look over there!"

Horrified, Tyrell obeyed his mother, but his body tensed up, bracing for whatever his mother was looking at. He knew it only had to be one thing. "Is it them? Are they coming?"

Tara commando crawled to the back of the car, and she pushed herself up with her hands. An intense pain radiated through her right arm, causing her to go down again. She cried out from the agony.

"Mommy, are you hurt?"

"I'm okay, sweetie." The pain nearly took her breath away, but she had to put up a brave front. Again.

The gurgling and growling grew closer. One of the monsters let out a blood-curdling shriek.

Tyrell went rigid. "Help me, Mommy! Help me!"

"Hang on, Ty!"

She pushed herself up on one arm and got to her knees. She sat up on her haunches, hunched over, and fumbled with his seatbelt. "Hold on, honey."

In the corner of her eye, she saw dead fingers gripping the edge of the car window. A head with raccoon eyes popped inside, looking first at her and then at Tyrell, baring broken teeth.

The belt buckle disengaged, and Tyrell fell to the car ceiling. Tara threw herself on top of him to protect him from the lunging zombie that was now part way into the car.

"Mommy, no!" He squirmed underneath her, but she did her best to cover him.

The zombie sunk his teeth down into her arm, and blood welled up around its torn lips. Tara cried out in agony, but she didn't dare pull herself away, lest she expose her son.

This wasn't supposed to happen. She was supposed to keep herself alive to keep Tyrell alive. The teeth sinking further into the flesh of her right forearm reminded her that this was no longer to be.

She heard a car engine race, tires skid to a stop, and a car door slam.

"Tara! Are you all right!"

Tara moaned as the zombie pulled away a chunk of her forearm and began to chew on it, its chomping wet and breathy. "Grab my feet! Pull me out!"

She felt hands—human hands—grab her ankles and pull. Tara grabbed onto Tyrell, and both of them were dragged out of the car together. Tyrell was embracing his mother, crying.

Lena was standing over them, the shotgun from the police car lying at her feet. "Are you guys okay?"

*

There was shrieking from inside the overturned car. Lena quickly crouched, grabbed the shotgun, and aimed it at the car window as Tara and Tyrell squirmed away from the car.

A head peeked out from the car window. It looked up, opening its mouth to shriek, but Lena pulled the trigger. The zombie's head burst open, spraying its blood and brains all over the side of the car and the pavement.

Lena was not experienced with guns. The kickback from the shotgun caused it to fly out of her hands, and she stumbled backwards, almost losing her balance. Her ribs hurt from where the stock banged into her. She clutched her ribcage.

"She's been bitten."

Lena turned around a saw Mrs. Holly standing there, pointing at Tara. Lena looked back at the squad car. Robbie and Lenny were looking out the back window, but thankfully the car doors were shut. There were no other zombies by the car.

For the moment.

Tara was cradling her forearm. Tyrell was watching her, tears streaming down his face. He knew she had been bitten, and he knew what it meant.

"Give me the shotgun," said Tara through gritted teeth.

Lena looked at her perplexed. There were more snarls coming from inside the upside-down car.

"Now!"

Lena grabbed the shotgun off the ground behind her and handed it to Tara.

"Go by Mrs. Holbrook, Tyrell."

"But Mommy…"

"Do as I say!"

Lena reached down and snatched him away, unsure of what was about to happen.

Tara held the shotgun in her good arm. She lay the broken, bitten arm down on the pavement and placed the end of the barrel on the crook of her elbow.

Lena knew what she was about to do and pulled Tyrell away, shielding him from it with her body.

*

Tara took a deep breath, gritted her teeth, and pulled the trigger. The shotgun jumped back, out of her hand, nearly breaking her right index finger on the trigger in the process. Her elbow exploded on the pavement as she felt her tendons snap.

She sat up, her arm still dangling as it had not become completely severed. As her head swam and adrenaline pumped throughout her body, she knelt down on her dangling forearm and pulled, screaming, as she separated herself from her damaged forearm.

She stumbled away from it, slamming her face onto the pavement as a second zombie emerged from the car window. It grunted, seized Tara's severed forearm, and pulled it back inside the car.

*

Lena passed Tyrell off to Mrs. Holly, who embraced him firmly as his body shook from sobbing. Lena grabbed Tara under the armpits and hoisted her to her feet. Lena threw Tara's good arm over her shoulder and walked her over to the police cruiser as Tara bled all over the pavement.

Mrs. Holly was standing there, eyes alert. They eyed Tara's torn arm. "She needs a tourniquet, or she'll bleed to death." When Lena looked at her, stunned, she added, "I'm a retired nurse, remember?"

Lena nodded, thankful for that fact. She was also grateful that Mrs. Holly had apparently snapped out of her shock.

Mrs. Holly walked up to Tara and examined the bloody nub at her elbow. "I'll need a belt or a long piece of fabric."

Tyrell took off his T-shirt and shoved it into Lena's arms. "Here. Use this."

Lena took it and handed it to Mrs. Holly.

"Lay her down," said Mrs. Holly.

Lena helped lower Tara to the pavement and lay her down on her back.

Mrs. Holly knelt beside her, her knees complaining, and slipped Tyrell's T-shirt around it. She tied it high up on Tara's arm, close to the armpit. "I'll need a dowel, and something to secure it once I'm done twisting."

Lena got to her feet and reached inside the squad car. She emerged with a few zip ties and a retractable baton. She handed them to Mrs. Holly. Her eyes darted over to Tara's overturned car. Whatever was inside was still inside, feasting on Tara's severed forearm.

Mrs. Holly tied the zip tie around the T-shirt next to the first knot, but left it loose. "We occasionally used to see these kinds of wounds when I worked in the ER." She then tied a loose square knot, slipped the retracted baton inside it, tightened the knot around it, and began to twist. Tara winced and yelped, trying to sit up.

Mrs. Holly looked up at Lena. "Help me hold her down."

Lena got to her knees and firmly pressed Tara's torso back to the pavement, holding it there.

Tyrell knelt next to his mother's head. "It's okay, Mommy. They're trying to help you." He stroked her hair.

Lena had to fight back tears as she watched Tyrell try to comfort his mother. The back door to the squad car opened behind her. "What's happening, Mom?" asked Robbie.

"Get back inside the car and look out for more zombies!" she yelled over her shoulder. She heard the door slam shut.

When Mrs. Holly finished twisting, she held the dowel in place. She slipped it under the zip tie. "Tighten the zip tie."

Lena reached out and tightened the zip tie around the baton, holding it and the tourniquet in place. Tara was now still.

"She's in shock," said Mrs. Holly.

"Let's get her in the car," said Lena.

Lena stood up and helped Mrs. Holly to her feet, her knees creaking. Lena grabbed Tara under her armpits and dragged her over to the rear driver's side of the squad car, Tyrell following beside her, still stroking his mother's hair. Lena thought it was quite the pitiful sight.

Mrs. Holly opened the door and helped Lena slide Tara into the back seat. "Slide over by her feet. Keep them elevated," she told Robbie and Lenny. "Let her head rest on the seat on the other side."

"Wait a minute," said Tara. "What if she wakes up as…?"

Mrs. Holly frowned. "You mean what if her field amputation didn't prevent the spread of the virus?"

"Yes. I don't want her waking up a monster in the back seat with Robbie and Lenny. We'll have to put her in the trunk."

Mrs. Holly shot her a look of disapproval. "I don't know if that's such a good idea."

"I'm not taking the chance with my son in the back seat. End of story."

Mrs. Holly nodded, but she didn't like it.

Lena reached inside the car, grabbed the keys, and dragged Tara back around to the trunk. She opened it, juggling Tara with her other hand. There were blankets inside over the spare tire.

"Help me get her in."

Lena grabbed the blankets, holding onto Tara with her other hand. She threw them onto the pavement and held Tara with both hands again.

Mrs. Holly grabbed Tara's legs. They slid her inside, her legs bent at the knees to fit her inside.

"What are you doing?" asked Tyrell. "Why are you putting her in the trunk?"

Lena crouched down beside him and looked into his eyes. "Your mom took off her arm to stop the spread of the infection. If it didn't work, she'll wake up a zombie. We can't have her in the car with us if that happens."

"She'll be perfectly fine in the trunk," added Mrs. Holly. "We need to leave now. It's dark, and it's unsafe to stay here out in the open like this."

"Get in the back with Robbie and Lenny," said Lena. "We'll make sure your mom is nice and comfortable, and then we'll get out of here."

Mrs. Holly grabbed the blankets from Lena. She rolled a couple of them up and slipped them under Tara's legs to elevate them. Then she covered Tara with the third blanket.

Lena slammed the trunk shut. She ushered Tyrell into the back seat. Then she and Mrs. Holly got back into the car. Lena put the key in the ignition and killed the lights. She began to drive back into town, back to the police station to get Tara help and figure out what to do next.

CHAPTER 11

Chief Holbrook was rallying the troops. "We need to barricade the front doors! Pacelli, I want you and another spotter with rifles on the roof! I want a bird's eye report of what's going on in the streets!"

The several officers left in the station were taking stock of weapons and ammunition. Reports and updates were coming in from various state and local agencies, as well as federal—anything from the Department of Health to the Department of Defense.

Holbrook was trying to get status reports from the officers out on the streets. The response had been eerily underwhelming. There were mostly a few officers who had found a nook to hide in after their patrol had been overwhelmed by the dead.

He hoped Becky was one of them. He hadn't heard from her since the attack on the beach. He had already lost her sister to the dead two years ago. He didn't want to lose her, too.

His cell rang. He pulled it out of his pocket, saw who it was, and answered it. "Are you okay, hun?"

"We didn't make it out," said Lena. "The army raised the bridge. Stonewall's been overrun."

"I know. We're getting reports in from everywhere that the whole Eastern seaboard is under attack. Get back here, to the station."

His radio crackled. It was Pacelli. "There's dead everywhere, Chief."

"Hold on a second…" Holbrook put down his cell and got on his radio. "Roger that, Pacelli. Keep me posted. Don't fire unless any try to get into the station."

"Roger that, Chief. Over and out."

Holbrook picked up his cell. "Everyone all right? Did you run into any trouble?"

There was a pause. "We picked up Lenny and Tyrell Bigelow. We've got Tara in the trunk. She's in bad shape."

Holbrook knew why she was in the trunk. "She was bitten."

"Yeah, but she blew her arm off with your shotgun to try and stop the infection."

"Jesus," gasped Holbrook. "She's going to bleed to death."

"Mrs. Holly put a tourniquet on her to stop the bleeding. She needs medical attention."

"We're cut off," said Holbrook. "You can get to the mainland by way of Oceanside Terrace, but they're overrun, too." He heard Mrs. Holly talking to Lena.

"Hello?" said Lena.

"I'm still here, hun."

"Mrs. Holly said that her neighbor two doors down is a retired surgeon. Dr. Potts. If we can take her there, she may have a chance."

"I don't like you driving around town while it's infested with the dead. Plus, we don't even know if this Dr. Potts is home, or even alive for that matter."

There was silence on the other end. "I can't just let her die, Jim. I've got to do something. She's a hero...her son's already lost his father." She said that last part in hushed tones.

"I'm going to try calling his landline," said Holbrook. "Let's see if he's even home before you go out of your way."

"We're safe as long as we're driving. We're in town again. The dead seem to be dispersed pretty evenly. As long as they don't bunch up, I think we're okay for the moment."

"Okay. Mrs. Holly doesn't happen to have his phone number on her?" He heard Lena relay the question.

"No, she doesn't."

"What's this Dr. Pott's first name?" He heard Lena repeat the question to Mrs. Holly, who answered her.

"Harold."

"Good. I'll call you back in a few minutes. See if you can find a place to hide."

"Okay. Love you."

"Love you, too." Holbrook hung up. He knew that name, Harold Potts. He had no idea the man was a retired surgeon.

He grabbed his Smuggler's Bay phone book off the table behind his desk and rifled through it until he found a Harold Potts. The street matched. He punched the number into his cell. The phone rang.

"Hello." The voice sounded faint and hoarse.

"Hello, is this Harold Potts?"

"Yes...it is...Who's this?" The man sounded elderly.

"This is Chief Holbrook of the SBPD."

"Hello, Chief."

"I understand you're a retired surgeon?"

"Yes...Chief, the dead are back. They're everywhere."

"Yes, I know Harold. We have a wounded woman. She attempted a field amputation with a shotgun."

"My goodness."

"Yes. There's a tourniquet on her, but she needs medical attention."

"I'm sorry, Chief...but I'm not equipped to do anything..."

"Dr. Potts...Harold...if we don't help her, she's going to die."

"What about the hospital in Stonewall?"

"Sir, we're cut off from the mainland. Have you watched the news?"

"Yes, I have."

"Then you know the whole East Coast is overrun."

"Yes...I do."

"You are our only hope. This woman is a hero from the last attack. She lost her husband in it, and her son will be an orphan if he loses her. He's only seven years old."

Silence on the other end. That last part apparently got to Harold.

"I'll need some supplies."

"Yes!" Holbrook grabbed a pen and paper. "Go ahead." He started writing down a list of things, such as peroxide, antibiotics, needle, threat, and gauze. When Harold had finished the list, Chief Holbrook put down his pen and ripped the list off his pad, shoving it into his pocket. "Thank you, Dr. Potts. We'll be there real soon."

"I'll expect you. And call me Harold."

"Yes. Thank you, Harold." Holbrook terminated the call. He dialed Lena, and she picked up on the second ring.

"Hello?"

"I got a hold of Harold Potts. You're going to go to his house, but first you need to pick up some supplies. He said you could get them at the CVS."

"In the middle of the zombie apocalypse?"

"Lena, he's retired. He doesn't have the equipment in his house. I'll go with you."

"No, you need to be at the station. I can handle this."

"Are you sure? The dead are everywhere."

"It'll be easier if I head straight there. We'll be there in a few minutes."

"I'll text you the list of supplies. Don't stop the car unless it's safe. Call me when you get there."

"Got it."

"And Lena…"

"Yes?"

"Be careful. I don't want you getting killed over this."

"I'm not some helpless damsel. Don't worry, I'll be careful." Lena terminated the call.

* * *

Marie was next to the Frog Bog, crouched behind one of the pillars. The rest of the gang were all behind her, waiting for her next instructions. Vinnie and Dharma nervously eyed the pier, keeping an eye on the advancing dead from the Raging Rapids. They tripped over bodies, falling to the pier, but they kept getting back up and were closing the distance.

Marie looked towards the left. The boardwalk was largely empty, except for a few of the dead shambling. They seemed to be heading in the same direction, towards one of the storefronts. She looked the other direction. Down the boardwalk, there were several zombies milling around, but most had apparently taken to the streets.

Marie turned back to the group. "Okay, we're clear to the left. But, we're going to have to pass a small group, but they're all headed for the same storefront. Probably cornered some poor soul…We stay all the way to the left, hugging the fence, behind the benches."

Everyone in the group nodded. Marie took the lead, circumventing the Frog Bog and the Water Gun Race booths, sticking to the left. The others followed behind her. The coast was mostly clear, except for the few dead now staggering over to…

Oh, shit, thought Marie.

Dharma gasped and grabbed Vinnie's arm, nearly yanking him off balance. "The sunglass store!"

Marie stopped and turned to the group. "Dharma, are you sure your parents are in there?"

Dharma looked panicked. "I think so. I'm not sure."

Nancy frowned. "Why else would those zombies be all heading for the booth? They have someone cornered."

Dharma now grabbed Marie's arm. Her eyes pleaded with her. "We have to help them!"

"I can take Ali and the rest to Vinnie's pizzeria," offered Salvatore. "You guys can help Dharma's parents."

Marie didn't like the idea of being separated from her children again. "We go to the pizzeria first, then a few of us will double back to help Emily and Ira."

Dharma squeezed her arm tighter. "They might be dead by then!"

Vinnie looked up and down the boardwalk. "We're sitting ducks if we're just going to stand here and argue. You guys go ahead, get to the pizzeria. Dharma and I will figure something out."

This time, Salvatore touched Marie's arm. "Really, Mom. I can do this. You help Mr. and Mrs. Ross."

The young girls they picked up back at the pier watched him with a mixture of anticipation and admiration, especially the older one. They looked like they wanted to be anywhere on earth but where they were now.

Marie gave him a long look. She didn't like it, but she knew he was right. Hell, she was impressed that he was stepping up, although she was certain hormones had more to do with it than heroism. "Here, take my gun." She tried to shove it in his hands.

Salvatore pushed it away. "No. You're going to need it."

Marie nodded, her face solemn. "You be careful. Get right to the pizzeria. Don't stop for anything."

"Knock on the back door," said Vinnie. "They won't be able to lift the security gate without making a lot of noise and leaving themselves vulnerable."

Salvatore nodded. "Okay," he said to his sister, the girls, and Nancy. "Let's go."

Marie, Dharma, and Vinnie waited, watching Salvatore lead them down the boardwalk, hugging the fence. They passed the sunglass store without being noticed by the dead inside.

After they had gotten away without incident, Marie turned to Dharma and Vinnie. "Okay. We creep up slowly and real quiet-like. Let's see if we can get a look inside."

Just then, Marie's cell phone rang. She quickly grabbed it and answered. It was Salvatore. "What?"

"The dead are pounding on a closet door. Someone's in there, trapped."

"Okay," said Marie. "Get to the pizzeria. Text me when you get there." She hung up and set her cell phone to vibrate. She wanted to get the text, but she didn't want her phone ringing at an inopportune time, alerting the dead.

"Who was that?" asked Vinnie.

"Sal," said Dharma.

Marie nodded. "He said they've got someone trapped in a closet."

Dharma nodded. "The supply closet. My parents must've run in there to get away from them."

"So, what's the plan?" asked Vinnie. "We only have one gun."

"We cause a distraction," said Marie. "Lure them away. Then one of us can get whoever's in there out."

"I'll cause the distraction," said Vinnie. "I'm fast."

Marie nodded. "You have to lead them out. Stay close enough to keep them on you, but far enough out of reach." She knew it had to be Vinnie. She was too out of shape to run with him, and Dharma wanted to rescue her parents. "I'll help Dharma."

"Got it."

They crossed the boardwalk to the storefronts without incident. They crept up to the store to the right of the sunglass store unnoticed. There was a zombie stumbling around a few storefronts down to the right. It saw them, shrieking in response, but it was moving slowly.

Marie leaned in close and whispered. "Don't worry about that one yet. It's alone. I'll deal with it if it gets close. Focus on our task at hand."

Vinnie and Dharma nodded. As they mentally prepared themselves for their perilous task, they didn't notice the young dead girl dressed in pink walk up the ramp from the beach. She limped over towards them, eyes fierce and teeth bared.

"Fooooooooooood!"

Marie, Vinnie, and Dharma all jerked their heads towards the other side of the boardwalk and saw the young dead girl pointing at them.

Marie was stunned. "Did that thing just talk?!"

"I didn't know they could do that," said Dharma.

"They *can't* do that," said Vinnie.

But, they didn't have any more time to discuss it. The dead from inside the sunglass store came spilling out onto the boardwalk.

"Oh, shit," gasped Vinnie.

Marie raised her gun hand, training it on each zombie as it passed them. They hadn't been spotted yet.

The little dead girl in pink pointed at them and shrieked. The other dead began to turn and look.

"We've got to get the fuck out of here!" said Marie.

"My parents!" insisted Dharma.

They had nowhere to run but inside the sunglass store. Marie ran inside first. Vinnie grabbed Dharma by the hand and they followed.

Dharma shook her hand free and ran towards the door, pounding on it. "Mom! Dad! It's me, Dharma!"

Vinnie and Marie were looking around the hut for something, anything, they could use. They traded looks, and then, in some unspoken agreement, they shoved the two, large wooden center displays towards the entrance, toppling them over. Dozens of designer knockoffs spilled to the ground.

The closet door opened, and Emily and Ira Ross emerged, throwing their arms around Dharma, startling her. Dharma quickly pushed them away to get a good look at them. "Are you guys okay? Were you bitten?"

"No," said Ira, watching Vinnie and Marie barricade the entrance to the store. "Are you okay?"

Dharma nodded. "Thanks to Vinnie and Mrs. Russo."

"Oh, thank God!" gasped Emily.

The dead were converging on the store, crunching the cheap sunglasses underneath their clumsy feet. The toppled displays blocked the bulk of them, but several were slipping in along the sides. The rest were crawling over.

"We've gotta get out of here!" shouted Vinnie.

Marie plugged one in the head on the right, then one on the left, its fingers nearly grazing her arm. She backed away as they dropped to the floor, tripping up the dead pushing in from behind them. It bought them an extra few heartbeats.

Ira pointed to the back of the store. "Everyone, out the back door!"

There was a glass door behind the counter with the cash register. There weren't any zombies at the door. Emily went first, throwing it open. One-by-one, they exited the hut, descending a small set of steps, and landing on the sidewalk below.

The dead were right behind them, shoving the door open. They all tried to squeeze through the narrow doorway simultaneously, which slowed their pursuit. It looked like a Three Stooges gag. It was almost comical.

Marie looked around. The dead were everywhere, wandering the streets of Smuggler's Bay. *Jesus, there are so many of them. Where'd they all come from?*

Vinnie pointed down the street to the left. "Let's go. My pizzeria's three blocks over."

He took the lead, dashing down the sidewalk, Dharma, Ira, and Emily in tow with Marie bring up the rear. She was huffing and puffing. Her face was red and slick with sweat.

There were screams in the near distance, some living, the others from the dead. There were empty police squad cars scattered along the street, but no cops in sight, except for a few bodies in various phases of consumption. Three blocks into town, Vinnie saw a squad car with flashing lights creep past. He pulled out his cell phone and dialed his father, who picked up on the third ring.

"We're two blocks away," said Vinnie.

"Come in through the back. Marie's kids and Nancy are here."

Vinnie hung up the phone, but he kept it in his hand.

They reached the back of his father's pizzeria. Vinnie's father opened the back door and waved them over. "Hurry up!"

Vinnie, Dharma, Ira, Emily, and Marie all entered the pizzeria, and Vinnie's father quickly closed the back door, locking it.

* * *

As Becky's brain processed the warning from the other side of the wall, she felt arms wrap around her body, squeezing her arms against her sides. She tried to struggle, but she was shorter and lighter than Sam.

He lifted her off her feet, pulling her away from the wall, and whispered in her ear. His voice was breathy, his breath warm and moist. "He told you, didn't he?"

Becky stopped struggling and tried to remain calm. Maybe she could talk her way out of it. "He told me he was all right. That's all."

"Liar." Sam's grip didn't loosen any.

"No, really. Why? What do you think he said?"

"He told you about me. About what I did."

Becky relaxed her muscles, creating a small gap in his embrace. But, he was like a boa constrictor, tightening his embrace, squeezing the breath out of her.

"Sam, I have no idea…" she gasped. She had no wind for speech. It was a matter of seconds before she was going to pass out.

Remembering her training, she swung her head back, and the back of her skull smashed the bridge of his nose.

He whimpered and loosened his grip, allowing her feet to touch the ground. She placed her right foot behind his and shoved backwards, kicking off the table with her left foot.

Sam lost his balance, tripped over her foot, and instinctively let her go. He went crashing to the ground, clutching his nose.

She whirled around. "That was a big mistake."

Sam's eyes were watering. "You fucking cunt," he spat into his cupped hands. "You broke my nose!"

There was the pounding of dead fists on the door and window. They had heard the ruckus outside.

She was alone in a room, unarmed, with an apparent rapist in the middle of the zombie apocalypse. She couldn't allow him to get back up, and at the moment, she wasn't worried about police brutality. She started kicking him in the head and in his ribs. He curled up, yelling and crying out with each blow.

The pounding outside became louder and more forceful. The large window was rattling. It was going to break.

Becky shoved the dresser away from the door and got behind it as the glass of the large window shattered. The dead pushed their way through the shards of broken glass and vertical blinds, descending on Sam.

He disappeared under a heap of zombies, screaming in horror as they tore him apart. More of the dead came through the window, joining the feeding frenzy. The sounds Sam made were something Becky would never forget as long as she lived.

She peeked through the peephole as two zombies inside the room reached out for her, stopped by the dresser. The coast outside the door looked clear, as the dead were all converging on the broken window.

She unlocked the door and pulled it open, but the edge of the door caught the edge of the dresser. As hands swiped at her, she shoved the dresser with her hip, bumping it until the edge of the door cleared it. She flung the door open and dashed outside, stopping at the fence by the pool.

A dead woman lunged at her, but she sidestepped and punched it in the head. She backed away as it tumbled to the ground.

A hand clapped down on her shoulder. Becky turned and raised her fist to strike.

It was the old man next door. Recoiling, he had his hands up, shielding his face. "Hey, hey, it's okay!"

She lowered her fist, and he lowered his hands.

He was cringing. "I'm not going to hurt you."

"Thank you for warning me about Sam."

"I have a car, but we have to get Erin." He pointed to the room across the way.

Becky nodded. "Let's go."

They rounded the pool, and the old man jumped ahead, banging on the room door. "Erin! Erin, it's Larry! Open up!"

They waited, but there was no response.

"Back up," said Becky.

Larry did as he was told.

Becky took a couple of steps back and kicked the door. On the third kick, it swung inward, pulling off part of the door frame.

Larry slipped by Becky as she kept a lookout. He re-emerged from the room. "She's unconscious."

"Great," said Becky. Just what she needed. They needed to make a quick getaway, and they had to deal with an overdose.

She entered the room and saw Erin unconscious on her bed in her clothes. She was pallid and drenched in sweat. The room was a total pig sty. She walked over and checked her pulse. "She's in bad shape."

"I'm not leaving without her," insisted Larry.

"Grab her feet."

Larry ran over and grabbed Erin's feet. Becky grabbed Erin under her arms. They lifted her off the bed. She was light, thankfully.

Becky led the way to the door. Fortunately, the dead were still preoccupied with eating Sam.

"Where's your car?"

"Right here, in the lot. The old Dodge."

They lugged her out the front gate, which was unlatched. Becky pushed it open with her hip.

"Over here." Larry led them over to a large, rusted, old car. He lowered her feet and fished his keys out of his pocket. His hands were trembling. He opened the front door and unlocked the back. He opened it, and Becky dragged Erin's limp body over to the back seat. Together, they shoved her inside lying on her back, her knees bent and lying sideways to make room.

Becky closed the back door and held her hand out. "Keys."

"Well, I-I thought I'd drive."

"Keys."

Larry begrudgingly handed her the keys.

"Thank you." Becky rounded the car and slid into the driver's seat. She reached across and unlocked the passenger door. No power locks. It was an older model.

Larry let himself into the passenger seat. "Don't smack her up. She's all I got."

Becky arched an eyebrow. "Larry, anything I'd do to this car would be an improvement." She turned the ignition, the engine reluctantly turned over, and she pulled the shifter into reverse.

They backed out of the parking lot, knocking over two dead—a woman and a boy. She felt their bodies crunch under the wheels. She put the car in drive and turned left to head down the street.

Larry turned around to give Erin a look. She was still unconscious. "Where are we going?"

"The police station."

"What the hell are we gonna do there?"

"There's police there. Weapons. Radios."

"How many cops do you think are left after the first wave?"

It was a legitimate question, and something Becky hadn't wanted to ponder. "I don't know, but at least we'll have supplies and communication."

"I don't want to die in no police station. I would've rather died back in the room."

"We're not going to die, Larry. Not if I can help it."

"Well, that's reassuring."

"Sarcasm isn't going to help us, Larry."

"It's about all I got left."

"That's not true." She turned to look him in the eye. "You were in the military."

"Army. I was in Vietnam, right in the shit."

"You have training. You know how to fire a gun."

"I was hit, right in the leg." He pointed down at his knee. "I was running through that God-forsaken jungle when I felt my leg get taken out from under me. It was like I was hit by a lead pipe. I received an honorable discharge. Still get nightmares."

Becky smiled. "Well, there's one good thing about this situation."

"What's that?"

"You won't get shot."

"No, just eaten alive. If I'm lucky."

Becky punched him in the arm. "See, Larry. That's the spirit!"

"Yeah."

* * *

Lena pulled into the CVS parking lot. She crept into a handicapped parking space, right in front, and put the cruiser in park. She left the engine running.

There were zombies wandering up and down the street in front of CVS, but none seemed interested in them at the moment. Lena eyed the front entrance to the store. The lights were on, but she didn't see anyone inside. However, her angle didn't afford her a complete view of the store.

"I'm g-g-going with you," offered Lenny.

Lena looked at Mrs. Holly, and then at Lenny. She smiled. "I appreciate your offer, Lenny, but I need you to stay here and watch Robbie and Tyrell."

Lenny was going to insist, but he looked at the two boys in the back seat with him. They looked scared. He appeared to change his mind.

"I'll come with you," said Mrs. Holly.

Lena shook her head. "No, I need someone who can drive this car…in case I don't come out."

Robbie's eyes were watering. "Mommy…"

"It'll be okay, honey," said Lena. "It's just in case."

"I don't want you going in there."

"I have to, Robbie. For Tyrell's mom. She needs my help."

"You don't have to go in," said Tyrell, resigned. "She's probably dead anyway." He choked on those words as if they were poison in his mouth.

Lena's eyes narrowed. "Don't you say that. You're mom's tough. She's a real warrior. When I got out of town the last time the dead attacked, she was here fighting. She fought for your life, and now we're going to fight for hers."

Tyrell looked down for a moment, ashamed. "Thanks, Mrs. Holbrook."

"Don't thank me now." Lena checked her phone. She got Jim's text. It was a short list: advanced blood stop hemostatic gauze (as much as possible), sterile gloves, alcohol (as much as possible), tweezers. "Thank me when Dr. Potts saves your mom."

Lena looked around. The parking lot was clear. "Okay, Mrs. Holly. Let's switch places."

They both got out. Mrs. Holly came around the front of the police cruiser and slid into the driver's seat.

"Keep the engine running," said Lena.

Mrs. Holly nodded and closed the door.

This was it. Do or die. Lena was going to get the supplies and get out. She was doing it for Tara Bigelow. That woman saved lives during the last attack. She helped counsel survivors afterwards as the town rebuilt itself. It was time someone did something for her.

Lena texted her husband. 'At CVS. Coast clear. Going in.'

CHAPTER 12

Unarmed and terrified, Lena Holbrook stepped up to the electric doors. They opened. Air conditioning and light music wafted out to greet her, an odd juxtaposition to the chaos happening outside.

Lena took a deep breath, cell phone in hand, and stepped inside.

The store was surprisingly tranquil. And empty.

There were no cashiers up front. There were no customers visible. Other than the soft music piping over the speakers, the place was silent.

Lena passed the cash registers, looking up at the aisle labels, but careful to check down the aisles as she passed. It looked as if the place had been abandoned. Maybe, in all of the tumult, everyone had fled.

But, that meant they knew about the dead, which meant the dead had to have been inside the store. Which meant that maybe they still were.

She grabbed a small basket off the top of a stack and passed the greeting cards and the toy aisle. She passed the magazine rack on her left and the display of printer cartridges on her right.

There was an aisle for soaps and shampoos. Then she saw it in the back. 'First Aid, Bandages.' She turned left, passing the soaps, creams, and shampoos, her ears pricked for any sounds.

She reached the first aid aisle. She found bottles of rubbing alcohol. She grabbed several and threw them into her basket. She found regular gauze and bandages. They weren't hemostatic, but she grabbed a few boxes anyway. She threw in two packs of sterile gloves.

She searched the shelves, but she didn't find any hemostatic gauze. She checked one more time, and then she figured she had to check the pharmacy. It was a specialty item and was therefore probably kept back there.

She strode to the end of the aisle, turned right at the antacids display, and headed for the pharmacy. She passed cereals and pretzels on her right and stopped in front of the small pharmacy counter. She looked left and then right. There continued to be no one inside the store.

She stepped up to the counter and took a gander at the back. There didn't appear to be any pharmacists on duty. The pharmacy looked abandoned, like the rest of the store.

"Hello?' she called out, just to be sure.

She waited, muscles tensed, listening and looking.

When there was no answer, she placed her basket on the counter. She hoisted herself up, sat on the counter, and swung her legs around to the other side. She slid off the counter and into the pharmacy.

There were rows and rows of shelves holding medication. She scanned them, shelf by shelf, looking for the hemostatic gauze. She passed over antibiotics, hypertension pills, and finally saw the gauze.

She held out her shirt, placing as many boxes as she could into it. Then, she waddled over to the basket and began to unload her cargo when something collided into her back.

The basket toppled over, spilling its contents onto the floor on the store side. Hands reached for her neck, and she heard grunting and growling in her ear.

Lena pushed off the counter with both hands, shoving the zombie backwards as it grasped her around the neck. She heard teeth snap shut, but its grip on her neck appeared to be blocking its own bites.

She wriggled around, trying to shake loose. It shrieked into her left ear, causing it to ring. She placed a foot up on the counter and shoved herself backwards. This time, the zombie lost its footing and tumbled backwards, taking Lena with it, into a shelf of medications.

She got her footing and lunged forward, gradually pulling loose from the zombie as she slipped out of its grip. Once she was back at the counter, she turned to look at it. It was likely a man, but in a severe state of decay, missing its arms from the elbow joints.

Lena still felt its grip on her neck. She reached up and grabbed the slippery hands. The flesh was soft and rotten under her fingers. She peeled them off and threw them down. They hit the white tile floor with a wet splat.

"Yuck!" Lena grimaced and hopped the counter as the slimy dead man kicked backwards, trying to stand up by leaning on the shelves. Its stubbed arms waved around in futility. He looked like a zombie T-rex.

Once over, Lena scrambled to put everything back into the basket. Just as she put in the last container of gauze, she heard two loud honks outside. Then she heard the front doors open.

The horn honks were Mrs. Holly warning her.

She walked along the back of the store by the antacids, watching the angled mirror above the display. She looked up in time to see a shape enter the store and vanish behind the greeting cards. *Shit.*

The zombie in the pharmacy let out a shriek, and it was immediately answered by another shriek from somewhere inside the store.

Lena clutched the basket close to her. She needed to get back to the police cruiser. Her eyes swept her surroundings, searching for a weapon. She saw canes hanging down the aisle next to the cereal and chips.

She crept over to the aisle, quietly slipped one of the canes off its hook, and hefted it in her right hand. Her left hand held the basket of supplies. The cane was long, but it was too light to do any damage as a bludgeoning weapon. At best, she could use it to keep the other zombie at a distance.

She tiptoed up the aisle towards the front. She figured that if it was heading down the greeting card aisle towards the back, she could circumvent it by going up front.

The pharmacy zombie shrieked again, followed by some strange guttural sounds. Once again, it was answered by a similar shriek, but different guttural sounds. *Holy shit. These bastards are talking to each other.*

She didn't remember Jim ever talking about these things communicating. She was suddenly reminded of that scene in that dinosaur movie with the two velociraptors talking to each other as they stalked two children.

She made it to the front, away from the calls of the second zombie. She peeked around a display of hanging ballpoint pens. The path to the front door was clear.

Lena took a deep breath, steeled herself, and darted across the front towards the exit. She passed the candy aisle, the magazines, and the printer cartridges.

She passed the registers on her left and was passing the greeting cards on her right when something heavy tackled her, sending her flying in front of the aisle with the beach toys, which was the last aisle before the door.

The thing wheezed as it writhed on top of her, leaking all kinds of bodily fluids. On her stomach, Lena winced and squirmed under it, moaning in disgust and horror. The basket full of supplies lay five feet to her right. It had landed on its side, and all of its contents had spilled out across the floor.

Lena rolled over, pressing her cane sideways against the zombie, shoving it off of her. It squealed as it was rolled. She got a good look at its face, or what was left of it. It was bloated, sagging skin clinging to its skull, but its face was almost entirely shapeless. Its eyes were nearly swollen shut, but it watched her through narrow slits.

She hit it in its face with the cane, but the cane was too light. It only served to enrage it further.

Lena scrambled away from it, giving it a parting kick in its jaw, dislocating it. She crawled over to the basket, turned it right side up, and began to pick up all of her spilled items.

The zombie now lunged forward at her on its hands and knees, reaching out for her. She swiped at it with her cane, but the zombie caught it and ripped it out of her hands. It threw the cane off to the side and scurried towards her, snarling.

Lena looked up to her right and found a children's red plastic shovel. She snatched it off its hook and swung it at the monster, hitting its face. But, as it was only plastic, it didn't have much stopping power, and the creature scampered towards her again.

She threw the shovel at it, snatched a can of aerosol suntan lotion, and sprayed the zombie right in its eyes. It screeched and recoiled.

"Yes!" shouted Lena. "Take that, fucker!"

As if in answer, it projectile vomited blood at her, covering the front of her blouse and pants.

Lena cried out and shivered in revulsion. She wiped her blood-soaked hands on the seat of her pants, and grabbed a long, foam pool noodle out of a cardboard display box. She started whacking it on the head. The zombie slowed its advance and swatted at it, like a cat would a string.

Frustrated, Lena chucked the noodle at it and grabbed a beach umbrella. She turned it in her hands, pointing the semi-sharp end that goes into the sand at the zombie. It pushed forward, opening its mouth. She shoved it right in with all of her might, ramming it home.

The zombie gagged as the umbrella shaft slid down its throat. It picked its right hand up off the ground and tried to swat the umbrella away, but it was jammed in its throat good.

Lena got to her feet, grabbed the basket, and tried to run around the abomination. Seeing her run, it turned its head to follow her, tripping her up in the other end of the umbrella. She tumbled to the floor, managing to keep the basket upright and hugging it close to her like a wide receiver guarding the ball as he's being tackled.

The zombie fumbled for Lena, but the beach umbrella got in its way, preventing it from grabbing a hold of her. Lena rolled over on her side and gave the top of the umbrella a swift kick, driving it further down the monster's throat. It tried to screech, but it was stifled by the blow. Instead, blood flowed around the white, pink, and purple umbrella as a projectile vomit attack was interrupted.

In a last-ditch effort, it tried to get up. However, as it stood up, its head was forced into vertical alignment with its throat by the umbrella. As it stood in front of her looking like an undead sword swallower, it looked up at the ceiling. It couldn't track Lena, and it stomped its feet in frustration like a two-year-old throwing a tantrum.

Having neutralized the monster, Lena realized that she had forgotten the tweezers. She found the correct aisle, pulled a few off of a hook, and threw them in the basket.

The zombie in the pharmacy howled at her in rage.

"Oh, shut the fuck up!"

As she crossed the front of the store to exit, she saw her other undead friend stumbling around in the aisle, banging into the shelves and displays.

She gave it a wave and left the store.

She went straight to the police cruiser, checking the parking lot. There were several zombies walking on the grass, stomping on the small decorative bushes, but they were far enough away to not be an immediate threat. When they saw her, one let out a shriek, and the small throng picked up their pace.

Mrs. Holly got out of the car and walked over to greet Lena. She looked Lena up and down, gawking at the blood on her shirt and pants. "Oh dear. Are you all right?"

Lena shoved the basket into her arms. "Never better. The blood's not mine. Let's get to Dr. Potts."

Mrs. Holly didn't budge. "Are you sure you're all right?"

Lena looked down at herself. "I wasn't bitten, if that's what you mean."

Mrs. Holly only nodded. She rounded the car and got into the passenger seat. Lena saw the small throng now trudging their way across the parking lot. She gave them the finger and slid into the driver's seat.

Robbie leaned forward in the back seat, a mixture of relief and concern on his young face. "Are you okay, Mom?"

"One of the pharmacists gave me hard time, tried to eat me. Then there was another guest."

"I honked the horn to warn you," said Mrs. Holly, looking sheepish. "I didn't know how to work the siren...It's my first time riding in a police car."

Everyone laughed, allowing a brief moment of levity to break up the madness. It was a much-needed release. Lenny wasn't sure why they were laughing, but he joined in anyway.

When they had finished their chuckle, Lena's expression sobered as she backed the cruiser out of its parking spot. "They can talk to each other."

"Who's that?" asked Mrs. Holly.

"The zombies. The one in the pharmacy called out to the other one, telling it where I was."

Lena swerved and mowed down three of the approaching zombies, missing one.

"That's new," said Mrs. Holly.

Lena nonchalantly stopped the car, threw it in reverse, and took out the last zombie she had missed. She looked in the rear view mirror at Tyrell. "Now let's get your mom fixed up."

Tyrell nodded, regarding Lena with what she thought was a mixture of relief and admiration. She put the cruiser in drive and exited the parking lot.

* * *

As Vinnie and company filed into his family pizzeria, his father shoved heavy boxes back in front of the glass door.

Vinnie helped his father. "You know this won't keep them out."

Marco wiped his brow. "I know. It's more so they don't see the light, and it muffles the sound so they don't know we're here."

There were shrieks outside in the distance, the shrill cries of the dead.

After they finished blocking off the back door, Vinnie joined the rest of his company in the back of the pizzeria. The booths were half occupied with various people, and Pedro was up front cooking.

Vinnie's mother, Maggie, came running over. She threw her arms around him. "Oh, thank God you're all right."

"Jesus," said Vinnie, "you're staying open?"

Nancy nodded, impressed. "Now Marco's a true business man after my own heart. That's how it's done. Business interruption, my ass."

Marie rolled her eyes, but she averted her gaze when Nancy caught her. She pretended to look around the pizzeria. When she saw her kids, she ran over to them.

Alessandra was standing up, playing with her hair, a nervous habit she had since a little girl. Salvatore was sitting in a booth across from the two girls they picked up at Blackbeard's Pier.

Marie hugged Alessandra, squeezing her tight.

"I'm okay, Mom."

"I know, honey. So am I."

Alessandra saw Ira and Emily Ross and smiled. "You rescued Dharma's parents."

Marie nodded. She looked over at Salvatore, who was too busy playing it cool for the older girl to acknowledge her. "Hey, big man."

Salvatore managed a smile. "Hey, Mom."

"I see you managed to get everyone here safely."

He pointed to the younger of the girls. "Mom, this is Bethany." Then he pointed to the older girl. "And this is Jackie." He blushed when introducing Jackie. "They're from New York. They're here visiting their aunt and uncle."

Marie thought he was so cute, she wanted to eat him up. "It's nice to meet you gals. I'm glad we were able to get you to safety. Well, I'm famished. Fighting zombies makes me hungry."

Marco walked up to Marie and placed a hand on her shoulder. "You want a slice?"

"I was hoping for a calzone."

Vinnie's mother smiled. "Done. I'll go tell Pedro, and he'll hook you up." She gave Vinnie's shoulder a squeeze before going up front.

Vinnie settled into a booth across from Nancy. He noticed everyone was speaking in hushed tones. There was intermittent pounding on the metal security gate.

Up until this point, he hadn't had time to process the loss of his friend, Mike. His father returned to the table, sliding two plates holding pepperoni slices right in front of him and Nancy.

Nancy looked up and smiled. "Thanks, Marco."

"There are drinks in the fridges up front. Help yourselves." He returned to making the rounds, checking on everyone.

Nancy grabbed the powdered garlic, applying a liberal amount on her slice. She picked up her massive Jersey Shore slice, folded it lengthwise, and tipped it back as she raised it to her mouth, careful not to lose any of the tasty grease. She ripped off a large chunk and chewed it loudly, smacking her lips indulgently.

Vinnie sat there staring at his slice, as if it was going to bite him.

"What's wrong?" asked Nancy with her mouth full. "Aren't you hungry?"

Vinnie shook his head. "I don't have much of an appetite right now."

Nancy chewed a bit more and swallowed. "I could use a beverage, you know."

Vinnie gawked at her, incredulous. Her boyfriend had just been torn apart by a horde of the dead, and now, not only was she stuffing her face, she was ordering him to go fetch her a drink. "Excuse me?"

"You heard me. Iced tea would hit the spot."

Vinnie looked at her, dumbfounded. When he saw that she wasn't budging on the matter, he got up and walked wearily over to the fridges up front.

Dharma was tending to her mother and father. She saw Vinnie and looked concerned. She excused herself from her parents and began to walk over to Nancy's table.

Nancy shook her head. She scrunched her face up, saying, 'Don't worry, I got this.'

Dharma paused, gave Vinnie another worried look, and returned to her parents.

When Vinnie returned, holding two iced teas, he placed them on the table. "Anything else?"

Nancy looked up at him. "Sit down, Vinnie. I wanna talk to you."

Tired and resigned to their current situation, Vinnie did as he was told. He slid back into the booth across from Nancy and waited.

"I know you're upset about Mike."

Vinnie shrugged, the pain evident on his face. His lip twitched. "Of course. Aren't you?"

Nancy narrowed her gaze. "Now that's not fair, Vinnie Cantone. I'm actually very upset about it, but losing Mike doesn't stop my necessity to eat."

Vinnie shook his head. His face contorted as he fought back the tears. "That was a horrible way for him to go. Those poor kids."

Nancy nodded. "It *was* horrible. Remember, I saw the whole thing. I wanted to help him, but he just gave me this look, as if he had already accepted what was about to happen. He wanted me to get out of there.

"There was nothing I could do for him, so I escaped while I could. It was what he wanted."

Vinnie stared at his pepperoni slice on its plate. "After everything he'd been through last time...everything he survived...he had to go that way."

"This is going to sound strange, Vinnie, but he died doing what he loved. Helping the children. He died on the damned carousel he adored so much."

"It was useless," insisted Vinnie. "It was all for nothing. All of it. Two years ago and now. What's the fucking point?"

Nancy reached across the table and placed her hand on his. The gesture made Vinnie uncomfortable, as it was very uncharacteristic of Nancy. "Vinnie, the point is that we're still here. The dead attacked two years ago, a superstorm nearly wiped Smuggler's Bay off the map, my pier was nearly washed into the ocean, and we're still here.

"Marie Russo lost her husband, but she's still here. So did Tara Bigelow. And Lenny Krueger lost his mother."

"What's the point of still being here?" said Vinnie, disgusted.

Nancy took another bite, chomped on it loudly, and washed it down with a slug of her cold iced tea. "The point is, we are here for people who need us. People we love. Marie and Tara are here for their kids. You're here for Dharma and your parents.

"And, you were a good friend to Mike. His best friend. He loved you. You know that."

Vinnie nodded, his eyes welling up.

Dharma walked over to their booth and slid in next to Vinnie, bumping him over with her butt. "How's everyone holding up?"

Vinnie wiped his eyes. "We were just talking about Mike."

Dharma frowned and put her arm around Vinnie's shoulders, giving him a hearty squeeze.

Marie approached the booth. "What's the plan? This is great and all, but what's our strategy?"

"Strategy?" asked Marco. "I was planning on staying here and eating pizza until we're rescued."

"Who says we're going to be rescued?"

"Marie, let's not think like that," said Ira.

"No, she's right," said Nancy. "The last time we barely made it out alive. We were waiting on top of a collapsing structure, surrounded by zombies, and the outbreak was much smaller than this."

Marie nodded in agreement. "Vinnie and I saw the police barricade. It was overwhelmed almost immediately. So was the National Guard. So, we can't expect any first responders to help. Tell them, Vinnie."

Vinnie nodded, looking down at the table. "It's true."

"There's got to be help out there," pleaded Emily.

Vinnie shook his head. "Listen…all we hear are the screams of the dead. I haven't heard a police siren since the beginning. No more gun fire. Just the dead now."

"Help will be sent," said Marco, sounding hopeful. "They'll send in the Army."

"The Amy has its hands full," said a woman in the next booth, Millie Fogherty. "I caught a glimpse of it on the news. It's not just us."

Salvatore and the girls were on their phones.

"It's true," said Salvatore. "The entire eastern seaboard is overrun."

Emily looked panicked. "Well, if that's the case, we're screwed."

Ira pulled her close, embracing her. He was trembling.

"Not necessarily," said Marie.

"What are you suggesting?" asked Emily. "We are in no position to fight back."

"I'm sure we're not the only survivors," said Nancy. "We need to make contact with the others, somehow. Find out who's left."

"How do we do that?"

Dharma perked up in her seat. "Look, between each of us, we know lots of people in the Bay. Nancy knows almost everyone. I say we call our phone contacts in our cells and start a chain."

Nancy nodded. "That's right. We'll call our immediate contacts, they call theirs, and on and on. They'll all report back to us."

"Once we get a sense of who's left and where," added Marie, "we can coordinate a response. Without food to hunt, these things are going to wander around aimlessly. They'll spread out. Some might even move on."

"Where are they going?" asked Ira. "We're on a barrier island."

At the sound of the word 'food,' Vinnie perked up. A chill went down his spine. "That's right. There was a little zombie girl. She...she spoke."

There was a collective gasp.

"What?"

"What are you talking about?"

"He's right," said Marie. "One of them spoke. These things are mutating. They're communicating, or at least some of them are."

"And you think we can fight them?" asked Marco.

There were shrieks and more pounding on the metal security gate.

"They're not that smart, though," said Vinnie. "They know we're in here, but they don't think to check the back door. So even if they talk, it's not like they're strategizing or anything."

"Yet," added Nancy ominously.

"If they spread out over the Bay, we can pick them off in small groups," said Marie.

"I don't mean to sound difficult," said Emily, "but with what?"

"I have weapons at home. The police station, I'm sure, has weapons."

"The National Guard left a ton in their little staging base," said Dharma.

"Hell, there're weapons lying around in the street," said Vinnie. "The police barricade. It's right here."

Emily stood up, her voice becoming a bit raised. "This is nuts. I don't know if I can be a part of this."

Dharma stood up and hugged her, trying to calm her.

Nancy shook her head. "What's nuts is waiting here to die for help that likely isn't coming."

"But what if this is it?" asked Emily, her tone becoming frantic. "What if this is the end? Of it all?"

Ira put his hand on her shoulder, "Honey, please. We have to stay calm." Emily shrugged it off.

Vinnie slid out of the booth and stood up. "We've survived an awful lot. These things have come before, and we're still here. We've all lost loved ones, but Smuggler's Bay is our home.

"I don't know about you, but I'm not willing to just give up and let these things get us. Let's say that the mainland is overrun. We're a barrier island, like you said, Mrs. Ross. It's a smaller geographic area with a smaller population. The tourists haven't arrived yet, so it's just us locals. There's going to be fewer of these things here than say Newark or Paterson."

"What are you saying?" asked Maggie.

"We can take back the island and seal it off."

"We can raise the drawbridge," said Marie.

"But what about the neighboring towns on the barrier island?" asked Dharma.

"I know lots of people," said Nancy. "I can get a sense of who's left. We can rally our numbers, organize."

"We can do this," said Vinnie. "But, we need to get started *now*. There's a lot to do, and we don't have tons of time."

Dharma smiled at her man. Her parents watched him in awe. No more worrying and living in fear. Vinnie was back.

"Well, let's get going," said Nancy. "Everyone start calling their contacts. Marco, we're going to need pens and paper."

Marco distributed pens and order pads, and everyone (including Emily Ross) began calling the contacts on their cell phones. They were surprised at how many survivors they were able to reach, and they started tabulating numbers and locations.

Dharma began to construct a crude map of the Bay on the back of a paper plate, indicating the locations of survivors and their numbers.

It was here, in a pizzeria, on the first night of the second wave that the Jersey Shore resistance began. Not with the police, or the military, but with average, pissed-off citizens who were tired of being knocked down yet again by an old enemy.

Little did they know that in scattered spots in several towns along the long barrier island that was the Shore, other groups were doing the same, regrouping and coordinating their response.

CHAPTER 13

Becky and Larry were a block away from the police station when Erin had come to. She coughed in the back seat.

Larry turned around. "Erin, are you okay?"

She sat up, white raccoon eyes wild, her teeth bared. She let out a shriek that nearly caused Becky to crash the old clunker.

"Jesus Christ!" shouted Larry.

Erin leaned forward and grabbed him by the throat, snarling and grunting as she tried to pull him close.

"Help!" Larry pushed against the seat with both hands, trying to keep away from her snapping jaws.

"Shit!" Becky had no weapon. "Hold on!" She gunned the engine, pushing the gas pedal to the floor. She had a straight run down the major thoroughfare. The car picked up speed. It was big and heavy, but it was a large engine.

"What are you doing?"

"Buckle up," said Becky.

Larry grabbed the seat belt and leaned forward, struggling with the buckle. Erin was now crawling over the front seat.

"Hurry up!"

"I'm trying!" shouted Larry, feeling Erin's clammy fingers on his back. There was a shriek, and his back was covered in blood and vomit.

Becky punched Erin in the side of her head, and it hit the window. Erin, however, was unfazed. "Fuck it."

Just as Larry snapped his belt buckle, Becky slammed on the brakes with both feet, and Erin went flying forward into the windshield.

As the car skidded to a halt, Erin's head slammed the windshield. Being made of safety glass, it didn't break. Instead, it broke down into a spider web cracking pattern.

Fortunately, the glass wasn't the only thing that cracked. The impact of Erin's skull with the glass did the trick. She fell between Becky and Larry and was still.

"Jesus!" shouted Larry. "You could've killed me."

"*I* just saved your life. *She* was trying to kill you. You've got to keep these things straight, Larry."

She slowly turned the car around and headed back towards the police station. They were almost in front of the station. She swerved, taking out a few zombies, and pulled up onto the curb right in front, stopping the car.

"Get out," she told Larry. She opened the driver door and stepped out of the car.

"Jesus H. Christ," she heard from the roof. Pacelli was looking down at her. "Chief's gonna be glad to see you." He picked up his radio. "It's Becky. Let her in."

Larry got out of the car and was looking around. The dead had spotted them and were beginning to converge.

"Come on, Larry." Becky ran up to the police station, Larry following right behind her, and an officer let them in. It was Martinez.

"Where's the chief?" asked Becky.

Martinez locked the door and ushered them away from the glass. "Inside, taking inventory of our numbers and coordinating with the State. The Army sealed off the island." He looked at a blood-soaked Larry. "Hi."

Larry introduced himself. "Larry Mendoza."

"He saved my life," said Becky.

"Thank you for that, Larry," said Martinez.

They marched into the station. Becky saw Holbrook in his office. He was on the phone.

"He's a vet," Becky told Martinez. "And not the kind that heals animals."

"Really," said Martinez. "Thank you for your service."

Larry couldn't believe it. Here they were in the middle of the zombie apocalypse…

When Chief Holbrook saw Becky, his face lit up. He opened the door to his office, and she waltzed right in.

Larry made to follow, but Martinez stopped him. "No civilians."

Larry was taken aback. "What am I supposed to do?"

Martinez flashed him his million-dollar grin. "Do you like coffee, Larry?"

*

"Okay. Good. Let me know when you are there and safe. Okay. Love you, too. Bye." Holbrook hung up the cell phone. "Becky, I'm glad you're alive."

Becky was on his desk phone trying to call her husband, Greg. She nodded. "That was Lena? She's still out there?"

"I tried to send her out of town, but the Army raised the drawbridge and sealed us off from the mainland."

"I know," said Becky. "It was all over the news. The entire east coast is overrun."

Greg picked up. "Becky?"

"Yeah, it's me. Are you all right?"

"Fine, but there're zombies everywhere. Where are you? I tried to call your cell."

"I'm at the station. I lost it, but I can't go into that now."

"I'm glad you're okay. I was worried sick."

"Greg, do you remember what we practiced?"

"Yeah, shelter-in-place. I already filled both bathtubs, and I have the attic stairs pulled down. James and Trisha are here. The zombies got into their house."

"Greg, this is very important…were either of them bitten?"

"No, thank God."

"Good. I need you to wait there. You should have enough protein bars and bottled water to last a while."

"What's going on, Becky? The news said the whole eastern seaboard is under attack."

"I don't know yet. I've got to go. Stay put until the authorities arrive."

Greg paused. "I won't leave without you."

"Greg, if they come, promise me you'll go with them."

"But what about you?"

"I'm fine. I'm at the police station. We're hunkered down with plenty of guns and ammunition. Chief Holbrook's got it all under control."

There was another pause. "That's not what the news said."

Holbrook reached for the phone. Becky handed it to him.

"This is Chief Holbrook. Becky's okay. We're in a safe, defensible place. But, she's going to get careless if she's worried about you the whole time. We don't want any accidents."

"I don't want that either," insisted Greg.

"Then do what she says and stay safe. If the authorities come for you, go with them. We have your cell number. We'll keep in touch."

"Okay, Chief. Whatever you say."

Holbrook hung up the phone. "Don't worry, he listened to me."

Becky sighed in relief. "How's Lena? Do we need to go get her?"

"She's fine. She picked up some passengers. Do you know Tara Bigelow?"

"The shrink?"

"Yeah. She's in their trunk. She was bitten on her forearm and decided to do a field amputation close range with my shotgun."

"Holy smokes."

"Lena's heading to a retired surgeon to get her help. She just picked up supplies at a CVS. Barely made it out."

"It's really bad out there, Chief. What's the plan?"

"We're cut off, at least for the moment. I'm trying to find out who we still have. There aren't many cops left. The National Guard was wiped out. It won't be long before those things try to get in here."

"Who do we have here?"

"Pacelli's on the roof, spotting. Just you, me, and Martinez. Who's your new friend?"

"I holed up at the Nautilus and had a run in with one of the welfare housing cases."

Holbrook shook his head. "Hopefully not this one."

"No, Larry helped me out of there. He's okay. Ex-military. We can use him."

"Okay, so we have you, me, Pacelli, Martinez, and…"

"Larry. Larry Mendoza."

Holbrook shook his head and placed his hands on his belt. "Not enough people. There are a hundred of these things out there."

"So, what do we do? We can't just wait here for these things to barge in and eat us."

Holbrook thought for a moment. He had received some specialized training in anti-zombie tactics after the last attack. "We have to keep these things occupied and find a way to thin their numbers."

He stepped outside the office. Martinez was standing next to Larry, who was seated and sipping coffee from a paper cup.

"Martinez, get over here! And bring Larry!"

Larry looked at the chief and then Martinez, who shrugged. Larry put his coffee down on the desk and stood. They both walked into Holbrook's office.

"Chief?"

Holbrook was pacing. He had a plan up his sleeve. "Martinez, you're going to drive a cruiser. Lights, sirens, everything. We're going to be the Pied Piper.

These zombies will follow us, and I'm going to hang out the window and pick them off a little at a time."

"What about the rest of us?" asked Becky.

Holbrook turned to Larry. "You know how to fire a rifle?"

"Sure as shit, Chief."

"Good. I want you two up there with Pacelli covering me. You're going to pick them off from the roof."

"Do we have enough ammo?" asked Becky.

"We have some. Enough to thin their numbers a bit."

"Then what?"

"With fewer of them around, we can go out scouting for survivors. They'll be easier to manage, or avoid."

"Do you expect these things to just follow behind you in a neat line?" asked Larry. "What if they bunch up and try to overrun you?"

"That's why you'll be up on the roof providing support," said Holbrook. "Take out those that aren't falling in line."

"They'll be coming at you from all sides," said Becky. "You'll need a second car to help contain them, corral them. I can drive, and Larry here can shoot."

Larry winced at the idea. "I don't know…I kinda like the roof idea better."

Becky shot Larry a biting look.

Before she could retort, Holbrook cut her off. "He's right. He can take the roof. Pacelli will go with you." He got on his radio. "Pacelli, we have a plan. I'm sending an Army vet to relieve you."

"...Okay, Chief."

Holbrook placed his hand on Larry's shoulder. "Thank you for this. Now don't fuck it up." He turned to Martinez. "Show him to the roof."

Martinez gestured for Larry to follow him, and they both left Holbrook's office.

Becky sighed. "Do you think it's a good idea to leave Larry up there alone to watch our backs?"

"You said he saved your life. You don't trust him?"

"What if he's...mentally unstable?"

Holbrook leaned on his desk. "Becky, not all vets are emotionally disturbed. In fact, most aren't. He just fell on hard times, had a bit of bad luck. Happens to lots of good people."

"Yeah, I guess."

"Did he give you any reason not to trust him?"

"No. I suppose not."

"There, it's settled then. Besides, he's a civilian. We can't ask him to put himself in harm's way. He's better used up on the roof."

Martinez returned with Pacelli.

Pacelli looked dubious. "Chief?"

Holbrook stood up off his desk. "Martinez is with me, and you're going to be with Becky. One drives, the other shoots. We're going to flash the lights and hit the sirens, get them to follow while we pick 'em off. Thin their numbers."

Pacelli nodded. "Right on."

"We have to get outside to the cars, first," reminded Becky. "How many we got left?"

"Exactly two," said Holbrook. "Martinez, you and Pacelli round up as much ammo as we got left and pack it up. Does Larry have enough up on the roof?"

"Yeah, I was mostly scouting. Didn't really expend much. Only when one or two of those zombies were making their way to the station."

"Good. We meet by the door by the parking lot in five. Time to kick some ass."

* * *

Lenny Krueger jostled back and forth in the backseat of the police cruiser as Mrs. Chief swerved to either avoid or hit the creeping dead wandering the streets. He knew they were on their way to Dr. Potts's house. He didn't know who Dr. Potts was, but he knew he didn't like doctors because they usually stuck him with needles and made him bleed into a thin glass tube. Or they stuck their fingers in his ass, which he thought was the strangest thing any had done to him. Dr. Atari did it to him when it burned every time he had to pee. What his ass had to do with burning pee was beyond him.

Dr. Tara was the only doctor he liked. She was nice. She never tried to hurt him. She only talked with him, and he always felt better after their meetings.

As Mrs. Chief stopped short in front of what must've been Mr. Potts's house, jumping the curb and skidding on the beige and white gravel, Mrs. Chief shouted, "Everyone out! Now!" She grabbed the basket of supplies, flung her door open, and darted out of the car.

Lenny always did what he was told. He jumped out after Tyrell, Robbie, and the ghost of Billy, of course. Mrs. Chief shoved her basket of medical supplies into Lenny's hands. "Hold this." Then she popped the trunk.

Mrs. Chief and Mrs. Holly rounded the car and began to hoist Tara out of the trunk. Mrs. Chief grabbed her under her arms, and Mrs. Holly grabbed her feet. They hobbled back around the car, leaving the trunk open.

Billy stretched as Mrs. Chief, Mrs. Holly, and everyone else ran up to the front door of the house.

Lenny hesitated, turning to Billy, scolding him. "C'mon, Billy! We have to g-g-get inside! It's not s-s-safe out here!"

Billy turned his head sideways, checking out Mrs. Chief, grinning. "That's a nice ass, if I ever saw one."

Mrs. Chief turned on the front stoop and yelled at Lenny, not seeing his imaginary friend. "Lenny! Get over here! NOW!"

Not liking being scolded, Lenny jumped and hopped to it as several zombies milling around across the street took notice. One of them screeched. Another zombie appeared from between the houses on their side of the street. It hunched over and projectile vomited blood through the ghost of Billy.

Billy looked down at himself. "Well, that was rude." He turned and flipped off the offending zombie. "Kiss my ass!"

An old man opened the front door. "Hurry up! Get inside!"

Mrs. Chief ushered everyone inside as Billy taunted the zombie. The zombie, a teenage girl limping on a broken ankle, passed through the apparition, taking no notice of Billy. He smacked its ass as a parting shot, his spectral hand passing through it.

Mrs. Chief entered the house, and the old man slammed the storm door shut, locking it. He quickly shut the wooden front door, engaging the deadbolt lock. There was pounding on the screen door and screeching just outside.

Lenny was relieved when he saw Billy pass right through the door, brushing himself off.

Mrs. Chief smiled. "Mr. Potts, I presume?"

The old man was short in stature, thin to the point of waifishness, and his head was topped with wispy white hair. He nodded solemnly, as if accepting a grave duty with great reluctance. He looked at Dr. Tara. "I take it this is the patient?"

"Yes."

"Put her on the dining room table." He led the way into the next room. Mrs. Chief and Mrs. Holly hoisted her up onto the table, laying her on her back.

Lenny grimaced as he saw Dr. Tara's bloody nub lying on the table. He saw what Dr. Tara did to herself, and he hadn't been able to begin to comprehend it.

Dr. Potts saw Lenny standing there in the archway, holding the basket of supplies. He walked over to him. "May I?"

Lenny nodded, and Dr. Potts took the basket in both hands. He brought it over to the dining room table. He pulled out a cardboard box, ripped it open, and slipped on rubber gloves. He muttered words like, 'avulsion amputation,' and 'nerve and vascular tissue,' but Lenny had no idea what they meant. He looked to Robbie and Tyrell, to see if they understood, but they looked as lost as him.

Dr. Potts shifted Dr. Tara's body on the table, adjusting her head and saying things like 'airway control' and 'body temperature.' The first term reminded Lenny of airplanes and the airport, but he had no idea what that had to do with what was happening here.

Mrs. Chief stood to the side, hand over her mouth and eyes glued to Dr. Tara. She didn't seem to follow what was happening either. Lenny looked at Billy, who was leaning against the wall and picking his teeth with his fingernail. He shrugged. "Beats the shit outta me, kid."

Lenny was beginning to question if this Dr. Potts was even speaking English, and then he saw Mrs. Holly. Every time the old man said one of those gibberish words, she nodded as if she understood what he was saying.

This reassured Lenny. At least someone knew what was going on. Then he remembered Mrs. Chief referring to Mrs. Holly as a nurse back in the car when she explained to Robbie and Tyrell why Mrs. Holly was twisting something around Dr. Tara's stub.

Dr. Potts looked over his shoulder, and what he said next Lenny understood. "They shouldn't be watching this."

Mrs. Chief nodded and walked over to Lenny, Tyrell, and Robbie, all standing in the archway, looking on in horror. "Lenny, I need you to take Tyrell and Robbie into the other room. Maybe put on the TV."

"But I want to watch," protested Tyrell.

Mrs. Chief took a knee and placed her hands on Tyrell's shoulders. "Honey, Dr. Potts needs to concentrate if he's going to help your mom. It won't do her any good if you stand here and watch."

Tyrell's face began to contort, as if he was going to cry. Mrs. Chief hugged him. "I'll let you know what is happening, but you can't be here now. Okay?"

Tyrell, a tear escaping his right eye, nodded.

The ghost of Billy elbowed Lenny in the ribs. When Lenny looked at him, Billy was nodding to Dr. Potts. "Check out his arm."

Lenny looked over at Dr. Potts. His short sleeve shifted, and Lenny saw what he thought was a bite mark.

"Lenny."

Lenny's eyes widened as the implications of that bite mark dawned on him.

"Lenny!"

Lenny snapped out of his head and saw Mrs. Chief glaring at him. "*Now*, Lenny."

Lenny paused a moment, remembering what he was instructed to do, and waved an arm. "Follow me. We'll w-w-watch television."

He went into the living room, Tyrell and Robbie following behind him. Billy brought up the rear. Lenny turned on the television, and it immediately went onto the news. He grimaced and changed the channel to a western. A man dressed entirely in black was having a shootout with what had to be the 'good guy,' clad entirely in white.

Satisfied, Lenny placed his hands on his hips and nodded. "See, cowboys!"

Robbie and Tyrell sat down on the couch. Robbie was watching the movie, but Tyrell kept glancing in the direction of the dining room, which was now out of view.

Billy sauntered over to Lenny and leaned in, as if to intimate something private. "Lenny, you saw what I saw."

Lenny waved a dismissive hand. He didn't want to think about the bite mark and what it meant.

"Don't you shush me," said Billy. "I don't think the old lady or Mrs. Chief even noticed it. You have to tell them."

Lenny shook his head. "No, it'll be all r-r-right."

Tyrell looked up at Lenny, looking perplexed, wondering who he was talking to. Lenny smiled at him, and Tyrell looked back at the television, continuing to shoot the occasional glance in the direction of the dining room.

"No it won't be all r-r-r-right," pressed the ghost of Billy, mocking Lenny's stutter.

"Stop making fun of me," muttered Lenny so that it was barely audible. "And you're g-g-going to scare the k-k-kids."

Billy, exasperated, shook his head. "You know what's going to scare the kids? When the good doctor turns and tries to fucking eat them."

Lenny shook his head and whispered, "That's not going to h-h-happen. Not this t-t-time."

"Lenny, he's going to hurt everyone. What kind of a shit show superhero are you if you let that happen?"

"He's helping Dr. Tara."

Billy was now standing directly in front of Tyrell, but Tyrell paid no mind, as he didn't see him. He continued to look through him at the television. "Right now, he is. But, what is he going to do when he turns into one of them monsters?"

Lenny considered this for a moment. Was it true that neither Mrs. Chief nor Mrs. Holly noticed the bite mark on Dr. Potts's upper arm? Maybe he did have to say something.

The ghost of Billy was now dressed as a cowboy, frilly sleeves and all, doing his best John Wayne. "You know what you have to do, pilgrim."

Lenny swallowed hard and nodded. Billy was right. He had to tell Mrs. Chief. He turned to Tyrell and Robbie. "I'll be right back."

He walked through the living room and back into the archway of the dining room. He saw Dr. Potts placing pads on Dr. Tara's stub. They were wet and sticky, as if turning to gel. Mrs. Holly was standing to the side with tweezers in her hand. On the table in front of her was a folded paper towel, stained red, with bloody bits of something on it. The scene caused Lenny to freeze in the archway, fighting back nausea.

Mrs. Chief looked over at him, and she pursed her lips. "Lenny, what are you doing?" She marched over to him and shoved him out of the room. "I told you to stay out. You need to keep the kids calm."

"Mrs. Chief, I-I-I'm sorry."

Hearing the sincerity of his apology, she softened. He was about to say something else, but she cut him off. "It's okay." She squeezed his arm. "I know you're worried about Tara."

"Yes, but…"

"We all are. I promise that I'll let you guys know what's going on, but now's not the time."

"B-b-but, Mrs. Chief…"

"No 'buts,' Lenny. Stay in the living room."

Lenny nodded and put his head down. He walked back into the living room as Mrs. Chief returned to the dining room.

Tyrell was studying Lenny's face. "What's wrong, Lenny?"

Lenny wanted to tell somebody about the bite mark, but Tyrell was just a kid. He was tasked with keeping them occupied and calm. If he told Tyrell about the bite mark, it would frighten him. Lenny didn't want to frighten Tyrell.

Lenny shrugged. "Nothing. Everything's ok-k-kay." He gave one of his signature thumbs up. His performance seemed to do the trick, as Tyrell drew his attention back to the television.

Lenny stood there, smiling, but dying a thousand deaths on the inside. He didn't know what to do.

"Good job, Lenny," chided Billy. "Now you're all going to get eaten alive."

In the dining room, Lenny heard a cell phone ring and then Mrs. Chief's voice. "Hello? Nancy? My God, where are you?" Mrs. Chief stepped out of the dining room and into the kitchen. "Are you okay? Yes, I'm in a safe place...yes, Robbie, my neighbor, Lenny Krueger, and Tyrell Bigelow are all with me...his mother's hurt really bad...we found a doctor who's working on her now...uh huh...yep...sure...I can call him...wait, even better, here's the number. You can speak to him yourself. So we're not playing a game of telephone...are you ready?..."

Lenny heard her read off a bunch of numbers. He recognized it to be a phone number, but he didn't know whose number it was.

"Okay...okay...yes...great." Mrs. Chief must've hung up, because when she entered the living room, she was shoving her cell phone into her shorts pocket.

She addressed Lenny and the kids, managing a smile. "Good news." They all looked up at her, expectant. "That was Nancy from Blackbeard's Pier. She's actually at Marco's Pizza on the boardwalk. She's okay, and she's with Vinnie, Dharma, and a whole bunch of people. They made it out okay."

Lenny, Tyrell, and Robbie all smiled at this morsel of good news. At least there was something positive. Lenny had, for the moment, forgotten the looming threat in the dining room, a ticking undead time bomb waiting to go off.

Billy shook his head in disapproval, but he was quickly distracted by Mrs. Chief's legs. He wolf-whistled and shook his head. "Damn, Mrs. Chief, if I wasn't goddamned imaginary..."

CHAPTER 14

Chief Holbrook was hanging out the rear window of the police cruiser popping off shots at the trail of zombies they had rounded up. Martinez crept down the Main Street, going slow enough for the staggering dead to keep up, but fast enough to keep them trailing behind.

As dead emerged from their flanks, Pacelli would run interference in his police cruiser, and Becky hung out the back window taking shots. Across the back seats of both vehicles were extra clips and ammunition.

Holbrook had run out of ammo and ducked back inside the car to reload when his cell phone rang. He pulled it out of his pocket, expecting it to be Lena. "Hello?…Nancy? …uh huh…Where are you?..." Martinez turned around to look at Chief.

Holbrook sat down, keeping his eye on the dead through the rear window. "…uh huh…yeah…we're working on thinning their numbers…okay, we can do that…yep…bye." He hung up his cell.

Martinez looked at him in the rearview mirror. "Chief?"

"That was Nancy Rizzuto. She's at Marco's Pizza with a bunch of survivors. She said Marie Russo has weapons at her house, and they want to help, but there are too many dead."

Confused as to why Holbrook had stopped shooting, Pacelli called Martinez on the radio. "What's going on? Are you guys okay?"

Holbrook waved a hand, indicating that he wanted Martinez to hand him the radio. Martinez passed it back to him.

"Pacelli, slight change of plans. We have a bunch of survivors holed up in Marco's who want in on the action. We need to provide a diversion so they can get out and get to some weapons."

"Chief?"

"Marie Russo has a stash in her house, and frankly, we need all the help we can get right now. Follow my lead."

"Roger that, Chief."

Holbrook dropped the radio and pointed ahead over Martinez's right shoulder. "Make a left on Mariner Avenue. That'll put us two blocks away from Marco's. Then we'll turn onto Surf and round up some zombies and lead them away."

"Got it," said Martinez.

He turned left onto Mariner, and the dead followed.

Holbrook marveled at how they just followed the car like lemmings, wondering if it was the flashing lights or the sirens. Or maybe both.

Any that tried to branch off from the herd or flank them were swiftly taken out by Pacelli and Becky.

As they turned left onto Surf, Martinez gasped as he saw the abandoned police barricade. "Jesus."

Some of the cars even still had their lights flashing. There was blood spatter on the car windows, and guns littered the asphalt.

"Where are the bodies?" asked Martinez.

Then, almost as if in response, zombies poured out from the boardwalk ramps and in between buildings. Scattered amongst them were half-eaten, reanimated cops.

"There's your answer," said Holbrook. "Wait a minute..." He looked out the window as zombies began to approach from all sides, pounding on the car and pressing up against the car windows like rabid fans swarming the limo of a rock star.

Holbrook pulled out his cell phone. He redialed Nancy. "Hello...Nancy...listen, we're right in front of Marco's...you don't need to go to Marie's...there are plenty of weapons on the ground...yes...uh huh...we could use a few more cars...you'll need a driver and a shooter in each...right...creep and shoot...we can divide and conquer...that's right...okay...bye." He hung up and shoved his cell back in his pocket.

"What now, Chief?"

"We're going to lead as many of these zombies away from Marco's, and we're going to get more back up. If we can split them up and take them out, we might actually have a chance of clearing Smuggler's Bay."

Martinez nodded. "Fuckin' A."

*

Nancy stood up and addressed the room. "Okay, I just spoke with Chief Holbrook. He needs pairs of drivers and shooters to operate abandoned police vehicles. He said there're plenty of guns lying all over the ground. They could use the back up."

"I could drive," volunteered Vinnie. He was a car guy, and he always wanted to drive a police cruiser.

"Me, too," said Marco. When Vinnie looked at him, Marco shrugged. "There's no way I'm letting you go out there alone."

"Me neither," said Dharma. "I'll drive, too."

"No, you're not," said Emily. "There's no way. You're staying in here where it's safe."

"That's the point," said Dharma. "It's not going to be safe. Not unless we try and take the town back."

"I'm not crazy about you two going out there either," said Maggie to Marco and Vinnie.

"We don't have a lot of time to argue this," said Nancy. "Dharma's right. Okay, now we need three shooters."

"I'll do it," said Marie.

"Me, too," offered Salvatore.

Emily expected Marie to protest, but Marie didn't.

Marie nodded. "That a boy, Sal."

Emily couldn't believe what she was hearing. "Marie! You're okay with your son going out there?"

Marie shrugged. "He's a good shooter. He's been to the range. I'd rather he help out than wait in here to be a hot lunch."

Emily threw up her hands in exasperation. "I don't believe this. Everyone's lost their damned minds."

Nancy raised her right hand. "I'll be the third shooter. The chief said he's passing by now, so we've got to move fast. Drivers, grab the first available squad car you can find. Shooters, pick up as many guns as we can."

"Wait a minute." Marco walked over to the closet in back and opened the door. He pulled out three pizza delivery pouches. "We can shove a bunch of guns in these."

"Good idea," said Nancy. "Okay, let's get ready."

Emily hugged her daughter. "Please, Dharma. Don't go out there."

"I have to," said Dharma softly. "Besides, I can't let Vinnie go out there alone."

"He has his father with him," insisted Emily, pleading.

"Marie and Vinnie both risked their lives to help me save you and Dad. I can't not help them now."

"Let her go," said Ira softly. "She's right."

Emily realized that she had lost the argument. She squeezed Dharma one last time. "You be careful out there."

Dharma smiled. "I will."

*

Holbrook leaned forward, reached over the seat, and picked up the radio. "Pacelli, come in."

"Roger, Chief. There're too many of them here."

"Tell Becky to stay inside the car. We're just leading them away. Some of the survivors are going to grab some cruisers and join us. Divide and conquer."

"Roger, Chief."

They pulled away from Marco's, pushing their way through the swarm of zombies that hovered around both cars like a cloud. Holbrook looked out the back window, and he pulled out his cell. He dialed Nancy again. She picked up.

"Okay, you should be clear."

*

Vinnie and Marie were at the front of the queue lined up by the back door of Marco's. Behind them were Dharma and Nancy, and then Marco and Salvatore. Marco and Vinnie cleared the boxes away from the door.

"Remember," said Nancy, "drivers will grab a police car. The shooters will grab as many guns as they can."

Everyone nodded.

Marco called over Maggie. "You close and lock this door behind us. You don't open it up for anyone."

Maggie nodded. "Got it."

Marco kissed her and pushed the door open, and the three pairs dashed out. There were a few straggling dead lumbering around. When they saw the people dash out, one of them shrieked. They all began to converge on the survivors.

Vinnie, Dharma, and Marco all dashed for the nearest police cars, tugging on the driver door handles. Vinnie's and Dharma's were open, the engines left running.

The first squad car Marco tried was locked. He ran down past Vinnie's and Dharma's and found one that was unlocked. He slid into the driver's seat and found the keys in the ignition. He prayed and turned the key. The car started. "Thank Christ."

Marie, Nancy, and Salvatore scrambled to pick up guns, shoving them into red Marco's Pizza delivery pouches.

One of the dead got a little too close for comfort to Marie, and she plugged it in the head. Nancy and Salvatore were able to dodge the others, narrowly avoiding bloody projectile vomit, holding up the large pouches as shields.

Salvatore smiled at a zombie, an old man with tattered clothes, his pants torn off and his penis wagging in the wind. He flipped it the bird.

"Stay focused," snapped Marie. "Stop fucking around."

Salvatore wiped the smile from his face. He picked up a shotgun, cocked it, and fired point-blank into the bottomless zombie's face, exploding its head off its shoulders.

Vinnie, Dharma, and Marco flipped the lights on their pilfered cars. After they had gathered enough weapons and ammo, the three shooters paired up with their drivers.

Marco took off first, followed by Vinnie, and then Dharma. Marco got on the radio. "Chief Holbrook, this is Marco Cantone. We're rolling. Over."

There was a pause, and then the radio crackled. "Very good. Everyone accounted for with all their fingers and toes?"

"Yes, Chief."

"Good. We're going to lead them back around in front of the police station. I want one of you down a side street facing the opposite direction. When we bring them by, hit the sirens and draw some away. This isn't a race. Creep and shoot. Take out as many as you can."

"Got it," said Marco.

"Roger that," said Vinnie.

"I'm on it," said Dharma.

Marco, being out in front, turned down Ocean Ave. Vinnie turned down Bay Street, and Dharma took off down Cove Street. Meanwhile, Salvatore, Marie, and Nancy were in their respective back seats dumping their guns out of the pizza delivery pouches and onto the back seats. They began sizing up their stash, assessing their ammo situation.

When the drivers each made it to the end of their side streets, they each made three-point U-turns and faced the other direction, backing up so that the trunks of their cars were jutting out a little onto the boulevard in front of the police station.

Vinnie looked in the rearview mirror and saw a scraggly old man on the roof of the police station with a sniper rifle.

Marco saw it too. He got on the radio. "We're in position, Chief. There's a man with a rifle on the roof of the police station. He doesn't look like one of yours."

"Roger that," said Chief. "That's our sniper. We're coming around, passing in front of the CVS. About to make a left onto Main Street. When we pass by, hit the lights and sirens and start creeping up your streets. Some of them should break off and follow you."

"Everyone got that?" asked Marco.

"Yup," said Vinnie.

"Got it," said Dharma.

They waited, engines running.

*

Vinnie checked his gas tank. The car had been left running, so it was half full. He hoped he wouldn't have to stop for gas. He got on his radio. "Everyone check their gas. Mine's half-empty."

"You would be a half-empty kinda guy," quipped Dharma. "I'm going to say that I'm half-full."

"I'm at three-quarters," said Marco.

Vinnie turned to Marie. "Are you ready?"

Marie smirked. "I was born ready, Vincenzo." She held up a police pistol. "Just don't get nervous and take off too fast. We need to keep them close so I can get some headshots."

"Got it," said Vinnie. "I'll keep 'em close." He was glad he paired off with Marie. She was a genuine bad ass. He felt confident having her as his shooter.

Holbrook came creeping up Main Street with his trail of undead lemmings behind him.

"Here we go," said Vinnie.

Marie lowered her back window. She stuck the top half of her body out. There was a zombie ambling out from behind a few garbage cans, toppling them over. It saw Marie and staggered over to her, reaching out for her.

"Look out!" said Vinnie.

"I see him," said Marie, her voice calm and casual.

It was a pregnant woman, but her skin was bloated and green. Her abdomen was torn open, and there was a zombie infant hanging out, raccoon eyes, swiping its hand. The sounds it made were indescribably horrific.

"Holy shit," winced Vinnie.

Marie trained the gun on the woman zombie's head, let it walk right up to her, and pulled the trigger. The zombie woman dropped to the ground face first, covering the zombie baby. "Got it."

A few moments later, Chief Holbrook passed Dharma. She flipped on her lights and sirens and began creeping up the block she was on. Nancy hung out of the back window. They disappeared from view, but Vinnie heard Nancy popping off shots.

Holbrook's car passed Vinnie and Marie.

"Okay," said Marie, banging the roof of the car with her free hand.

Vinnie hit the lights and siren. He lightly pressed the gas pedal, creeping forward, checking the rearview mirror. A throng of dead broke off from the main trail and followed. The old man on the roof of the police station was firing down at zombies on the street.

Marie was firing, too. Her shots were controlled. She took her time and chose her shots. Vinnie saw zombies dropping to the street, one by one.

Just then, he thought of something. He got on the radio. "This is Vinnie. What happens when we get to the end of our side streets?"

"That's a good question," said Marco.

"You'll need to split up," answered Holbrook. "Marco, you turn left. Vinnie, you go up the ramp of the boardwalk and continue on the boardwalk.

"Dharma, you go right. Turn right onto Decatur as I come up left onto Mariner. This way, we don't run right smack into each other."

"Right," said Dharma.

As Vinnie crept up the street, he visualized their paths in his head. The whole thing reminded him of a video game. They had to drive, passing each other, but without intersecting paths.

Marie ducked back inside the car to grab another gun. "Slow down a little. Let 'em get a little closer."

"Got it."

Marie popped back outside and continued shooting.

Vinnie was approaching the end of his side street. "We're almost at the end."

There was no answer from Marie. She was concentrating, dropping a zombie with almost every shot. Vinnie thought the woman was amazing.

He crossed Surf and approached the wide wooden ramp leading up to the boardwalk. The ramp was built specifically for police vehicles to access the boardwalk. As he climbed the incline, Marie paused her shooting.

She popped back inside the car, tossing the gun aside and grabbing a third. "This is tedious."

"Slow and steady," said Vinnie. He turned right onto the boardwalk. The trail of dead followed. Marie popped back outside the car and resumed shooting.

There were a few zombies ahead of them, staggering down the boardwalk. They were all walking towards their car.

"Marie, we've got a few coming at us!"

She must've turned to look. She ducked back inside, grabbed a fourth gun, flipped off the safety, and handed it to Vinnie. "Here, take them out."

Vinnie accepted the gun. "I don't know, Marie. I can't shoot."

"Sure you can," she said. "Just point it at them and pull the trigger. Try to get 'em in the head."

Before he could argue, she was back outside, picking off their tail.

Vinnie checked the rearview mirror. He saw that the herd was indeed thinning out. He looked out the front, and he got goosebumps. One of the zombies approaching was that little girl. The one that spoke.

He lowered his window and waited until they got closer. The little girl seemed to fall back, allowing the other two, a man and a woman, to go ahead.

Vinnie slowly swerved right, allowing him a shot at them. He took a deep breath, held it, and squeezed the trigger. His first shot missed both zombies. The second shot grazed the man's shoulder. It's jaw hung, dislocated, tongue squirming around.

Vinnie decided that it wasn't the biggest threat, so he focused on the woman. Her eyes were narrowed, her expression primal. She shrieked at him. He squeezed the trigger, hitting her in her right breast. Vinnie grimaced, apologizing under his breath.

Marie ducked back inside the car. "There're only a few left." She reached for another gun. "Last one."

Vinnie took another shot and hit the zombie woman in the throat. "Marie, I need help."

"You can do it," she insisted. "Don't fuck it up." She disappeared back outside.

Vinnie narrowed his eyes, trying to visualize the target. The female zombie was so close now that she was almost able to take the gun out of his hand. He leaned his head sideways out the window, resting it on his shoulder.

The zombie reached out for him. He squeezed the trigger. He hit her in her right eye socket, and she dropped to the boardwalk, his arm passing over her head as the car crept forward. He took aim at the man, squeezed the trigger, and dropped him, too.

"Marie, I did it!" As the man dropped, the little girl came dashing out from behind him. Vinnie squeezed off two more shots. Either she was moving too fast, or he panicked.

The little girl reached out and grabbed his gun arm. Her grip was unnaturally tight. Vinnie tried to jerk his arm into the car, and he let go of the wheel. The girl was trying to bite his arm.

Vinnie reached out with his other hand, grabbed her by the hair, and held her head away from his arm as she snapped her teeth like a hungry piranha.

As he leaned out the window, his right foot depressed the gas. The police car veered to the right, crashing into a heavy metal T-shirt shop. "Shit!"

Marie nearly fell out of her window. "What the...?"

The little girl, still holding onto Vinnie's arm, was dragged. Vinnie stepped on the brake. The car crashed through a glass counter and came to a stop.

The little girl was hung up on the broken metal frame and jagged shards of the glass counter. As her fingers slid down and off his arm, they pulled the gun out of his hand. The little girl growled and swiped her arms at the car.

Vinnie turned around toward the back seat. "Marie, you all right?"

She wasn't in the car.

Vinnie looked through the rear window and saw her lying flat on her back on the boardwalk just outside the store. There were only several zombies left, but they were converging on her. She kicked at them, firing her gun.

"Marie!"

Vinnie tried to open the driver side door, but it wouldn't open more than a few inches. Something was blocking it. He slid over to the other side and got out.

"Marie!" He clumsily staggered over the partially intact portion of the glass counter, crunching broken glass under his feet. He winced as he felt jagged glass bite into his shins, but he didn't let it slow him down.

As he rounded the car, he saw Marie throwing her gun at one of the zombies. She kicked her legs at two that were trying to get on top of her. "No! Stop it!" she shouted.

Vinnie started waving his arms at the dead surrounding her. "Over here! No! Over here!"

The two at her feet grabbed her ankles and were shoving her legs apart, sliding in between them.

"No! Please! No! Stop it!"

Vinnie rushed the pile, tackling two trying to approach her from the side. They went crashing down to the wooden planks, Vinnie on top with an arm over each zombie.

He pushed himself up on his hands and sat on his haunches in time to see the dead swarm her. She kicked her legs and shoved their faces away with her hands, but they pushed their way in.

Marie tried to squirm and wriggle away as she disappeared under the pile. Her hand jutted up from under the heap, trembling and spastic. Her angry protests turned to cries of pain as they sunk rotten teeth into her flesh.

"No! Noooo!" Vinnie stood up. *Not her. Marie is invincible. She's a hero. She's a mother.* All of these thoughts raced through his mind. He wanted to rush the pile, but his legs wouldn't cooperate. He couldn't see her face, but he heard her muffled cries. It was already too late.

The dead backed away from her twitching body, pulling out her entrails with greedy hands. Her neck was torn away, and her arms and legs bloodied. They feasted on her innards as she watched, eyes bulging in terror, until her life faded from her body.

Vinnie backed away from the frenzy, shaking his head in denial of what he was seeing.

"Fooooood," said a guttural voice from behind him.

Vinnie turned to face the little girl. "You! This is your fault!"

She screeched at him and flashed a sinister grin.

He wanted to bash her fucking brains in with every ounce of his being. She growled at him, taunting him, laughing and wheezing.

Vinnie felt fingers on his back. The bitch was trying to distract him.

He shrugged them off, but the weight of their bodies collided with him, pushing him forward.

He stumbled, falling to his hands and knees on the boardwalk. He felt the weight of bodies on his back as he pushed up, resisting them. He crawled forward, trying to shake the zombies off, and they shrieked as they clung onto his back and legs.

"You bitch! You fucking little bitch!" He commando crawled, kicking his legs, propelling himself towards her with all of the hate and anger he could muster. It welled up inside him like a geyser.

This isn't supposed to be happening. Images of Dharma ran in his mind's eye, her smile, her laugh. He was supposed to be with her, protect her. They had plans.

The little girl looked on, pleased at her handiwork.

There were the screech of tires on wet wood and the sound of car doors opening. "Vinnie!"

He heard popping sounds. Suddenly, he felt a bite of pain in his left quad. The load on his legs got lighter as he squirmed away, but the pain in his left leg was blinding.

He rolled over onto his back, kicking away two zombies that were lying on top, and saw Dharma standing there, hands over her mouth in horror. Nancy stood beside her, one eye closed, arm extended, pistol out in front of her and trained on him.

"Jesus, are you all right?" asked Nancy.

Vinnie nodded.

Nancy turned to the dead feasting on Marie and shot each one in the head as they slurped down her flesh and innards.

Dharma ran over to Vinnie, got down on her knees, and hugged him close to her body. His face was smothered into her T-shirt as her body shuddered. She was sobbing.

He pushed his face away so he could breathe. "I think one of them bit me on the leg."

Dharma gasped. "What? No! No, it can't…shit! No!"

Vinnie pushed himself away from her, but she pulled him close again. He looked down at his left leg. Blood was pooling on the wooden planks underneath it.

Nancy knelt down next to him. "Let me see."

Vinnie hesitated, resigned to the fact that he had been bitten, but Nancy rolled him over onto his stomach. He grunted from the pain that ignited from being manhandled as it shot up his leg like lightning.

Dharma stood there sobbing. "No, no, no, no…"

Vinnie felt Nancy pull up his left short leg. Her finger grazed the surface of the wound. Then it probed it, sending another wave of pain shooting up his leg.

Vinnie felt hot, and the world around him swam. Nancy rolled Vinnie onto his back again. He swooned, feeling light-headed.

Nancy arched an eyebrow. "I have good news and bad news."

"What?" was all Vinnie could manage.

Dharma knelt next to him, her eyes searching Nancy's face. "What's the good news?"

Nancy smiled. "The good news is, he isn't bitten."

Dharma let out a high-pitched squeak, causing the little dead girl hung up on the broken counter to grunt in displeasure. She pulled Vinnie close, squeezing him.

"What's the bad news?" he gasped, as Dharma squeezed the wind out of him.

"I shot you in the leg."

Dharma loosened her grip. "She had to. They were going to bite you."

Vinnie ignored the bad news. He lay in Dharma's arms looking up at her, smiling like an idiot. *God, it was good to see her face.*

Dharma looked down at him, confused. "Well, you don't have to be *that* happy about it."

"I'm just happy to see you," said Vinnie, his eyes dreamy. "You came back for me."

"Of course," said Dharma. "I always have your back."

"He's going into shock," said Nancy. "We have to get him into the car and keep him warm."

Dharma looked down at Vinnie. "I need you to sit up, honey." She and Nancy helped him sit up. They each grabbed him under an arm and hoisted him to his feet. Vinnie helped, but he felt weak.

Dharma slung his right arm around his shoulder and began to walk him to their police car. They walked past Marie's torn body.

"I'm sorry," muttered Vinnie. "It's my fault."

"Shhhhh," whispered Dharma. "Not your fault. The dead did this."

Nancy ran into the store, to the right of Vinnie's crashed police car. She grabbed a couple of Baja beach blankets. She started to follow Dharma and Vinnie when she heard a wheezy cackle from behind her.

Nancy looked down at Marie's gored body and turned on the little dead girl. She walked up to the girl as the girl swiped at her, but stopped just short of the little monster's reach.

"Marie, what are you doing?" asked Dharma from behind her.

The little dead girl grinned at Nancy. Her eyes were alert.

"You," said Nancy through gritted teeth. "You started all of this."

The little dead girl growled at Nancy, snapping her teeth. "Foooooooood."

Nancy leveled her gaze at the little abomination. "Yeah, I remember you. You're April Traub, that little girl from the Pier. *My* pier."

"Foooooood!"

Nancy raised her gun, pointing the barrel point blank at the little girl's head. The girl shrieked and laughed in defiance.

Nancy shoved the barrel of the gun into the girl's mouth. The girl bit down on the metal. Her hands seized Nancy's arms. Her fingers tried to claw at Nancy's skin, but having been an active little girl, her finger nails never had the chance to grow long.

"You're looking a little anemic," said Nancy.

The little dead girl shrieked, but Nancy pulled the trigger. The girl's head dropped.

Nancy pulled the pistol barrel out of her mouth, wiped it on the side of her pants, and walked back to the police car.

Dharma was standing by Vinnie, who was now lying in the back seat covered in blankets. She watched Nancy with a worried expression.

"Let's get out of here," said Nancy. "Vinnie needs medical attention."

* * *

Lenny was pacing around the living room. Both Robbie and Tyrell were fast asleep on the couch. His eyes were heavy and his body weary. He looked at the clock. It was 4am.

Finally, Mrs. Chief came walking into the living room. She, too, looked tired, but she was smiling.

"Is everything okay?" asked Lenny.

"Dr. Potts said Tara's been stabilized…" Mrs. Chief saw Lenny's confusion. "She's tired, and she needs to rest, but she's probably going to be okay."

Lenny released the tension he was holding in his shoulders. He smiled. "Thank g-goodness."

Mrs. Holly entered the living room, also looking a bit worse for the wear. "The doc's exhausted, but I think he did it."

Mrs. Chief looked at the clock as she rubbed her neck. "What time is it? Christ, he's been at it all night."

Dr. Potts walked into the living room looking positively drained. "It's been a long night. Your friend needs rest. Speaking of which, I'm going to go to bed. You're all welcome to stay as long as you like. There's food and iced tea in the fridge."

"Thank you for everything," said Mrs. Chief.

Dr. Potts staggered a bit as climbed the stairs. He grabbed the railing for support.

"Are you all right?" asked Mrs. Holly.

Dr. Potts smiled. "I'll be fine. Ol' grandpa ain't what he used to be." He climbed the steps as if his feet were made of lead.

After he disappeared upstairs, Mrs. Holly yawned. "And I have to use the facilities." She disappeared into the kitchen, where there was a power room off by the back door.

"Dr. Potts didn't look so good," said Mrs. Chief. "Poor man. We woke him up in the middle of the night with supplies from CVS and asked him to perform emergency surgery."

Lenny didn't quite understand what she was talking about. He felt a tickle in his bladder. "I have to use the b-b-bathroom."

Mrs. Chief smiled at the announcement, although Lenny wasn't sure why. She looked towards the kitchen. "Mrs. Holly's in there. Can you hold it?"

Lenny shook his head, his expression apologetic. "It's an emergency."

"I assume there's a bathroom upstairs. I'm sure Dr. Potts wouldn't mind."

Lenny nodded, gave the thumbs up, and he began to round the coffee table.

Mrs. Chief stopped him, placing a hand on his shoulder. She gave it a friendly squeeze. "You did good, Lenny. Thanks for keeping the kids calm."

Lenny looked Mrs. Chief in the eye. He felt his eyes welling up. He always appreciated praise, but it meant a lot coming from Mrs. Chief. "My pleasure."

He looked over at Billy, who was also asleep in the armchair. Lenny waved a dismissive hand, chortling. He grabbed the railing and began his climb up the stairs.

Lenny entered a short hallway. He walked tentatively, not knowing exactly where he needed to go. He found the bathroom on the right, the door ajar. He stepped inside, flicked on the lights, and closed the door behind him.

It was a large bathroom with faded floral wallpaper. Some of it curled back at the seams with age. There was a low bathtub, a pedestal sink, and a toilet. Across from the toilet was a towel rack holding two large bath towels. Above the toilet hung a small hand towel.

Lenny turned and saw a doorway leading to Dr. Potts's master bedroom. Dr. Potts was lying on his bed in his clothes, legs splayed out. His face was pale and his brow sweaty.

Lenny didn't know what to say to the man—he didn't even know if he was awake—so he went to his go-to response. He smiled and gave a thumbs-up. "Good…job."

Dr. Potts didn't respond.

"I have to go to the bathroom," added Lenny, excusing himself.

Lenny closed the door for privacy, locking it.

He turned sideways, passed the sink, put down the toilet seat, stood with his back to the toilet, dropped trou, and sat.

Lenny heard the doorbell ring. Then he heard Chief Holbrook's voice. It sounded like the kids woke up. "Daddy!"

He listened to the sounds of the reunion out in the living room as he tinkled. Lenny wanted to join them, but nature was calling. Everyone sounded happy.

Was the zombie attack over?

When Lenny had emptied his bladder, he stood up, pulled up his underwear and pants, and flushed. He washed his hands with soap. After drying his hands, he opened the door and stepped out into the hallway.

He closed the door behind him and was startled when he turned around and saw Dr. Potts standing right in front of him.

Dr. Potts stood there, swaying back and forth, shoulders slumped, and wheezing. His eyes had dark shadows around them. His face looked ashen and angry.

"Hi," squeaked Lenny, unsure of what to say.

Dr. Potts sneered, flashing his teeth. Lenny thought he looked like a wild animal. A chill shot down Lenny's spine as he realized that he had forgotten about the bite on Dr. Potts's upper arm.

"D-D-Dr. Potts?"

Dr. Potts reached out for Lenny, seizing him by the throat. Lenny tried to cry out, but Dr. Potts's grip strangled his airway. Lenny clawed at Dr. Pott's arms, but the old man's grip didn't relent.

Billy Blake drifted into the hallway. Lenny reached out a hand to try and get his attention.

When Billy saw what was happening, he practically did a double take. He began to wave his arms around. "Hey, you dead bastard! Over here!"

Dr. Potts's grip loosened as he turned his head to look at Billy.

Billy walked right up to the old man. "You leave my friend alone, you crusty old fuckbag!"

Dr. Potts released Lenny. He shrieked at Billy, lunged, passed right through him, and fell down the stairs as Lenny rubbed his hurting throat.

There were screams downstairs.

Lenny heard Chief Holbrook shout, "Everybody get back!"

There was a horrible, animalistic shriek. Then there were two gunshots and a heavy thump.

CHAPTER 15

Over the next several days, Holbrook rounded up whatever police were left and organized and armed any and all survivors. They swept the town, block by block, dispatching the last of the dead wandering the streets. They stabbed the temples of any of the recently deceased so that they wouldn't reanimate, and the bonfire was reignited on the beach to burn the remains.

More weapons were scavenged, supplies were gathered, and food stores were inventoried. Holbrook put lookouts on the bay and along the beach, but no more dead were washing up on shore to cause trouble. There were armed checkpoints at the town limits on either side.

The mayor was missing and presumed dead, so Holbrook took charge for the time being. He communicated with the neighboring towns, lending support as well as receiving support. Stonewall and several towns inland were lost to the dead. Smuggler's Bay was effectively cut off.

Holbrook walked the boardwalk, surveying the operations. The boardwalk had become the nerve center for survival operations. Many businesses, particularly eating establishments, remained open. People still needed to eat, and while some remained cloistered in their houses with doors locked, others sought company and found strength in numbers.

The Smuggler's Bay boardwalk cam perched atop the Blackbeard's Pier Arcade had gone viral, piping out live images of pedestrians milling about, as they always had, as if nothing had happened. Then again, when cut off from the rest of the world on a barrier island, what else was there to do? It was human nature to seek out normalcy in times of crisis.

Pacelli was strolling down the boardwalk, stopping at storefronts, jotting down notes on a clipboard. When he saw Chief Holbrook, he smiled and made his way over, clipboard tucked under his right arm.

"Afternoon, Pacelli."

"I have the latest inventory, Chief."

Holbrook nodded. "Give me a snapshot."

Pacelli consulted his clipboard. "The A&P is still open. We have supplies from six pizzerias, a dozen restaurants, and three pubs that are still in operation."

"That's good in the short term," said Holbrook. "I'm worried about when we lose power."

"Right," said Pacelli. "Without power, there's no refrigeration. Food is going to spoil, and we don't want people getting sick."

"What about non-perishables?" asked Holbrook.

"The A&P, pharmacies, and convenience stores have candy bars, beef jerky, canned nuts, dried fruit, soda, and bottled water. Without the tourists in town, it should last a while."

Holbrook nodded. "Good. That'll do for now. I have calls in to the OEM. The governor has already requested federal disaster assistance."

"How long will that be?"

"Don't know. I assume they're assessing the situation as we speak."

The Bay sanitation workers continued their usual duties, cleaning up the garbage and detritus from the prior night's attack. The beach was closed, but the lifeguards served as medics and auxiliary police. Some worked out of the pharmacies and urgent care facilities, doling out medications. Others gathered and inventoried the weaponry left behind by the National Guard on the boardwalk. Captain Mac Cochran oversaw their operations and communicating with the Coast Guard.

Nancy saw Holbrook and Pacelli and walked over to them. "Chief. Officer Pacelli."

Pacelli acknowledged her with a nod.

"How is everyone doing?" asked Holbrook.

Nancy put her hands on her hips. "People are scared."

Holbrook flashed a weary grin. "I don't blame them."

"They want to know when it's all going to be over. This isn't like two years ago. It's different this time."

Holbrook nodded. "Yes, it is, but it's amazing how people are carrying on."

Nancy nodded. "I have the arcade open, but Chief, I've got to be honest. I'm wondering if it's even worth charging money anymore. What if this is it? What if this is the end?"

"Don't talk like that, Nancy."

"With all due respect, Chief, I'll talk any damned way I see fit."

He smiled at this. Outsiders or the few residents who didn't know her well often didn't know how to take Nancy. Holbrook knew her personality well and appreciated her often blunt candor, particularly under the current circumstances.

"Don't let others hear you talk like this," he insisted.

"I'm not the only one," said Nancy. "We're holding out, but no one knows how much longer. Any word from the State or Feds?"

Holbrook shook his head. "I was just telling Pacelli. Not much yet."

Nancy chortled, but it was a bitter sound. "Damned government. Our tax dollars at work."

"No one expected this, Nancy."

"Christ, I remember when our biggest worry was a terrorist attack. Hey, Chief, I'm thinking of calling together a meeting of the Bay's Business Association."

"For what?" asked Pacelli.

Nancy's eyes grew fierce. "For what? People are scared, you dolt. It'll help. We can talk it out. Support each other."

Pacelli groaned. "C'mon, guys. What's the point of any of this?"

"She's right," said Chief. "If people have nothing to do, panic will set in. We can't have that. Any way people can feel productive is a good thing right now."

"Well, I'm off," said Nancy, looking impatient. "I have phone calls to make. Too much to do."

Nancy acted as his "Deputy Mayor" of sorts. It made sense. She was organized, task-oriented, and she knew damn near everyone. She was a natural leader.

She placed Dharma in charge of entertainment, to occupy the children. The Blackbeard's Pier Arcade was open, along with a handful of rides for the younger children. However, Nancy kept the carousel dark. Holbrook figured it was out of respect for Mike Brunello.

"Do you really think any of that's going to help?" asked Pacelli.

"You forget, I was NYPD during 9/11. New York City didn't entirely shut down after the attack. Remember that massive blackout along the East Coast?"

Pacelli nodded. "Yeah, people thought that was terrorism."

"I was stranded out on Long Island," said Holbrook. "The highways were at a standstill. I got off and parked myself at a diner. After calling Lena to see if she was okay and tell her where I was, I went inside. The owner was selling ice cream, all you could eat for a few bucks."

Pacelli chuckled.

"Hell, it was going to waste anyway," said Holbrook. "So, I sat at the counter, ate more ice cream than was decent in one sitting, and made conversation with the man sitting next to me. It's what people do when things like this happen."

"If you say so, Chief."

"I do." This gave Holbrook an idea. People had questions. When was help coming? Were they safe? How long would supplies last? What about Stonewall? Would there be an evacuation to inland, away from the zombie threat?

He knew what he had to do. He hated doing it, but there was no mayor. He supposed he could get Nancy to do it, but she wasn't right for the task. The town needed reassurance, inspiration. He had to call a town meeting.

He picked up his cell and dialed Nancy. Cell service was still up, as the dead had no interest in machinery, like cell towers.

She answered. "Miss me already, Chief?"

"Nancy, I want you to put the word out. We're having a town meeting at St. Barnabas church. Five o'clock."

"Why the church? Shouldn't it be city hall?"

Holbrook thought about it for a moment. "City hall's too small. Besides, the church is a sanctuary. It's a place where people go for assurance. It just seems right for what I need to do."

"Consider it done." She hung up.

*

Tara was recovering at her home under the careful watch of her son, Tyrell, and a lifeguard named Joel. She was still weak, and she was experiencing wicked phantom pain, but she was stable and recovering slowly.

She spent her days watching television, monitoring the news stations and reporting back to Holbrook. She needed to feel busy, like she was contributing.

Tyrell wandered into her bedroom. "Mom, what are you doing?"

"Watching the news, honey." She was on her laptop, searching the internet for any breaking news. Joel sat next to her bed in a chair, his eyes glued to the television.

"Can I watch with you? I'm bored."

Tara smiled. She normally would have said no, but he knew what was going on. He was a part of it. Keeping him from the news wouldn't have preserved any innocence. Besides, she'd rather him sit beside her, inside, rather than going outside unsupervised.

"Sure, honey."

Tyrell hopped up onto the bed and scooted next to her, placing his back against the headboard. "Whatcha lookin' at, Mom?"

"It's getting tougher and tougher to find any news," said Tara.

"Why?"

"They're no longer broadcasting. They had to evacuate to be safe." At least that was what she hoped happened. Either that, or they were killed by the dead. "I'm looking at sites on the internet, where news is being reported from safe zones."

Many of the major stations in the tri-state area had gone dark in the past twenty-four hours, as they were located in population-dense cities infested with the dead. Fox News and MSNBC went dark when New York City overrun. CNN went dark when Atlanta fell. The BBC was still broadcasting, which was what Joel was watching on the television.

The zombies had spread rapidly, and it had soon become clear that Smuggler's Bay was not the only area under siege. The attacks, however, seemed to be limited to the United States.

The news had been throwing out all kinds of theories. One "expert" posited that a Russian spy vessel had been spotted just off shore from New Jersey two years ago, and it might have had something to do with it. It was presumed, at the time, that they were just there for surveillance purposes, but now people were speculating that they were introducing biological agents into the water. Another so-called expert accused the United States Government of experimenting on the elderly with some mind control technology, as many of the outbreaks had originated in nursing homes and assisted living facilities.

One thing was for certain, the tin foil hats were on, and every paranoid asshole with access to the media was offering up their half-baked conspiracy theory as to why the zombie attacks were happening.

The advance of the dead was stopped at Ohio, Kentucky, Tennessee, and Alabama. The more heavily populated areas, like New York City and Philadelphia were becoming impenetrable bastions of the dead. There were mass evacuations. However, just as in Smuggler's Bay, the authorities had been quickly and easily overrun. The virus spread faster than it could be contained, and the death toll was in the millions.

The CDC now reported rapid transmission of the Z Virus, with infection occurring within an hour of exposure. In fact, victims had begun to reanimate as they were being eaten alive. This was no longer a pandemic. It had become a war of attrition, where the dead were almost instantaneously recruiting the living to their ranks.

*

At five o'clock, the town had begun to filter into St. Barnabas, taking their seats in the pews. Holbrook was up front at the podium, microphone on. Monsignor O'Donnell stood in the aisles, greeting guests with a handshake and some kind words.

When the influx of people appeared to slow to a standstill, except for a few stragglers, and the pews were filled (some people even stood along the wall) with people looking at Holbrook with eager anticipation, he cleared his throat.

The din died down and was replaced with silence as all eyes were forward and undivided attention was given to their beloved police chief.

Holbrook glanced at Lena and Robbie, who sat next to Nancy in the front row. Lena smiled, her eyes met his, and it was enough to bolster Holbrook.

He adjusted the microphone. "Thank you, all, for coming." His voice echoed around the church. He looked down at the empty podium. He hadn't brought any notes, but he had given much thought about what he was going to say, and he believed it best to speak unrehearsed.

"Let me begin by saying that I'm proud of all of you. In less than twenty-four hours, you've all pitched in and kept this town going."

Someone shouted, "It's because of you, Chief!"

There were murmurs and heads nodding in agreement.

Holbrook put up his hands, in humble denial of the claim. "No, no. It's because of all of you. I couldn't do it without all of you."

The church quieted down again.

Holbrook cleared his throat awkwardly and continued. "Throughout the day, I've been approached with many questions…How long is this going to last? Are we still safe? Is anyone coming to help us?"

There were whispers of agreement. People were nodding and buzzing with outrage and fear.

"The truth is, right now, I don't know. I don't have the answer to those questions. We've lost our mayor and town council. I'm doing my best to help you keep this town alive. To keep each other alive."

There were cheers and shouts of enthusiasm for Holbrook's sentiment.

"The fact is, we were attacked by the dead for a second time, and this second wave was much worse than the first. The dead have returned in numbers that defy logic. They mutate and turn faster. Some are even communicating with each other.

"Right now, I have more questions than answers. But, one thing is clear…we need to keep this town running. We need to take care of ourselves and each other. There has been contact with state and federal government agencies, but no one is relaying a plan or course of action."

More murmurs from the crowd, but instead of enthusiasm, it was agitation. He had touched a nerve.

"Some would say, at least for the moment, that we are cut-off. Alone. But not me."

More buzzing and mumbling. People shifted in their seats. There were coughs, and somewhere in the back a baby cried.

"We're not alone because we have each other. We've survived catastrophe before, and yet we still stand, picking up the pieces, honoring our dead, and soldiering on.

"I believe in this town. We are a strong community that time after time has defied the odds. Pulling together, we look out for one another. I believe that we can weather this storm until help arrives. We are not weak, we are not helpless, we are strong."

There were cheers again from the pews, nods of agreement, even whistles and fist pumps.

"All I ask is for your continued cooperation. We are in this together, and together we'll see our way out of this."

Applause erupted inside the church, and people stood in ovation. Holbrook blushed at the response. However, it wasn't just embarrassment he was feeling.

There was also guilt. Guilt for promising them safety and success when there was no guarantee of it. He assumed the authorities would, at some point, step in. They had to. He remembered how long it took for FEMA and various other government agencies to respond to the attack and superstorm two years ago. They had been unprepared for it, and this second wave was even worse.

He looked over at Lena, who mouthed the words 'I love you.'

*

Chief Holbrook stood next to Monsignor O'Donnell, shaking hands, giving as well as receiving words of encouragement from people as they exited the church. Lena stood next to him, delivering greetings of her own as Robbie hid behind her, overwhelmed by the attention.

Holbrook leaned over and muttered to Lena, "So this is what being a politician feels like."

Someone caught his eye in the crowd, causing him to miss Lena's retort. It was Mac Cochran. His expression was that of urgency.

Holbrook excused himself and met Cochran halfway.

"Chief, I have to talk to you."

"Mac, what is it?"

Mac pulled Holbrook aside and leaned in, speaking in a hushed tone. "Chief, the Coast Guard has detected a boat loitering about twenty miles out."

"So, what? What is it? You seem spooked."

Cochran looked him in the eye. "It looks to be Russian, Chief."

"Russian?" Holbrook asked a little too loudly.

Cochran winced, but no one seemed to hear it.

"Are you sure?" asked Holbrook.

"Positively. It's one of those spy ships."

"What are they doing here, now?"

Cochran shrugged, looking nervously around him. "Don't know, Chief. It's not the first time."

Holbrook pulled him close. "Keep an ear out, and keep me posted."

Cochran nodded and navigated through the crowd to the exit. Lena slid beside her husband, grabbing him by the arm. She looked concerned. "Jim, what was that all about?"

Holbrook smiled. "Cochran's been in contact with the Coast Guard. He was filling me in on what's going on."

"What *is* going on? Is everything okay?"

He managed his most sincere smile. "Everything's fine, honey."

"What about dinner?" asked Robbie. "Is Daddy going with us?"

"Daddy has work to do, dear," said Lena. "There'll be other dinners."

Holbrook kissed Lena. "No, I'll be there. Six o'clock."

"Yay!" cheered Robbie.

"Are you sure?" asked Lena.

Holbrook checked his watch. "Yeah. I have a few things to check on, then I'll head home for a bit."

* * *

Vinnie limped his way on a wooden crutch towards Blackbeard's Arcade. He hobbled in through the front and looked around. There were some children playing on the machines, but it was mostly empty.

Dharma was standing next to Salvatore behind the prize counter. She smiled when she saw him, but Salvatore averted his gaze. The expression on his face soured.

Vinnie hopped over to the counter. "Dead in here." He winced at his own choice of words.

"It's dinner time," said Dharma. "People are home or out at restaurants."

"The pizzeria's slow," said Vinnie.

Salvatore ignored Vinnie and turned to Dharma. "I'm going to play some pinball, if that's okay."

Dharma hugged him. "Sure, that's fine, sweetie."

Vinnie stood there looking wounded as Salvatore trudged off to the pinball machines in the back corner. "He hates me."

Dharma looked sympathetic. "Oh, he's upset his mom died."

"He thinks it's my fault."

"You know it wasn't, Vin."

Vinnie's eyes darted back and forth to make sure no one was within earshot. "Do I? I feel horrible. Marie was a force of nature. She was a hero. And, now she's dead thanks to me, and her kids are orphans."

"It's not your fault. It was those monsters."

"I should've been more careful. I should've told her to get back inside the car."

"You had no idea that little girl zombie was going to attack you. You said so yourself, she almost bit your arm."

"Yeah, but Marie would've still be alive."

Dharma scowled. "Don't talk like that. *I'm* glad you're alive."

Vinnie looked around. "Where's Alessandra?"

"She's with Nancy."

"Really?"

"Yeah, Nancy's taken a real liking to her. She's using her as her little assistant."

"She feels bad for her," said Vinnie.

"She's empowering her," insisted Dharma.

Vinnie looked over at Salvatore, who was sullen as he played pinball. "I apologized go him, profusely. I just don't know what else to say."

Dharma came around the counter and hugged Vinnie. "There's nothing you can say. This isn't about you or your guilt. This is about a kid grieving his mother two years after losing his father."

"I guess you're right."

"You guess?" She punched him in the arm.

"Okay, okay. You're right," he conceded.

"He'll come around. Give him time."

"I hope so."

* * *

As days passed, Holbrook tried his best to remain optimistic, if not for him, then for the others. For Robbie and Lena.

It had been a week, and they hadn't lost power. Because of new theories that the virus was present in the local water supply, they used bottled water and soft drinks rather than the local water supply as a precaution.

The boardwalk businesses continued to pull together to pool food and resources, but without incoming shipments, the supply was dwindling. Holbrook and Nancy had introduced the idea of rationing to Marco, and he agreed.

The arcades were used to occupy the children and keep them entertained, but it was lights out at night. Over the course of the week, they had discovered that the lights had attracted some of the dead from across the Bay, who strolled up onto the beach in search of a hot meal. They had been dispatched by Holbrook's patrols, but it was a warning to be more cautious.

Everyone chipped in, each to his own ability. A handful of retired engineers helped monitor the water supply, sanitation systems, and damaged structures. They inspected gas and power lines for safety. The local teachers did their best to teach the children, even though it was summer. The children of Smuggler's Bay were less than enthusiastic about it, but it kept them busy and out of the hair of the adults helping run the town.

It was a quiet Friday morning, and Holbrook was patrolling the bay side with Becky when they heard the staccato chopping of helicopters. They looked up to find six Blackhawks and two Chinooks passing overhead.

"What the...?"

"It's about time," said Becky.

After a few minutes, Holbrook's radio crackled. It was Pacelli. "Chief, Pacelli here."

"Go ahead, Pacelli."

"Chief, we got some army copters landing on the beach."

"I know. We saw it. I'm on my way."

*

By the time Holbrook made it over to the boardwalk, the army was setting up on the beach. There was an officer pointing here and there, issuing orders, and his men went about their delegated tasks with urgency.

Pacelli and Lena, on boardwalk patrol, were waiting for him at the boardwalk stage on Mariner Avenue. As Holbrook walked up to them, he saw Lena's face. She looked concerned.

"What's going on?" asked Holbrook.

"I don't know," said Lena. "They just started running around."

They watched as several men started erecting tents. A small party walked off towards Blackbeard's Pier and started surveying the construction equipment. Smuggler's Bay survivors gathered at the edge of the boardwalk, watching the goings on with great interest. Some people even cheered

"They're setting up a staging base." Holbrook looked at the apparent officer in charge and sighed. "Well, let's go make friends."

Lena turned to Pacelli. "Stay here. Keep the boardwalk patrol alert."

Pacelli nodded and marched off.

Holbrook smiled. Lena had really come into her own since the attack. She became tougher, more resourceful. She took charge with such confidence that even his men took orders from her.

Holbrook and Lena walked down the wooden ramp to the sand below and began trudging over to the officer directing everyone. He shot them a glance, but ignored their approach, remaining focused on his work.

When they got close, the officer finally regarded them, though not warmly. "Who are you?"

Holbrook extended a hand. "Jim Holbrook, police chief."

The man shook it. "Colonel Waters, US Army. Who's in charge?"

"I guess that's me," said Holbrook.

"Not anymore. I'll take it from here."

Holbrook wasn't crazy about his demeanor. "What took you guys so long?"

Waters shot him any icy glare. "There's a war going on, or maybe you haven't heard."

"Colonel, I don't know what you've heard, but we've been through war ourselves here. We lost many of our residents…family, friends."

Waters looked away from Holbrook, hands on his hips, surveying his operation. "Your efforts are appreciated, Chief Holbrook. I don't mean to sound otherwise."

"So, what's the plan?" asked Lena.

Waters regarded her with amused contempt.

Lena wasn't sure if it was because she was a woman or a civilian or both.

"The plan? The plan is to stage a resistance to the dead."

"You're using Smuggler's Bay as a staging base," said Holbrook.

Waters nodded. "That's correct. A barrier island is an ideal jumping off point for retaking the coast."

"That's great," said Holbrook. "How can we help?"

Waters levelled his gaze at Holbrook. "I'm going to need an inventory of your supplies—food, weapons, tools." He pointed across the beach to the pier. "I'm going to require use of that equipment as well."

"Sure thing," said Holbrook. "What for?"

"We're going to build an elevated, fortified base of operations."

"That's going to take a while," said Lena, confused.

"War is about the long game," said Waters. "We are not the cavalry riding in to wipe out the dead menace, Miss…"

"Mrs. Holbrook. Lena."

"…Mrs. Holbrook. This is not going to be quick, and it's not going to be easy." He turned to Holbrook. "How's your police force?"

Holbrook put his hands on his hips. "Most of them were wiped out in the attack. My current force is composed of several of the old officers, lifeguards, and a few civilians."

Waters nodded. "Good. It won't do us any good if there's no order."

"It was the best we could do under the circumstances, and it did the job," said Holbrook.

Waters listened, face stoic. "Well, we have a new job now, and that's to keep the island secure, hunker down, and fortify. Once that has been achieved, we're going to coordinate strategic strikes inland."

"That's great," said Holbrook. "By the way, do you guys know anything about that Russian spy vessel hanging around the shore?"

Waters paused, looking at Lena. Holbrook looked at her, too.

Lena sighed. She knew that meant this conversation wasn't for her ears, so she begrudgingly walked back towards the boardwalk, giving them their privacy.

"Yes, we're aware of the Russian spy ship. It's a Vishnya-class intelligence ship."

"What are they doing around here *now*?"

"Catching us with our pants down. Surveilling the chaos."

"Do you think they have any involvement in the attack?" asked Holbrook.

"We're not ruling it out," said Waters. "I don't mean to be rude, but I have to get back to work."

"I'm going to get that information you wanted, ASAP," said Holbrook.

"That would be appreciated, sir," said Waters. "I'll be in touch once we've established the staging area."

"I'll be around," said Holbrook.

Waters returned to directing his men, and Holbrook walked back up the beach to the boardwalk, where Lena was waiting for him.

"What a prick," said Lena.

"Nah, he's got his orders, and we need to help him any way we can. He doesn't have time for social niceties. Plus, he wants to make it real clear who's in charge now."

"And it isn't you."

"That's okay," said Holbrook. "I'm a police chief. He'll do a better job of leading the town."

"I suppose so," said Lena with some reluctance.

"If the news is correct, we've got a long haul ahead of us," said Holbrook. "There's been a Russian spy vessel lurking close to shore."

"I know, I saw it on the news." She looked away, at the beach. "It's what Mac Cochran told you about."

Embarrassed, Holbrook smiled. "I didn't want to alarm you."

"I'm not as stupid as you and your colonel buddy think I am."

Holbrook pulled her close and hugged her. "Don't ever think I feel that way. You're amazing."

She wanted to be bitter about it, but she melted in his arms. Who knew? Maybe before all this happened, everything she'd been through, she would've been so naïve. The dead had a way of hardening those who survived.

Holbrook looked at the people of Smuggler's Bay lined up along the boardwalk fence, waving to the soldiers, cheering them on. This was what they were waiting for, and he was glad it would offer them some solace.

However, Colonel Waters was right. It was just the beginning. Everything wasn't going to be okay. They would have to make it okay.

*

Vinnie limped over to the edge of the boardwalk using his crutch, Dharma by his side. They watched all of the activity on the beach. Vinnie was admiring the helicopters.

"Look at that," said Vinnie, watching the soldiers. "That's a welcome sight."

"What are they doing?" asked Dharma.

"Looks like they're setting up camp. We could use more help." He snapped his fingers, as if an idea had suddenly dawned on him. "Let's go bring them some pizzas."

Dharma smiled. "Good idea. Get off on the right foot."

Vinnie winced at the expression. "Really, Dharma?"

She smiled impishly. "Hop along, now."

"Please. Just stop."

"Shake a leg, mister."

"Oh, for Chrissake."

*

Lenny stood proudly behind the refreshment counter at Blackbeard's Pier, left in charge with Salvatore by Dharma. Since the arrival of the military, boardwalk traffic had picked up again. After gawking at the soldiers on the beach, some people came into the arcade to let off some steam.

Lenny was delighted when a few soldiers came into the arcade. A Colonel Waters had been asking to speak to the owner, which Salvatore indicated was Nancy.

In the CVS, Mrs. Holly and Tara ran the pharmacy as their own urgent care center, doling out medications and tending to the sick and wounded. Tara was doing much better, and she used her counseling skills to help those who were struggling with anxiety and acute stress syndrome.

Colonel Waters repurposed the construction equipment, once used to rebuild the pier and boardwalk, to create an elevated fortification as well as wooden barricades at the town boundaries.

Everyone carried on with their new normal, with a new sense of purpose and a new sense of urgency. There was no more daily grind in what became known as the Dead Zones. No more traffic, no more pain-in-the-ass boss, no more bills. The country thought it was going to be torn apart by politics, but Democrat versus Republican didn't matter anymore. It was no longer about getting more votes, filling more offices, or passing more bills.

Now, it was the living versus the dead, and the stakes were higher. The country now had to pull together in the face of a superordinate threat.

Becky had armed herself from the town's makeshift armory and slipped off in a row boat across the bay to find her husband in Stonewall, where they lived. He hadn't been picking up when she called him, and she was worried.

If he had been evacuated, he would've called her. The dead took her sister away from her. She wasn't going to lose Greg. If he was trapped inside their house, surrounded by the dead, she was coming for him.

She was coming for them all.

THE END

CHECK OUT OTHER GREAT ZOMBIE NOVELS

DEAD ASCENT
by Jason McPhearson

The dead have risen and they are hungry...

Grizzled war veteran turned game warden, Brayden James and a small group of survivors, fight their way through the rugged wilderness of southern Appalachia to an isolated cabin in the hope of finding sanctuary. Every terrifying step they make they are stalked by a growing mass of staggering corpses, and a raging forest fire, set by the government in hopes of containing the virus.

As all logical routes off the mountain are cut off from them, they seek the higher ground, but they soon realize there is little hope of escape when the dead walk and the world burns.

CHAOS THEORY
by Rich Restucci

The world has fallen to a relentless enemy beyond reason or mercy. With no remorse they rend the planet with tooth and nail.

One man stands against the scourge of death that consumes all.

Teamed with a genius survivalist and a teenage girl, he must flee the teeming dead, the evils of humans left unchecked, and those that would seek to use him. His best weapon to stave off the horrors of this new world? His wit.

CHECK OUT OTHER GREAT ZOMBIE NOVELS

RUN
by Rich Restucci

The dead have risen, and they are hungry.

Slow and plodding, they are Legion. The undead hunt the living. Stop and they will catch you. Hide and they will find you. If you have a heartbeat you do the only thing you can: You run.

Survivors escape to an island stronghold: A cop and his daughter, a computer nerd, a garbage man with a piece of rebar, and an escapee from a mental hospital with a life-saving secret. After reaching Alcatraz, the ever expanding group of survivors realize that the infected are not the only threat.

Caught between the viciousness of the undead, and the heartlessness of the living, what choice is there? Run.

THE DEAD WALK THE EARTH
by Luke Duffy

As the flames of war threaten to engulf the globe, a new threat emerges.

A 'deadly flu', the like of which no one has ever seen or imagined, relentlessly spreads, gripping the world by the throat and slowly squeezing the life from humanity.

Eight soldiers, accustomed to operating below the radar, carrying out the dirty work of a modern democracy, become trapped within the carnage of a new and terrifying world.

Deniable and completely expendable. That is how their government considers them, and as the dead begin to walk, Stan and his men must fight to survive.

CHECK OUT OTHER GREAT ZOMBIE NOVELS

DEAD PULSE RISING
by K. Michael Gibson

Slavering hordes of the walking dead rule the streets of Baltimore, their decaying forms shambling across the ruined city, voracious and unstoppable. The remaining survivors hide desperately, for all hope seems lost... until an armored fortress on wheels plows through the ghouls, crushing bones and decayed flesh. The vehicle stops and two men emerge from its doors, armed to the teeth and ready to cancel the apocalypse.

TOWER OF THE DEAD
by J.V. Roberts

Markus is a hardworking man that just wants a better life for his family. But when a virus sweeps through the halls of his high-rise apartment complex, those plans are put on hold. Trapped on the sixteenth floor with no hope of rescue, Markus must fight his way down to safety with his wife and young daughter in tow.

Floor by bloody floor they must battle through hordes of the hungry dead on a terrifying mission to survive the TOWER OF THE DEAD.

www.ingramcontent.com/pod-product-compliance
Lightning Source LLC
Chambersburg PA
CBHW020059180626
46812CB00006B/2394